"Every sound you make is sexy," Blade whispered.

At the base of her neck, his fingers splayed wide. His thumb rested in the hollow of her throat, feeling the erratic pulse there. His fingers tightened, as if to capture the eroticism she was exuding.

Rori felt his strong fingers wrap around her throat. The pressure, though not painful, reminded her of a recent nightmare—when a faceless man had attempted to strangle her. She waited for the fear to overpower her. She felt trickles of it, but it was soon displaced by an entirely different kind of fear. This one gushed through her like a tumbling tide; this one was based on the desire that ran rampant in her veins. Suddenly, all she remembered of the dream was the man's kiss... this man's kiss... and she would gladly give up all she owned for the brush of his mouth against hers.

But if he kissed her, he'd find out her secret. A secret that she'd rather die than reveal...

Dear Reader,

Welcome to the Silhouette **Special Edition** experience! With your search for consistently satisfying reading in mind, every month the authors and editors of Silhouette **Special Edition** aim to offer you a stimulating blend of deep emotions and high romance.

The name Silhouette **Special Edition** and the distinctive arch on the cover represent a commitment—a commitment to bring you six sensitive, substantial novels each month. In the pages of a Silhouette **Special Edition**, compelling true-to-life characters face riveting emotional issues—and come out winners. All the authors in the series strive for depth, vividness and warmth in writing these stories of living and loving in today's world.

The result, we hope, is romance you can believe in. Deeply emotional, richly romantic, infinitely rewarding—that's the Silhouette **Special Edition** experience. Come share it with us—six times a month! With this month's distinguished roster of gifted contemporary writers—Bay Matthews, Karen Keast, Barbara Faith, Madelyn Dohrn, Dawn Flindt and Andrea Edwards—you won't want to miss a single volume.

Best wishes,

Leslie Kazanjian,
Senior Editor

KAREN KEAST
Night Spice

Silhouette Special Edition

Published by Silhouette Books New York

America's Publisher of Contemporary Romance

To Mary Ben Cretenoid,
for being such a special friend.
And for M,
for always and forever

SILHOUETTE BOOKS
300 East 42nd St., New York, N.Y. 10017

Copyright © 1990 by Sandra Canfield

ISBN: 0-373-09614-3

First Silhouette Books printing August 1990

Printed in the U.S.A.

Books by Karen Keast

Silhouette Special Edition

Once Burned... #435
One Lavender Evening #469
A Tender Silence #536
Night Spice #614

KAREN KEAST,

a nature lover whose observant eye is evident in her writing, says if she were a season, she'd be autumn. The Louisiana resident admits to being an over-achiever, workaholic, perfectionist and introvert. Author of more than a dozen romances and two short stories, she likens writing a novel to running a marathon, noting the same determination and endurance is necessary to overcome the seeming impossibility of the task and the many obstacles along the way. Still, happily married for over two decades, she is thrilled to have the opportunity to write about the "joy, pain, exhilaration and sheer mania of love" and to be able to bring two lovers together eternally through her writing.

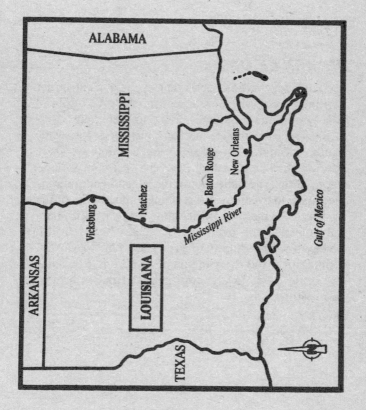

Chapter One

The slow, sexy love song slid into its final notes. Blending with it, as smoothly as cream in chicory coffee, came a deep, sultry, unmistakably feminine voice.

"That was an oldie, but definitely a goody, by the Captain and Tenille. C'mon, baby, do it to me one more time."

The imperative, part of the song, sounded like the disc jockey's personal plea. The words were said with the sizzling heat of a drop of water hitting a hot skillet.

"And this, all you Friday-night lovers, is Rori Kelsey coming to you from ninety-six point seven on your radio dial. That's KKIX—K-Kicks—right here in the heart of a shimmering, simmering, sweltering New Orleans. And this is Night Spice, the program guaranteed to season your night with romance, the program dedicated to the premise that one is such a lonely number.

"Speaking of numbers," the smoky voice continued, "the current temperature in the Crescent City is a muggy seventy-eight degrees, while the time is 11:35. Twenty-five minutes to go until the wrap-up of another show, another week. Twenty-five minutes to go until the bewitching hour of midnight. There's still time for you to call in a request for your favorite lady or favorite guy, and, if you don't have a special lady or guy...well, here's a song for you...especially from me."

As Rori manipulated Melissa Morgan's "Good Love" into play, she noticed that her hand was trembling. Not badly, but trembling nonetheless. In the four years she'd done the program she'd taken it from the bottom of the ratings to the tip-top, and she couldn't remember ever allowing her emotions to show, not even on that first scary broadcast. Usually she was at her steel-nerve best when on the firing line. Modesty aside, she knew that the attitude she projected, that she was sitting cozily in the home of each listener, was one of the reasons Night Spice was so successful. That, and the fact that nature had given her a voice to match the product—namely sensuality—that she peddled from nine o'clock to midnight every weeknight.

Clasping one hand in the other, she traced the source of the trembling. Part of it was fear—she couldn't deny it. Having her life threatened wasn't something to be treated cavalierly—yet, as one hour led into another through the long afternoon and evening, she'd found some other emotion taking precedence. It felt, tasted and smelled like anger, which in her practical book made it anger. What was it Stony was always saying? If it waddles like a duck and quacks like a duck, it probably ain't no Bengal tiger. Yeah, this was definitely a duck, webbed feet and all. She could feel the emotion building. How dare someone violate her privacy! How dare someone inject fear into her life! How dare—

At the thump on the glass front of the control booth, she jerked her head up. Her gaze met that of Stony Shanlon, the manager of KKIX, and her friend. He mouthed, "You're on the air," and pointed to the red flashing light that indicated she had an incoming call.

Rori instantly routed the call through her headset. "Night Spice," she said in a voice a newspaper had once described as sexy enough to make every good boy go bad. The same newspaper had written that her stunning beauty—the blue eyes and blond hair of a Nordic goddess—could make every bad boy proud he'd never been good.

The caller hesitated, and in that moment Rori's heart skittered. She felt another rush of anger. From now on, like it or not, everyone had become suspect.

"I, uh, is this Rori?" the man asked. Rori recognized the caller's nervousness, a nervousness she often heard from listeners phoning in. Her heart settled down, as she realized the call was genuine.

"Yeah, this is Rori. Who's this?"

"Ted."

"Hi, Ted."

"Hi. Look, I was wondering if you could play 'Somewhere Out There'? For Amy?"

"Sure thing. And thanks for calling, Ted. Have a good night."

"You, too, and, hey, Night Spice is my favorite show. And Amy's."

"Thanks, Ted. Thanks, Amy," Rori said, disconnecting the call and automatically pushing a button that would take the show to a pretaped commercial. Over the music that had already begun, Rori whispered seductively, "And now, let's share the night."

The commercial was for an internationally known perfume that had capitalized handsomely on the share-the-night slogan. According to the computer printout that Rori religiously consulted as a blueprint of each night's program, the tape was slated to run for thirty-eight seconds. That was the time she had to find the requested song. Swiveling in her chair, she searched the rotating iron rack behind her for the cart—slang for cartridge—that she needed. Because she encouraged callers to request only currently popular songs and because of her precise system of organization—a note on one of the many cork bulletin boards lining a wall of the control room threatened dire consequences to anyone who touched her rack—she had the cart in hand, and ready to play, in less than thirty-eight seconds. While she waited, her gaze slid to the stack of mail she hadn't managed to get through that afternoon. In fact, she hadn't gotten beyond the fifth or sixth letter.

I warned you to stop. Now I must stop you myself.

The words were indelibly etched in her memory, even though the police, hours before, had removed the typewritten threat. They'd also taken the two anonymous letters that predated the one she'd received that day. Those two letters, the first of which had arrived exactly two weeks before, had been nasty enough. One had read: *I'm watching you*, the other: *Stop corrupting*. Rori, though concerned, had tried to laugh them off. After all, they were not the first trash mail she'd received since she'd begun the show. People in high-profile jobs, especially one like hers, received their share of kook mail. Annoying as it may be, it was part of the territory.

Because of its bolder tone, though, she could not so easily ignore the third letter. When Stony had insisted upon calling in the police, Rori hadn't objected. Particularly since the newspapers were still full of the unsolved murders of three New Orleans women—all prostitutes, all strangled within a six-week span that had begun with the summer's heat wave, all with long, blond hair.

Rori fingered her riotous rabble of blond curls tumbling around her shoulders as she, ever the professional, keyed in to the fading commercial.

"Yeah," she said, her voice somewhere between a whisper and a sigh, "share the night with someone special. And here's a special song for a special lady. For Alice from Ted."

As the ballad waltzed onto the airwaves, Rori, in an action as automatic as breathing, slipped the headset to the back of her neck, angled her head toward the ceiling and exhaled a weary sigh. Only a few more minutes and she could call it a day, or rather a night. She could go home and shut herself away from the world. That thought led quite naturally to the advice Detective Pinchera had given her that afternoon. At the first opportune moment, she needed to have a dead-bolt lock installed. He'd said it calmly, but the words had sent dark frissons fleeing down Rori's spine. The thought that she might not be safe, even in her home, left her with a sick feeling. She took what comfort she could from the fact that all three of the anonymous letters had been addressed to the station. But wouldn't it be simpler than simple to get her home address? All anyone needed to do was check the telephone directory.

She was still trying to make peace with this troubling thought when the door to the control room opened and Stony, who, though he was only a few years beyond her thirty-one looked a good decade older, stuck in his prematurely balding head. "You all right?"

She glanced at him and lied, "Sure. Don't I act all right?"

"You just dedicated the song to Alice."

"So?"

"Her name's Amy."

Rori groaned. "Oh, God, I didn't. Tell me I didn't."

"It's no big deal—"

"Unless, of course, you're Amy," Rori bit out.

"Just correct yourself. And tell Ted the station'll pay for dinner for him and Amy. Hell, he'll be glad you made the mistake."

A look of self-disgust clouded Rori's face. She'd worked long and hard to get where she was, and here she was undermining herself with a sloppy performance.

"Hey," Stony said, interrupting her mental flogging, "cut yourself some slack. You've had a rough day. Oh, and by the way, I'm driving you home tonight."

Rori felt again the anger that had been building. "Look, I have no intention of altering my life-style just because some creep's sending me nasty notes. The jerk probably has the same mentality as an obscene phone caller. He has no intention of doing anything, he just wants to shake me up. And I refuse to be shaken." She prudently ignored the fact that her hand was trembling.

"Don't argue with me," Stony said. "You can't walk home in this heat."

"Since when did you become concerned about my walking in the heat?"

"Since tonight."

Rori frowned suddenly. "Why are you even here? You usually go home to Dottie and the kids at seven."

"I had things to do."

"Yeah, likely story." The discussion might have gone on, but the song ended. Rori dragged the headset into place and reached for the button that would put her on the air. Before she depressed it, she said to Stony, "We'll discuss this later. Now you'll have to excuse me while I throw myself at the feet of Ted and Amy."

"There's nothing to discuss," the station manager said as he closed the door behind him.

Within minutes, Rori of the already stupendous ratings had ingratiated herself with each and every listener. Her apology had been so sincere that Amy had called to say that hey, anyone could make a mistake. Amy and Ted, who turned out to be newlyweds, were thrilled with the free dinner. When Rori found out about the couple's honeymooning status, she threw in a gift certificate from one of the station's local advertisers, a lingerie shop that specialized in lacy garments just threads away from scandalous.

The rest of the show progressed normally, ending with a slow, soulful ballad by Lionel Richie. After that came the usual sign-off. "Well, late-night lovers, that's it for another night. The moon is high; the air is filled with lovers' sighs—and you thought it was the humidity! Until we meet again, Monday night at nine o'clock, be good to each other—be happy, be healthy, be in love." This last was so breathlessly rendered that it fairly floated on the airwaves.

And then the station stopped broadcasting.

Rori pulled off the headset and laid it on the console counter. As she combed her fingers through her hair, she saw one light, then another, fade within the studio. She heard the dim voices of the engineer and Stony, then Stony's footsteps outside the control booth.

"Let's go," he said. When she started to object, he cut her off. "Don't argue. I can be mean at midnight."

Outside, long night shadows draped themselves around the station's wrought-iron courtyard. Fern fronds, cascading in green confusion, whispered secrets to the creeping bougainvillea, while the tall ficus benjamina stood a poised sentry, its twined, leafy branches seemingly cocked to catch the faintest sound. The air, hot and humid and thick enough to slice, smelled heavy and dank. With danger? Rori had never thought so before.

Each weekday afternoon since she'd started the job, at precisely 2:50, she'd taken a cab to the station; each night, except for stormy weather, she'd walked the ten-minute trek from the station, which was located in the famed French Quarter, to her apartment, also in the French Quarter and only blocks away. She viewed the walk as therapeutic, a chance to unwind from the night's pressures. When asked if she wasn't taking a chance being out alone at night, she always replied that the French Quarter never slept. People were always milling around. However therapeutic, however crowded the French Quarter, Rori was suddenly relieved that her friend had railroaded her into accepting a ride. Though she hastened to tell herself it was only for tonight that she'd indulge in such pampering.

As she crossed the courtyard amid the shadows, breathing in the ebony danger, as she thankfully slipped into the passenger seat of Stony's car, the gravity of the day's occurrence struck her fully.

Someone had threatened her. Some stranger possibly meant her harm.

But why?

Even more important than that question was one other. Who?

At the moment KKIX left the air, a masculine hand with long, slender, bronzed fingers reached through the inky darkness to shut off the radio. The man lay sprawled across a rumpled bed in an attitude that suggested contempt for anything other than the most casual, a suggestion borne out by the fact that the bed hadn't been made since the morning before and the man wore a pair of gray drawstring sweat shorts, which he'd worn all day. As the silence closed in around him, he listened. Like a faint, frail echo, he could still hear the sultry, sexy, breathless, feminine voice.

"... be happy ... be healthy ... be in love ... in love ... in love ..."

He felt the same disbelief he experienced every time he listened to her, and he listened to her every night. He could not believe any woman could sound the way this Rori Kelsey did—like an angel and a tempting devil at the same time.

Angel?

Devil?

He mulled over the two words as he rolled from the bed and, barefoot, slipped to a window. From this third-floor vantage point, he stared into a pitch-black night dotted only with an occasional light from nearby apartments. Most of the apartments, however, in his building and the one across the way, were dark, their occupants settled in for the long, hot night.

Angel?

Devil?

Yeah, maybe that was the angle he was looking for. Allowing himself to hope, he slid through the bedroom's darkness into the kitchen, where he snapped on a light and, dodging balls of crumpled paper, threw his leg over a straight chair at a round table. His fingers automatically went to the keys of the manual typewriter. He began to type. Furiously. As though the idea had to be caught quickly or not at all.

She sounded like an angel, but there was something evil in the sticky sweetness of her voice.

He waited, restlessly, for the birth of another sentence to add to the first. Nothing came. Relax, don't panic, he told himself. Something'll come. Any minute now.

She sounded like an angel, but there was something evil in the sticky sweetness of her voice, he read as he absently trailed his fingers through the haze of hair matting his chest.

Still nothing came.

He reread the sentence, this time dragging the same hand through the dark hair of his head, hair mussed from countless finger rakings.

She sounded like an angel, but there was something evil—

"Dammit!" He jerked the sheet of paper from the typewriter, wadded it in his huge hand and slung it to the floor. It rolled to a spot within inches of a similar ball.

Scraping back the chair, he stalked to the refrigerator, yanked open the door—the few jars on the shelves rattled—and grabbed a cold can of beer. He ripped off the metal tab and slumped against the cabinet, downing a deep draft. Pleasant though it was, it did not wash away his frustration. It was a frustration he'd felt for so long that he was beginning to despair of ridding himself of it. It was starting to seem as much a part of him as his brown hair, his thirty-five years, which he wore reasonably well, he guessed, and his hungry disposition. His hungry predator's disposition, a friend had once called it.

Hungry predator's disposition.

It had served him well in his days as an investigative reporter, when he'd had to pounce on a story before someone else grabbed it away from him. He hadn't been an investigative reporter in four years, though. Unpredictable life had taken him in another direction. Then grim death had sent him in another. For nine months his life had been a sterile vacuum, filled with nothing but festering frustration and overwhelming, endless guilt. Try as he would to free himself, the hungry predator was trapped.

He swigged another couple swallows of beer, trying to empty his mind as he filled his stomach, hoping to find peace, even a moment's absolution, in numbness. He forced himself to think about the first thing that came to mind. The apartment. It wasn't necessarily furnished to his taste—too much chrome and glass, too much modish emphasis on black and white and canary yellow for a house that had been built in the 1840s—but he'd been lucky to sublease it. Especially on such short notice. Not in a long time had fate so conveniently played into his hands. His friend, the one who'd called his disposition hungry and predatory, had gotten an assignment that would keep him in Europe for the summer. He'd been more than happy to have a paying tenant to house-sit. So, six weeks before, at the beginning of a heat wave, his friend had moved out and he'd moved in—with one suitcase of clothes and a typewriter that should have been put out of its misery years before.

The old, three-story brick house had been restored and divided into ten apartments, each with a waiting list a mile long. Located in the French Quarter, the property was prime. As was the old house across the way. Both homes, within throwing distance of each other and sharing a courtyard, had been built for two North Carolina sisters whose father had given his permission for his daughters to wed men from New Orleans only if the gentlemen would agree to keep them together. History, perhaps helped along by the vivid imagination of rumor, read that the sisters were as different as day and night, one a gentle soul, the other a bona fide hellion.

Angel.

Devil.

The man's thoughts raced once more to the sultry voice on the radio. Like satin dragged across fevered skin, the voice whispered through his mind and senses, drugging him with its euphoric sweetness, its narcotic sensuality. And, like a narcotic, it had become addictive. He craved it in such desperate degrees that he should have been stunned. Instead, he felt nothing but need and want—desire that was expanding to include more than just the voice of this Rori Kelsey.

Guided by his hunger, the man, the can of beer still in his hand, stepped to the glass door leading to the apartment's wrought-iron balcony. He glanced across the courtyard to the companion house, to the third-floor apartment directly opposite to his own. He waited. Just as he did every night. When the light on the other side finally went on, the man doused the light to his apartment and, defying the stifling heat, slid open the door and stepped onto the balcony.

Rori flipped on the living room light.

For the first time since she had rented the apartment, the sight of the Pomele mahogany paneling didn't delight her, nor did the Travertine marble mantel or the way she had skillfully blended contemporary furniture with the few Victorian period pieces she could afford—all in a color scheme of tea rose and emerald green. The only thing that did delight her was the way the light hustled the eerie shadows to the far corners of the room.

Standing at the doorway, she surveyed the apartment before stepping in, an action that annoyed her even as she indulged in it. She would not allow some stranger to make her a prisoner in her home, she swore, closing the door behind her. As she made the vow, however, she was aware that tomorrow there would be another lock on her door, a stronger one, a safer one, and the thought sent a wave of relief lapping over her. She fought the urge to draw a chair under the doorknob. She also fought an urge to check the dark kitchen, open every closet door and look under the bed. If she gave in to the fear, there'd be no stopping it.

What she *would* give in to was the fatigue welling so heavily within her. What she needed was a good night's sleep, she thought, kicking out of her heels and padding in her stocking feet through the deep-pile carpet to close the draperies that stood open in front of the wide wall of glass leading to the balcony.

Midway through the living room, she unbuttoned her pencil-thin beige skirt and let it carelessly fall to the floor. She stepped out of it with only a hint of hesitation. Her legs, bare except for silk stockings, extended from beneath the French-cut opening of an ivory-colored teddy. Long and shapely, the legs had made it possible for her to model hosiery and underwear to pay for an education in radio communications. As she unbuttoned the beige crepe de Chine blouse, the rest of the low-cut, ivory-colored teddy came into view. With the blouse hanging open, Rori reached for the drape's draw cord.

She stopped . . . and let her eyes drift across the courtyard to the darkened apartment directly across from hers. He— whoever the man was—had obviously gone to bed. Curiously, the realization left her bereft. Tonight, with the weight of the world sitting squarely on her shoulders, his lights would have comforted her. During the past few weeks, a bizarre relationship had developed between them. Though not a single word had been spoken, a bond had been forged. At first she'd told herself she was interested in nothing more than his roses. Her own, despite her constant cajolery, compared unfavorably to the large, swollen blossoms decorating his balcony, blossoms that had not flourished under the gardening hand of the man who'd lived there before him.

In a candid moment, however, Rori had been forced to admit that it was the man who drew her. And why, she couldn't really say. True, he was unquestionably good-looking, with an athlete's lean, solid build, his muscles toned, his body tanned to perfection. But there was something more. Something about his eyes captivated her. They seemed . . . intense. That was the only word she could think of as apt.

He didn't merely see things, he visually devoured them as though trying to feed a painful hunger, as though he was unaccustomed to, intolerant of, playing games. He looked at her openly, blatantly, an action that normally she despised in a man. Somehow it seemed right for this one. To be honest, though she confessed it only marginally to herself, she liked the way his looking at her made her feel. It, he, made her feel alive, desirable, feminine . . . which was something she hadn't felt in a long while. For eighteen months, to be precise. Since she'd found her husband in the arms of another woman.

Suddenly Rori frowned.

Should she have remembered the stranger across the way when the police asked her about the people in her life? He *had* been watching her, which was precisely what one of the messages had alluded to, yet . . . Yet what? Wasn't the fact that he was so blatant about it enough to elevate him from suspicion? Wouldn't furtive glances have been more damning?

She frowned again, this time in disgust. This was exactly what she knew would happen—what she hated most about this whole thing. Everyone became a suspect: the caller who hesitated too long, the man who carried her groceries to the car, the man who delivered her mail, the butcher, the baker, the candlestick maker! The man across the way was just a neighbor. A neighbor who grew great roses. He'd never approached her. He never would. She had no wish for him to. And that was that. Verse and chapter.

Rori pulled the cord that slid the drapes shut.

Minutes later, as she tucked herself beneath white lace-edged sheets, however, she admitted that, stranger or not, she was comforted by the fact that a man she'd never met, and never would, was only a shout away.

From the depths of the balcony shadows, as though he had every right to be doing what he was, the man watched as Rori kicked off her shoes and walked toward the sliding glass door. Before she reached it, she had shed her skirt and unfastened her blouse, revealing a tantalizing eyeful of pale-colored teddy and paler skin. In those seconds before the drapes shut out the view—why had she hesitated?—he had a sensual impression of longer-than-long legs, a tiny waist and breasts that threatened to overflow their silky confines. He also noted the streams of curly blond hair that scattered and spilled in stylish disarray around her shoulders.

Her hair had first attracted him to her. He'd soon learned, however—from the maid who came with his friend's apartment—that the blond-haired woman across the way was the sensual voice on the radio. Her voice, sweet as honey, sexy as a wild fantasy, intrigued him. No, it did more than intrigue him. In some way he couldn't explain, it was going to free him from the trap in which he'd been ensnared for so long. She was going to be his salvation—professionally. And he did need to be saved. If someone didn't save him soon, he was going to go stark, raving mad. That is, if he hadn't already.

The sight of her in a state of dishabille only added to his madness. It also made him as hot as the night, and he felt his heartbeat tighten, quicken. Beads of sweat had popped the moment he'd left the air-conditioned interior for the cloying heat of the balcony. The salty droplets, influenced by his heated emotions, increased in number and ran in rivulets down his bare chest. He rolled the cold can of beer across his sticky skin, across pectorals religiously worked out; he allowed himself to whisper, "Ah," at the cool relief. Closing his eyes, he listened to the soothing babble of the little fountain nestled in the greenery of the lushly planted courtyard three stories below. The trickling, calming sound of the water acted as a balm to his inflamed body. Gradually, the image of shapely calves, flowing blond hair and the crescent halves of two full breasts receded, and he felt his heartbeat return to normal.

At first, out of profound guilt, he'd fought what she did to his body, but ultimately he'd had to accept it for the hard, painful fact it was. The unvarnished, unalterable truth was that a man didn't go without a woman for nine months and remain unmoved by the most beautiful woman he'd ever seen. Nature, which didn't care one whit about profound guilt, just didn't work that way.

As the man watched, Rori's bedroom light went on, then, seconds later, went out. He waited a little while longer, his eyes glued to the blackness at her window, before he dumped the remainder of the beer in the fragrant roses and stepped inside his apartment. The cool air swam over him, instantly drying the thick perspiration moistening his brow and chest. Negotiating the darkness, he headed for the bathroom, where he took a quick, cleansing shower. Once more finding his way in the dark, he toppled naked onto the rumpled bed.

As though he could see clearly, he angled his head toward the picture that rested on the bedside table. Despite the absence of light, he could see, deep in his mind's eye, the photograph of the woman. Immediately, as he always did, he felt pain. Guilt. And a thousand other negative emotions he'd stopped trying to catalog. The woman in the picture was beautiful, in a fragile, porcelain kind of way. Again, as though he could see clearly, his eyes lowered to the right-hand corner where the woman, in a handwriting as delicate as she was, had written an inscription. It was a message he knew by heart: To my darling husband, Blade, with all my love—Anna Marie. The words, proclaiming a love that at best was warped, had been written across an abundant mane of brilliant blond hair.

Rori's dream began just minutes after she fell asleep. She was in a sun-drenched field of flowers—red roses that grew by the thousands. Her neighbor stood in the middle of the field, basking in the sun, soaking in the sweet fragrance that swept the meadow.

"How do you grow such beautiful roses?" Rori asked him.

He leaned toward her and whispered something she couldn't understand. But then, maybe she couldn't understand because she couldn't concentrate. And she couldn't concentrate because he'd begun to stare at her. With his intense eyes. Eyes that suddenly made her warmer than the sunshine bearing down on her. She felt hot, weak, yet curiously filled with energy.

Suddenly he lowered his head and brushed his lips across her mouth so gently that it took her breath away. She wanted to cry at the beauty of it, because no man had ever kissed her so sweetly.

"No," she whispered, wanting his kiss more than anything, but fearing it.

"Why?" he asked, daring to kiss her again. This time she did feel her eyes tearing at the tenderness.

"Because I'm not what I seem. I'm a lie...a lie...a lie..."

The roses, their petals moving like velvety mouths, began to chant, "She's a lie...a lie...a lie..."

"She's a lie," her ex-husband said, appearing from out of nowhere. There was a woman by his side. A woman Rori had never seen. "She's the personification of femininity, yet she can't respond. Not even to her husband. She's cold as ice. Cold...cold...cold..."

The roses, as though an Arctic wind blew over them, froze and shattered into shards of red crystal. When her ex-husband began to make love to the woman, Rori ran across the slivers of glass, cutting her bare feet until they bled. Her neighbor, calling her name, started after her. She wanted him to catch her, yet she didn't. She didn't want him to know how flawed she was.

Abruptly, without warning, she grew afraid. Fear crawled up her spine, hastening her footsteps. She glanced behind her. Some faceless, shadowy someone was chasing her down the dark alleyways of the French Quarter. Someone who wanted to hurt her. From far away she heard the roses crying. Just as she heard herself crying. Then, just as she felt the faceless man's hands close around her throat, she awoke abruptly, a harsh scream spilling from her dry lips.

Nearby, Blade's sleeping body twitched with the onset of the nightmare. He moaned, trying to stave it off, but the misty dream, like a moorish fog, continued to descend. It was the same nightmare that had tormented his nights for the past nine months—the one he deliberately stayed awake to avoid. But there was no avoiding it now. It had dug in its sinister claws too deeply.

His fragile, beautiful wife—his Anna Marie—was dead and lifeless, her face pale and swollen from the cruel fingers of strangulation. Her head hung at an ugly, hideous angle; her blond hair, a macabre vision of loveliness, lay untouched. The room smelled of death—a sickly-sweet aroma that filled his nostrils and made his stomach churn.

Blade's body tensed, knowing what was coming next. He fought it by trying to drag himself awake. But he couldn't.

Instead, he helplessly watched as Anna Marie's corpse opened its eyes and fixed its gaze squarely on him.

"You killed me," her blue lips charged.

"No!" Blade cried, jackknifing to a sitting position as he fought free of the grasping dream. Cold sweat drenched his brow; his breathing rattled in the bedroom like a harsh hymn; his heart pumped with fast blood and heavy guilt.

Guilt.

God, how he hated that feeling! That cold, gray feeling. That no-matter-what-you-do-you-can-never-make-it-up feeling. But then why shouldn't he feel guilty? It was his penance.

Every murderer deserved to pay one.

Chapter Two

When the phone rang, Blade groaned an angry, sleepy protest. His eyes still closed, he groped for the receiver, found it and dragged it to his ear.

"Yeah?" he mumbled.

There was a hesitation, as though time had stubbed its toe. "Don't tell me you were still asleep."

Despite his drowsiness, Blade recognized the voice as Thad Abrams's. It took very little conjuring ability for Blade to imagine the editor of one of New York's most prestigious publishing houses in his swivel chair, his feet propped on the desk, a smoking cigar wedged in his fat fingers. Though the man gave the appearance of never having been excited in his middle-aged life, the truth was that in regard to books assigned to him, he was like a mother hen fussing over a brood of biddies. Blade knew, however, that the man's editorial skills were first-rate. They were one of the reasons Blade's three books, all best-sellers, had been so commercially successful.

"What time is it?" Blade asked, half his stubble-roughened face still buried in the soft pillow.

"Ten-eighteen your time."

Blade cocked one eye in the direction of the bedside clock and braved a look. The clock confirmed that it was, indeed, ten-eighteen, give or take a Saturday-morning minute. Out of habit, maybe as punishment, Blade glanced at the picture of his wife the way he had every morning for the past nine months—three-quarters of a year, a fraction of a hellish eternity. As always, she stared at him in silent reproof. As always, the nightmare lingered like a bad hangover.

"Up late, huh?" Thad asked.

Blade could hear the pleasure in his editor's voice. Thad no doubt assumed he'd been up late writing. Blade let him think it. There was no need to mention that he'd stayed up fighting sleep until the first light of dawn appeared, or that sometime shortly thereafter his body had simply given up the futile struggle.

"Yeah," Blade said, as he faced the inevitability of the day. He hauled himself to a sitting position and leaned against the bed's headboard. The sheet, the only cover he'd used during the hot night, crawled down his chest and pleated at his waist. "I guess this means you're working on Saturdays now."

"I came in to clear off my desk. I was out of the office yesterday. Besides, I wanted to call you on the watts line. I've tried a couple of times this week to get you."

"The phone's been out. They didn't get it repaired until Thursday afternoon."

"I thought it was out last week."

"It was. And the week before that. What can I say? I've obviously got a lemon of a phone."

"So, how's the book coming?" Thad asked, the phone already a forgotten issue.

Blade knew they'd arrived at the heart of the call. He admired the casual way Thad asked the question, as if he weren't waiting with bated breath to hear about progress on a book that had already missed one deadline.

"It's coming," Blade answered, thinking of all the aborted beginnings and the dozens of paper balls strewn around the kitchen floor. He excused the lie by telling himself that there was no need to excite his editor. His new deadline was the middle of October. It was only July. Surely there was still time . . . if only he could undam this damned writer's block! He thought of his blond-haired neighbor with her voice of molten gold, and of the book beginning he'd come up with last night. His mind was equally divided between thinking that the beginning was good, damned good, and wondering what Rori Kelsey was doing this sunny morning, when he realized that Thad Abrams had said something.

"Forget it," Thad said. "I must be out of my mind asking you what you think of it so far. You never think it's anything but a pile of crap. Somewhere along the way, however, the pile of crap always turns into a best-seller."

"Don't get cocky," Blade warned. "I may not pull off the miracle again." It might be a miracle to pull off a book at all, he thought, passing his hand over his face and trying to focus his bleary eyes. The sun was beaming brightly through the window, warming his thigh. It was going to be another hell-hot day. He'd bet good money on the temperature exceeding a hundred—

". . . a hundred bucks says you will. Because you figured out right up front what readers want. You never underestimate their love of violence—people love crime—and you never underestimate their intelligence. You never write down to them. Yeah, I smell another best-seller.''

"Maybe you just got a whiff of the garbage dump," Blade said. How long, he wondered, would it be before his editor tried to weasel the plot out of him? He knew the way he was keeping Thad in the dark about the book was enough to drive a saint to sin, but he also knew he was doing Thad a favor. If the editor knew there was no book, he'd be driven to more than sin. A nervous breakdown at worst. At best, he'd tug his chubby, chipmunk cheeks clean off his face, as though pinching and worrying the flabby folds of skin were just the things to ease anxiety.

"You sure you don't want to use me as a sounding board?''

If Blade could have remembered how to smile, he would have. "Yeah, I'm sure," he said, adding in an apologetic tone, "Look, I know I've been, and am being, impossible to work with. I appreciate the way you're giving me the space I need. I really do.''

"The only thing that matters is the finished product. Hell, that doesn't even matter! *You're* what matters. Getting your life back is what matters.''

"Yeah," Blade said, despairing that he ever would, but knowing the man on the phone meant what he was saying. Somewhere along the way, Blade and Thaddeus T. Abrams had become more than writer and editor. They'd become friends.

"I'll be honest with you," Thad said after taking a draw from his cigar, "I was worried about you. But I knew things would improve if you'd just get away from Phoenix for awhile. There were too many bad memories there. I knew if you got away, you'd be able to write again. Didn't I tell you that?''

"Yeah. You told me," Blade said, feeling guilty—so what was new?—that he'd let Thad believe he was on the mend. Just the way he felt guilty that he'd allowed the man to believe New Orleans had been a random choice. The truth was that he wouldn't have been able to explain his wish—no, more than a wish, a need—to return to the city where he'd met Anna Marie. She'd been happy here; they'd been happy here. Somehow, in some way even he couldn't understand, he'd hoped his return to New Orleans would perform an exorcism, negating everything that had gone so horribly wrong. If nothing else, perhaps it would remind him that there had been a time in his life when he and guilt hadn't been bosom buddies.

"Good news," Thad said, capturing Blade's attention again, "the book is scheduled for release next spring. Oh, by the way, the powers that be are talking about a tour to promote it."

"Lord, Thad, let me finish the book before we start promoting it."

Blade heard a panicked note in his friend's voice when Thad asked, "Everything is going all right, isn't it?" Ten to one, the man was pulling on his cheek until a whole winter's cache of nuts could have been stored inside.

"Thad, I said I'd have the book to you, and I will. Okay?"

"Yeah, sure. I'm not worried."

Well, you ought to be, Blade thought, but said, "Listen, about the tour, let's keep things as uncomplicated as possible. You know how I hate publicity."

"Will do. What have you decided about the house in Phoenix? You going to put it up for sale?"

An image of his wife, cold and lifeless, flashed through Blade's mind. On his empty stomach, the image threatened nausea. "I don't know. Probably."

"Well, I'm going to stick my Jewish nose in where it doesn't belong." Thad spent the next few minutes doing precisely that, though Blade took no offense. He was still too hung over from the restless night to take much of anything, except a few deep yawns. The general bent of his editor's opinion was to sell, sell, sell, fast, fast, fast. Blade had yawned again and was raking a hand through his tumbled hair when Thad asked, "By the way, what in hell is going on in New Orleans? The town made national news last night with those unsolved murders."

Blade's hand halted in his hair for a barely discernible second. "Yeah, well," he said, easing his fingers through the thick strands, "the world's a violent place."

"You can say that again," Thad answered, then poked his Jewish nose in the direction of the world's business. After waxing eloquently on the cure to universal ills, which seemed to center around tougher penalties for crime, he hung up with the admonition that Blade keep in touch. And keep writing. Because he could smell another best-seller.

Twenty minutes later, shaved and dressed in a pair of low-slung jeans, Blade followed the aroma of freshly perked coffee to the kitchen. A steaming mug in hand, he seated himself at the table and opened the morning paper. The *Times-Picayune*'s lead article was on the unsolved murders. Without stopping, even for a sip of coffee, Blade read every word.

A cup of lemon-spiced tea at her elbow, Rori read the morning paper. She had told herself she wouldn't look at the article on the murders, but she kept snatching peeks until she'd finished the piece. She wished she'd heeded her own advice. Reading the article had left her feeling antsy, unsettled—and wishing she was a brunette.

Don't be absurd, she told herself, rising and dumping the cold, untouched tea down the sink. The murders had nothing to do with the harassment she was receiving. All the victims had been prostitutes, a fact that eased her mind... until she considered the nature of the notes she'd received. Obviously their sender thought her a woman of less-than-high principles. Maybe in some twisted mind, her job was as immoral as prostitution. Rori's hand moved to the mass of wild, tawny curls cascading around her shoulders.

At a sharp noise from the living room, she jumped. Cursing her too vivid imagination, she pushed away from the cabinet and headed her feet, enclosed in canvas wedges, in the direction of the noise.

The locksmith, a clean-cut young man with an incongruous ponytail, looked up at her entrance. "Sorry about the racket," he said as he hammered out another deafening tattoo.

"No problem. I appreciate your coming on such short notice. And on a Saturday."

"That's my job," he said, squatting on lean haunches and making a couple of measurements before picking up a screwdriver and, with a seemingly effortless flick of his wrist, boring a screw into position.

Rori lowered her gaze to his hands. Strong hands. Hands that probably could throttle a throat... She let the threatening thought slither off before completing it. Instead, she focused on what the young man was saying.

"...the best. It's the safest lock made."

"That's good to hear," Rori said. She had given no indication why she'd requested the lock, so the man had no idea just how appreciated his recommendation of the product was.

"No, sir, no one's breaking in on this baby," he said. "It would be easier to punch a hole in the door."

"That strong, huh?"

He nodded. "Heaven and earth might move, but this door isn't going anywhere when this lock's bolted."

Rori allowed herself to take in, really take in, the hardware being installed. A rectangle of heavy-looking, shiny metal—brass, she thought—had been fastened to the door, unquestionably blemishing the glossy, fine-grained mahogany. Much larger than the original lock, it gave the immediate impression of being an anachronism, far too modern for its Victorian surroundings. Even from where she stood, she could see the dead bolt, a bar at least an inch and a half thick, jutting forward in search of the plate attached to the door frame.

Again, the grim reality of what was happening hit Rori. She was fortifying herself in her castle, hoping to keep the marauding vandals at bay. The dead bolt she was looking at might be the only thing between her and some wild-minded maniac. Suddenly the apartment's walls seemed to close in around her.

"I'll be out on the patio," she said, walking toward the sliding glass door.

"Sure," the young man replied. "I'll be finished here in a little bit." Just as Rori positioned her hand to open the door, he spoke again. "Can I ask you something?"

Startled, Rori turned.

"Are you that disc jockey on Night Spice?" he asked without waiting for an answer.

Relieved at the question—she wasn't certain what she'd expected—Rori smiled. "Yeah, I'm Rori Kelsey."

The guy grinned. "I knew it. The minute you opened the door and spoke. There's nobody in the world got a voice like yours."

Rori's smile widened. "I'll take that as a compliment."

"You can for a fact, ma'am." The grin grew. "Wait'll I tell the guys at the shop."

Embarrassed by the attention, Rori excused herself and slipped onto the patio. Despite her high-profile job, she was definitely a low-profile person. She liked her privacy—particularly since the divorce. Surely anyone could see at a glance that she was no longer whole, no longer the woman she'd once believed herself to be. She'd always thought it the cruelest of ironies that although she and her ex-husband had walked out of the marriage with exactly the physical possessions each had brought to it, Dwayne had gotten something of hers that was far more valuable. He had gotten custody of her confidence.

Rori tried not to dwell on the still raw and bleeding injuries of her divorce. She also quite deliberately refused to look at the neighboring apartment. It was only a brief glance away, but she averted her gaze. Instead, she gripped the iron railing, with its rich, lacy, filigreed design, and let the morning wash over her. It was going to be another scorcher of a day. Already the sun had traveled midway on its route toward high noon, though it would pick up strength as the day wore on, it was already powerful enough to pop perspiration on her brow. Beneath the T-shirt, which bore the call letters of the station and which she'd knotted at her waist rather than letting it fall loosely over her white shorts, she could feel drops of sweat gathering between her unconfined breasts. Just as she could feel the sun licking her bare legs with warmth.

Yes, it was going to be hot.

No, she would not look over to see if *he* was there.

She forced her mind to the subject of the weather. The muggy humidity was already making it hard to breathe. The air, like a chunk of concrete, sat suffocatingly still. Suffocating. As in choking. As in strangling. As in being strangled to death.

The dream flashed into her mind. Not that it had ever been far from it. Now, as she had in the black of the night, she could feel the strong, unyielding fingers closing around her throat, shutting out every drop of precious air. The same panicked feeling she'd experienced last night invaded her senses again. Her breath shortened. Her heartbeat sharpened. Her hands tightened around the wrought-iron railing.

Unable to stop herself, as though the stranger offered protection, she sought the apartment she'd been so willfully avoiding. The balcony was vacant. One part of her was relieved, another greatly disappointed. Taking a deep breath, she shoved the fear aside. Somewhere in the outfield of her mind, another part of the dream threatened her almost as much as the cruel fingers of the faceless man. It had something to do with the stranger in the nearby apartment...something that made her feel vulnerable... something that made the wall she'd built around herself seem less secure.

Annoyed with herself for dwelling on any aspect of the dream—after all, this was broad daylight!—she grabbed a pair of shears and began to trim the spent roses. Four enormous earthenware pots, each filled with a different colored bush decorated the balcony. As the shears snipped at the tattered remnants of a yellow rose, Rori wondered, as she had a dozen times, why the roses didn't look better. Too much water? Not enough? Too much sun, perhaps? No, the patio across the way had equal sun, yet the roses were so plump the stems could hardly support them. Maybe it was the fertilizer. Maybe she was using the wrong kind. Or not enough. As she continued to snip, she vowed to check with a nurseryman that weekend. Maybe he could point her in the right direction.

As she reached for a basket to collect roses for an arrangement, the feeling moved over her. It sweetly stung with all the subtle delicacy of a spider's lacy lair being drawn across her senses. And like an insect who'd come too close, she felt herself trapped in the gossamer threads. She was being watched. Something in that silent gaze compelled her to seek it out. She raised her head, then her eyes. Even before they connected with what she knew she'd find, her heart began a rushed rhythm.

The man stood on his wrought-iron balcony. No, Rori thought, the red rose she'd just plucked stalled in midair, he did a good deal more than just stand. His feet were planted at a bold angle that suggested domination, authority, command. She could easily have believed he was royalty surveying his subjects. Or maybe a man simply surveying a woman he wanted? At this last thought her already runaway heart bolted into a trebled beat.

Who was this man?

What did he want from her?

Why didn't she look away?

And why, why couldn't she remember what she'd dreamed about him last night?

Feeling the sun glaring on her back, she tried to remember the part of the dream before she'd grown afraid, the part that had had something to do with a field of red roses…and the man staring at her. God, even from the width of the courtyard, his eyes were magnificent, powerful, intense! She wished she could tell their color, but the distance didn't allow that kind of detail. Although it allowed observation aplenty—from his skin-tight jeans to the beer can he carried at eleven o'clock in the morning to his bare chest.

His bare chest.

She'd never before seen him without a shirt. It wasn't a sight she was likely to forget in the next hundred years. While she'd already accepted the premise that his shoulders were broad, she had miscalculated. Greatly. These shoulders spelled an awesome strength. Nor had she come anywhere close to guessing the quantity of hair on his chest, which was more than considerable. The crisp, curly brown-black mat, mingled with sweat, glistened in the crucifying heat of the Southern sun.

Why was the dream hiding at the edge of her memory? And why was it so important that she remember? Somehow, she knew it was a gentle counterbalance to the horror she'd dreamed later.

Gentle?

Yes. Intuitively, she knew he'd been gentle in the dream. Just as she knew he wasn't the kind of man who drafted poison letters. He wasn't the kind of man to waste time on threats. He was the kind of man to take action. Like now. Like the way his eyes relentlessly bored into hers, reducing her to the only object left on the face of the earth. As she watched him watch her, he raised the can of beer to his lips and drank. She could almost feel the cool liquid slide down her throat. She could almost see the moisture on his lips when he withdrew the can.

Lips?

She frowned . . . and fought a fluttery feeling. The dream had come a step closer. It took another, then another. Suddenly it came rushing back like the midnight tide of a wild sea. He had kissed her in the dream! Gently. Sweetly. So much so, he'd made her cry.

Vulnerable.

She felt vulnerable.

Helplessly vulnerable.

A rose fell from her fingers, plummeted three stories and splattered its velvet petals on the flagstone tiles below. At the same moment, the locksmith opened the sliding glass door, proclaiming that he'd finished installing the lock.

Rori whirled, telling herself that she had dropped the rose because the locksmith startled her. Not because she'd remembered the stranger's dream kiss. Not because its gentleness had eased a hurt she'd lived too long with and had never thought to have eased. Not because, as much as she wanted the pain to be healed, the thought of letting a man get close enough to try frightened her.

As the coolness of the air-conditioned apartment swirled around her and the locksmith smiled at her, Rori wondered when she'd become such a consummate liar.

Blade watched her disappear. He felt a keen sense of disappointment that she was gone. He also felt gratified that she'd been equally interested in watching him. The truth was that she was just as hot and bothered by him as he was by her. No man could misread those signals. Although it was quite possible she didn't even know she was giving them off, they were there. In the way her gaze didn't shy away from his. In the bold tilt of her heart-shaped face. In the unconscious toss of her hair, as though she was beckoning him nearer.

And why had she dropped the rose?

It was time for him to make a move. But it had to be the right move, he thought, emptying his beer into the pot of thriving roses. It had to be not only right, but perfect. Perfect like her beauty, like her voice. Perfect like the opening she'd unknowingly given him for the book. His eyes lowered to the shattered rose three stories below.

A sudden idea occurred to him.

An idea that was perfect.

* * *

Rori's doorbell rang at a little after four o'clock. She was in the midst of making out a programming schedule for the next week's work, something she often did on the weekend, much to the chagrin of Stony, who accused her of being a workaholic. He also accused her of deliberately spending Saturday nights alone. She couldn't argue either point.

Uncoiling the leg curled beneath her, she rose and walked to the door, where she cautiously called out, "Who is it?"

Only a sharp, clear silence answered her.

"Who is it?" she repeated, speaking more loudly. Though she hated herself for it, she could feel her heart pick up its pace.

Once more no one answered.

"Look," she said, taking her anger out on the unseen caller, "If you don't identify yourself, you can forget about this door opening."

Still nothing.

Pressing her ear against the door, Rori listened for any sound. She heard none. Surely perverts breathed heavily, didn't they? Or was that just obscene phone callers? Dammit! she thought, hating the sudden loss of control over her life. Knowing it was foolhardy, knowing, too, that she was doing it because she longed to hang on to some control, she defied common sense and cracked open the door.

"Look, I—"

She stopped. No one was there. Frowning, she was about to close the door when she saw the single rose lying on the hardwood of the hallway floor. Beside it, on the carpeted runner, lay a folded white note card. She bent, picked up both and stepped into the apartment...after taking a quick look down the empty hall.

The rose was bloodred, with petals as thick and perfect as if they'd been fashioned from the richest velvet. A heavy, sugar-sweet fragrance emanated from the delicate folds and danced alluringly beneath her nose. Rori's heart began to beat more rapidly, and she knew the rushed rhythm had to do with knowing whom the rose came from. Positively. Unequivocally. For confirmation, she flipped open the note card and read the boldly scrawled message: *To replace the one you dropped.* There was no signature. But then, why should he have bothered with one?

Rori's heart pounded a deep, blanketed thud-thud, as though the beats were being cushioned by the rose's velvet. Because her legs seemed weak, no longer willing to support her weight, she eased into the nearest chair.

He had sent her one of his roses.

She suddenly felt a bevy of contradictory feelings. On the one hand, she felt almost girlishly giddy, the way she had when her first tongue-tied beau had asked her out. On the other hand, she felt threatened. She and the stranger had been engaging in a silent affair for weeks. Affair? How odd that that word had come to mind, yet, try as she would, she couldn't deny its appropriateness. They *had* been having a silent affair. But it had also been a safe affair, harmless because of the distance they'd kept between them. Now, the distance had been shortened, the safety breached. The stranger was not a young, tongue-tied boy, but a full-fledged man. A man who would expect her to be equally a woman. If she wasn't careful, she stood to expose herself for the fraud she was.

Putting the stranger and the rose out of her mind— though she carried the rose to the kitchen with her—she returned to her work. Later in the afternoon, she turned down an impromptu dinner invitation from Stony. His wife, Dottie, got on the phone to put in her two cents' worth of pleading. Politely but firmly, Rori held her ground. Soon after, she tossed a green salad, reheated a cup of home-made soup and ate alone—the way she did most everything these days.

Ironically and with an emotional detachment that felt good, she wondered what Dwayne was doing this hot Saturday night. Probably preparing to pitch the sports news on one of the local television stations, then hit on the nearest woman he could find. She'd often wondered if their being in the same field—communications—had been part of their marital problem. Particularly since Dwayne had never seemed pleased with the level of success he'd achieved, believing she had eclipsed him. It hadn't taken a psychologist to know that their competition had not been healthy. At least, his competition with her. She sighed as she dawdled over her salad. Then again, maybe she was just looking for a convenient scapegoat for her own inadequacies. After all, it hadn't been Dwayne who'd been sexually dysfunctional.

Which brought the mental conversation she'd had earlier full circle, she thought, glancing at the rose. She would call a halt to this silent affair before it went a step farther. She would simply avoid her broad-shouldered, intense-eyed neighbor. That was the way to keep her emotions safe and sound. One humiliation per lifetime was all she could stand.

Hours later, however, as she crawled between the sheets and prayed that the dreams, the nightmare and the gentler one of the stranger's kiss, wouldn't return, the single red rose lay at her bedside.

Why had she laid it there?

It was a conundrum too complex to consider.

Blade worked on the book all afternoon—or tried to. Amid the ankle-deep hail of dozens of wadded-up pieces of paper, after he'd paced a hundred miles, back and forth, from room to room, he admitted that, without a miracle, he was never going to be able to write again. Except for the

opening sentence, which he became more and more convinced was damned perfect, not a word would come. Not a
lousy, stinking word!

As dusk began to fall, he talked himself into taking a
break on the theory that perhaps a rest would unleash the
words he knew were there waiting, if he could ever find a
creative bridge for them to cross. He hit the streets, trying
to walk off his pent-up frustration. Early on in his investigative career, he'd learned that walking helped him to unwind and clear his head. In the past nine months he'd logged
more miles than he could count—enough to fine tune the
muscles in his legs and put him in prime physical condition.

The French Quarter was just coming to life, but Blade
paid little attention to anything other than the placement of
one foot in front of the other. If he heard the shouts, the
laughter, the incessant, foot-tapping jazz coming from here,
there and everywhere, it changed not a grim line of his face,
eased not a wrinkle in his brow, lessened not a degree the
angle of his frown.

Within the hour, he returned to his apartment, ate a dinner he would have been hard-pressed to recall later, then
killed the evening by slow minutes and slower hours. Again,
he tried to write; again, he couldn't. At long last, exasperation sitting heavily on his senses, he cut off the lights and
glanced out the bedroom window toward Rori's apartment.

It was dark.

Was she asleep?

What had she thought when she'd found the rose?

He tried to imagine her reaction, but found that he was
tired of thinking, period. Sprawling across the bed, he threw
his arm across his closed eyes, seeking to empty his mind.
He was partially succeeding when the photograph of his wife

beckoned to him. In the darkness, he rolled his head toward it.

Why, Anna Marie, why?

He wasn't certain of the scope of the question he silently asked. Why had things turned out as they had? Why had she refused to trust him? Why hadn't he taken her more seriously? Why... He sighed. A thousand whys with not a single answer. And yet, one thing he knew for certain, even though he found it painful to admit. Their five-year marriage had been over long before she'd died. And that was another why that seemingly had no answer.

When Rori made up her mind, she could be as stubborn as a mule with a bad attitude. And she had made up her mind. She was not going to engage in eye contact with her neighbor again. The only thing was, it had been a lot easier to swear to it than to follow through with it—when he was perched on the balcony of his apartment, where he'd been for the past ten minutes, watching her fertilize her roses. She could practically feel his hot gaze blistering her back.

Ignoring the feelings tingling to life, Rori measured out the fertilizer the nurseryman had recommended and scattered it on the soil. She reached for a trowel. Out of the corner of her eye, she caught a glimpse of bare legs propped on what appeared to be a wrought-iron table. She quickly refocused her vision, though she could not entirely wipe out the image of well-muscled thighs.

She raked the soil. She watered it. She felt her T-shirt growing damp with perspiration, just as she could feel the lazy, hazy summer-day sun, of which the portable radio sang, tanning her shorts-clad legs.

Darn his hide, why didn't he just give it up? She wasn't going to look. She wasn't. And that was that. Final. Non-negotiable. As in, no way, José. Bending her elbow, she drew her arm across her forehead, wiping away the perspiration tunneling into her eyes despite the headband she wore. From beneath the shelter of her arm and the curls that fell from her unwilling ponytail, she peeked at him. She hadn't intended to; it just happened.

He was watching her. Thoroughly. Boldly. Making no pretense of doing otherwise. And unless she missed her guess, he knew she'd stolen a glance.

And then he did it. He levered his feet over the side of the table and stood, settling his gaze on her. His stare was so mesmerizing, so filled with power, that Rori lowered her arm, allowing herself, as though she had no will at all, to be drawn into it.

Did you find the rose? his gaze seemed to say.

She seemed incapable of anything, much less answering that the flower, now wilted, still lay beside her bed. She could not have explained why she hadn't thrown it away—any more than she could say why her heart was beating so profoundly.

Look away! she told herself. *Now! Before you get in over your head!* But even as she gave herself the command, she didn't look away. In the end, it was he who, without warning, broke eye contact and stepped into his apartment and out of view.

Rori breathed a sigh of relief. When she was thinking coherently again, she chastised herself for the inexcusable violation of her vow, and vowed anew to just stay the heck off the patio. Quickly, because the sun was riding high and hot, and because she was annoyed with herself, she fertilized the last bush. She was gathering the roses she'd cut, placing them in a latticework, thin-handled basket, when she heard the doorbell. She frowned. Leaving the basket of roses on the table, she walked through the apartment to the door.

"Who is it?"

Nothing.

"Who is it?"

Still nothing.

Suddenly she had the image of another rose lying on the hardwood floor, just waiting for her to claim it. It was an image that, despite her vow to forget the stranger, she found intriguing. She couldn't resist it. Throwing caution to the wind and the dead bolt aside, she opened the door just a fraction...her gaze going immediately to the floor.

There was no rose.

Instead, there were two feet, wearing huaraches, planted firmly, authoritatively where she'd expected to find the flower. Stunned, Rori let her gaze travel up the two bronzed, hair-dusted legs, over shorts as white as her own to a hand holding three cans of beer dangling negligently from a plastic casing. From there, as though she was a traveler who'd paid her full fee, she took the route over arm and shoulder and thick, wide chest, to the bluntly square chin, sloping cheeks and nicely shaped nose.

And then her breath ebbed away to only a sliver of air.

For she found herself staring into the eyes of the stranger. Eyes that were magnificent...powerful...unbelievably intense.

Chapter Three

Beer," Blade said, holding up the three cans with one strong index finger casually looped in a plastic ring.

Had he just announced that he was prince of some blue planet in a galaxy far, far away, Rori couldn't have been more surprised by his opening. So stunned was she that she stammered, "W-what?"

"Beer. The secret to raising roses is beer. Get 'em drunk and they'll bloom their little heads off."

Though his lips didn't so much as twitch with humor— why did she have the strong impression that smiling would be difficult for this man?—a certain spark did light his eyes momentarily. It faded as quickly as it had come, leaving his eyes once more a somber gray. Gray. Now she knew. His eyes were gray. A wood-smoke gray. A . . . haunted gray.

Haunted?

Yes, hidden in the dark depths of his eyes was a look that could only be called haunted, troubled, as though he stoically bore some great sadness. Somehow she knew she wasn't just being fanciful. The wounded creature in her could spot the wounded creature in him. She told herself that under no circumstances would she wonder about the why and what of his injury.

"Beer?" she repeated, focusing her attention.

"One can for the roses, two for the gardeners," he said, edging through the doorway. "As I said, the secret to growing roses is beer, coupled with benign neglect. The same is true for people, actually," he added cryptically. "The benign neglect part, that is. At least I have it on good authority that too much hovering isn't good. It suffocates, strangles."

The two words—suffocate and strangle—seemed to momentarily throttle the atmosphere, taking with them the last of the air, air that had become shockingly limited the second he'd walked into the room. Had she invited him in? She didn't remember doing so. But she must have, because he was standing in the middle of her living room. With all the commanding authority of a prince from a blue planet.

"Nice," he said, looking around the apartment. His eyes took in the rose-striped sofa, the spindly-legged chair she'd paid too much for at an antique shop on Royal Street but had never regretted buying, the small table with its ruffled floral flounce and plump crystal lamp. Beside the lamp sat a shallow bowl in which floated snow white, and lusciously fragrant, stephanotis blossoms. Rori's gaze followed her visitor's, taking in her surroundings as he did as though she'd never seen them before. "Nice," he repeated.

Her gaze wandered to his, stumbled, and for just a second she thought he was no longer speaking about the apartment but about her. It had everything to do with the way he was looking at her—particularly her hair. It had everything to do with the way she'd begun to tingle.

"You probably wouldn't get a horticulturist to agree," he said suddenly.

"W-what?"

"You'd probably never find a horticulturist to agree with my beer theory. At least one psychiatrist does, however, agree with the benign-neglect theory. As regards people, anyway." He nodded toward the sliding glass door and the balcony beyond. "Shall we?"

Rori had the crazy feeling that she was imagining all this, that the stranger wasn't standing in her living room, acting as though the two of them were long-time acquaintances, saying things that she only half understood at best. The glass door slid open.

"Damn!" He swore as the heat blasted him—them, for she found herself following him. "Is New Orleans always this hot?"

"We've had a record heat wave this summer," Rori heard herself responding, wondering why she wasn't asking questions instead of answering them. Questions like, Who are you? What are you? Why have you been watching me? And why are you on my balcony, uninvited guest that you are, squatting before my roses, preparing to pull the tab off a can of beer?

The curt clunk of metal tearing from metal rent the silence.

"I'm from Phoenix," the stranger said as he poured a dash of beer into each earthenware pot of roses. "It gets hot there, but the air is dry. This humidity'll kill you. How do you ever get used to it?"

"You don't."

"That's what my friend said," Blade answered, emptying the can of beer, setting it on the table next to the basket of roses she'd cut, pulling the tab off another can. This one he handed to her.

As though she were part of a foggy dream, she took it...and felt the chilled condensation moisten her palm. She heard herself ask, "What happened to the other man who had your apartment?"

"That's my friend. He's in Europe for the summer. I'm subleasing."

"Why?"

"It's hard to find an apartment—"

"No, why are you in New Orleans?"

Blade hesitated in the act of popping the other can. His eyes moved to hers. "I'm working here." At her silent question, he added, "I'm a writer."

"What do you write?"

This hesitation was longer, thicker, then he said, evasively, "This and that."

He cradled the beer can in his hand—his large, strong, bronzed hand, Rori noted, certain that at any moment the foggy dream would focus into reality. And when it did, she'd find herself alone...on the patio...in the heat. Maybe she was having a heatstroke. For that matter, maybe all the past weeks—the stranger, the stares, her speeding heart each time she saw him—was nothing more than a grand hallucination.

Holding the can up in a toast, Blade asked, "What shall we drink to? I know," he said, responding to his question before Rori could even pretend to ponder an answer. Tipping his can against hers, his eyes dark and smoky, he said, "To...hot."

In comparison to the word, which was delivered in a slow, sultry drawl, the sun knew absolutely nothing about warmth. But then, Rori had the curious feeling that the toast had absolutely nothing to do with the weather, but everything to do with that indefinable, strange, *hot* something going on between them. It was a feeling substantiated by the way his eyes, peering over the rim of his tilted can, roamed over her.

As the cold beer slid down his parched throat, Blade took in the rebellious curls escaping from the ponytail that swung at a jaunty angle each time she moved her head. The curls, a color between honey and toffee and streaked with lighter, buttery yellow tones, swirled in damp ringlets that clung to the nape of her neck, her temples, her peach-colored cheeks. From there, he looked into her eyes, which he couldn't have categorized if his life had depended on it. Except to say that they were blue. Which was like saying that the ocean was blue. Aquamarine. Her eyes were somewhere between green and blue, warm and hot, passion and lust. Dropping his gaze, he allowed his eyes to linger at the swell of her breasts, which were obviously full and bare beneath the T-shirt. Just as it was obvious that her long legs knew no reasonable end.

The unadulterated truth was that, at a distance, Rori Kelsey was the most beautiful woman he'd ever seen. Up close, he had no words to describe her.

As though she'd been brushed with fire, Rori burned in every spot his gaze touched. Her cheeks felt blistered, her eyes stung, her breasts . . . curiously, her breasts knotted as though thoroughly chilled. Abruptly she set her can of beer on the round redwood table.

"Who are you?" she whispered.

His eyes lowered to the lips that had posed the question. They were the most perfectly shaped lips he'd ever seen. The most sensual. And he wanted to do the most perfectly sensual thing to them. And then have them do it to him.

Once more dragging his eyes to hers, he said, "Blade. Blade Cavannaugh."

Blade Cavannaugh.

It seemed odd to have a name for the stranger. It equally seemed odd that he obviously didn't care to know her name.

Until it struck her that he probably already knew it. And had all along. That realization left her feeling...naked. As did the way he was staring at her. In the background the portable radio was playing something suggestively sensual about sexual healing. Rori suddenly had the overpowering urge to get away from this man, to a place where he didn't threaten to consume her, to devour her, with his eyes. And she had to go now, while she still had the power...and the will.

"I, uh, I need to get these in water," she said, noting the cut roses in the basket and using them as the excuse she was desperately seeking.

Blade said nothing, but watched as she gathered up the basket and entered the apartment. When she disappeared, he brought the can of beer to his lips and drank heartily but lazily, for he sensed that she needed a few minutes alone. Or, perhaps, it was he who needed the time alone. To deal with a heart that seemed intent on skipping every other beat.

"You forgot this, Rori," Blade said minutes later from the kitchen doorway. He held her can of beer.

Rori jerked her head upward, practically toppling the vase in which she was arranging the flowers. Her name on his lips, proving beyond a doubt that he did know it, startled her. Or maybe it was just the substantive way he filled up a doorway. She noted that his shirt had grown moist with perspiration and that it clung to his broad chest.

"You know my name," she said, trying to sound accusatory, but succeeding only in sounding breathless, for she could remember all too vividly the sight of him without a shirt...and the dark, copious hair that matted his broad chest.

Walking forward, he set the beer can on the countertop, then cocked a hip against the cabinet. He towered above her, making her model's height seem inconsequential. "I know lots of things about you, Rori Kelsey,'' he said so softly, so huskily that the rose in Rori's hand was totally forgotten. "I know you work for KKIX, that you host Night Spice, that you have the sexiest damned voice I've ever heard. I also know that you have a skimpy little teddy that drives me wild.''

Rori's heart had been increasing in rhythm with each disclosure he made. At the mention of the teddy, her heart stopped. Cold. She'd never dreamed that he'd taken, had the opportunity to take, such presumptuous liberties.

"You've...you've been watching me." Her voice was thick with incredulity, and she was suffused with a feeling she couldn't define. Fear? She'd have to think about that one. Irritation? She didn't have to think about that at all. "How dare—"

"You've been watching me, too," he pointed out casually, and with maddening truth. "We've been watching each other."

"Who are you?"

"I told you. I'm Blade—"

"What are you?"

"Just a man—"

"What do you want from me?"

He paused, lending just the right emphasis to his gravelly drawl. "The same thing you want from me."

Rori's heart slammed against her rib cage. Part of her reaction came from his nearness, another part from the picture that leaped to mind. It was an image of her flat on a bed, this man, unclothed and fully male, towering above her. "I...I don't know what you mean."

"Sure you do. You know that I'm attracted to you."

Rori heard a tiny, breathy sound and wondered if it came from her. She thought it had.

"And, furthermore, we both know you're attracted to me."

Rori swallowed hard. "Are you always so blunt?" she asked.

"Yes," he replied . . . bluntly.

"Are you always so instantly attracted to a woman you don't even know?"

"No." And that was the God's truth if he'd ever told it, Blade thought. "Are you always so instantly attracted to a man you don't know?" he countered.

"You're the one who says I'm attracted to you," she pointed out.

"Then deny it."

The command was a simple one. She should have been able to comply easily. Yet she couldn't manage a single word of disavowal. Instead, she seemed lost in the magnificence, the power, the intensity of his eyes.

"No," he said hoarsely, raising his hand and slowly, sensuously trailing the backs of his fingers down her upturned, very exposed neck, "I didn't think you could."

Rori shivered from the hot sensation skipping down the delicate skin of her neck. She heard an unfamiliar noise coming from her throat—a purr, a moan . . . something she was certain she'd never heard before.

The sound she made at his touch seemed to clip Blade at the back of his knees. "God," he whispered, "every sound you make is sexy!" At the base of her throat, he turned his hand and splayed his fingers wide. His thumb rested in the hollow of her throat, feeling an erratic pulse there that further destroyed him. His fingers tightened, as if to capture the eroticism she was exuding.

Rori felt his strong fingers wrap around her throat. The pressure, though not hurtful, reminded her of Friday night's nightmare—when the faceless man had strangled her. She felt a trickle of fear, but it was soon displaced by an entirely different kind of fear—one that gushed through her like a tumbling tide. This fear stemmed from the desire that suddenly ran rampant in her veins. Suddenly she could only remember the first part of the dream, the kiss, this man's kiss ... and in that moment she would gladly have given up all that she owned for the gentle, healing brush of his mouth against hers.

But if he kissed her, he would discover her secret. And she'd rather die than reveal her inadequacy. "I ... I think you'd better go," she whispered.

Hearing a note of desperation in her tone, Blade slowly released his hold on her. He stepped back, allowing his gaze to fall from hers.

Rori watched, even partially followed, as Blade turned and ambled toward the front door. There, he paused and looked at her. The message in his eyes was clear. Without the slightest doubt, they would be lovers. Not tonight. Maybe not tomorrow night. But one night. Soon. And no lock, however sophisticated, would be enough to keep him out.

Then he was gone, leaving Rori unsettled and frightened. Unsettled because she wasn't really certain what had just happened. Frightened because for one heartbeat she'd entertained the notion—the dangerous notion—that things could be different with this man.

The next two days were the hottest ever recorded in New Orleans. The sun, a searing sphere of orange, broiled everything caught beneath it. People, sweaty and panting, dragged their limp bodies from one air-conditioned setting to another while radio and television newscasts warned of the dangers of heatstroke. The newspapers warned of another consequence of the oppressive heat: crime rose in direct proportion to the mercury. Though the newspapers didn't come right out and ask if there would be another strangling of a blond-haired prostitute, the question was implied.

By Wednesday the Crescent City happily acknowledged two things. The temperature had lowered to a "cool" one hundred and one degrees, and there had been no serious incidence of crime. One city figure commented sarcastically that obviously the killer didn't read the newspaper... which was about the only real lead the police had.

On that Wednesday, Blade unhappily made two personal observations: his book, which had progressed no further than the first sentence, was about as cold as the weather was hot, and Rori Kelsey was avoiding him. Curiously, he found the first easier to deal with than the second. Perhaps because frustration with the book was old hat. Perhaps because he couldn't get Rori out of his mind. He couldn't forget the sea-blue of her eyes, the flaxen curls that had fought against the ponytail she'd forced them into, the pulse that had jumped against his thumb as his fingers had encircled her neck. The excited pulse. She was as drawn to him as he was to her—hell, she hadn't denied it when given the chance!—and just knowing that she was equally interested was a strong aphrodisiac. Too strong.

So why was she avoiding him? Why had she not once been on her balcony?

He knew the answer to that, too. He'd seen the desperation in her eyes, heard it in her voice. Whatever it was that was happening between them was moving too fast for her. It fell under the category of unbelievable, bizarre, scary. He understood, because he felt it, too. Still, it didn't change the fact that something was happening between them. Something that had never before happened between him and a woman.

Not even between him and his wife.

Anna Marie had inspired strong emotions within him, arousing his deep protective instincts. She had been a fragile, hothouse flower needing vigilant tending. She'd been a waif, a fairy, some frail creature not intended for this harsh world. And he had loved her to distraction—God, how he'd loved her!—but the pure animal magnetism of what had transpired on the balcony between him and Rori never would have happened between him and Anna Marie. Quite simply, Anna Marie wouldn't have understood that such a powerful need could exist.

But Rori Kelsey understood. She might be shocked by it, she unquestionably was rebelling against it, but she understood.

She understood.

Rori clearly understood what she was doing. She was blocking Blade Cavannaugh from her mind. She was working even longer hours than she usually did, out of the need to keep her mind occupied. She refused to consider the discussion that had taken place Sunday. Discussion? No, invasion was a more appropriate word. Blade Cavannaugh had invaded her apartment, her life, leaving behind memories she didn't want, feelings that frankly, she didn't know how to deal with. Nothing, no one, like Blade Cavannaugh had ever happened to her... and she didn't want him happening to her now. The solution was simple. She just wouldn't allow him entrance into her life. She'd block him out of her mind. In some far corner of her thoughts, she realized that working so hard not to think about her neighbor had created one positive side effect. She'd had little time to brood over the threatening letters, either.

At the moment she had time to consider nothing beyond the fact that the on-the-air button was glowing red. Easing into her professional persona, she said, "For you R and B fans, that was Anita Baker singing to us about sweet love.'' Rori whispered the last two words, making them sound like candy confections spun out of sugar and syrup. ''And you all know how sweet love can be. It can also be a little wild...a little tempestuous...even a little naughty—'' here her voice purred ''—and oh, so nice. Call and tell us about it if you're having a nice, sweet evening. And if you're having a wild, naughty evening—'' Rori's voice lowered dramatically to accommodate the sentiment ''—sorry we disturbed you.''

A flashing light indicated an incoming call.

''Night Spice,'' Rori crooned, ''you're on the air.''

''Hey, Rori,'' the young man said. In the background she could hear a chorus of male voices. ''This is Chi Beta Chi over at Tulane.''

Rori recognized the local university's fraternity. She'd spoken with the fun-loving guys before. ''Well, hello, Chi Beta Chi. You guys having a nice, sweet evening or a wild, naughty one?''

The chorus, filled with laughter and catcalls, surged louder. Over the din, the caller said, ''Wild and naughty. We're cuddled up beside textbooks. Listen, I'm calling to tell you we just voted you the woman we'd most like to be shipwrecked on a desert island with.''

Another voice shouted, ''Yeah, Rori, let's get shipwrecked together!''

Someone else cried, ''Before the chemistry exam tomorrow!''

Rori laughed, though as always she was uncomfortable with the disparity between her professional and private images. She lived with the secret fear that one day someone would be smart enough to see beyond the lie. Hoping that someday wouldn't be tonight, she said, ''I thought three out

of four college students preferred to be shipwrecked with a
leading brand of aspirin.''

Whoops and hollers followed.

"Thanks for the honor, guys," Rori said, "and thanks for
calling. Now hit those books." She broke the connection,
adding, "Here's a song for my friends at Chi Beta Chi. A
little something from Whitney Houston."

The strains of the currently popular song glided onto the
airwaves. Rori checked the computer printout. The song
would run for two minutes and thirty-seven seconds. Add
to that the thirty-one-second commercial, and she had all of
three minutes and eight seconds to call her own. She pulled
the headset onto her aching neck. It had been a long night—
made longer by the fact that she'd arrived a couple of hours
early. She'd told everyone that she'd come in to catch up on
some paperwork, but the truth was that she just wanted out
of the apartment. She wanted to get away from *him*.

Him.

He had a name now—Blade Cavannaugh—and somehow that seemed like one more intimate step taken. But
what exactly was it a step toward? Nothing, she told herself
hastily, now as grateful that her free time had run out as
she'd been grateful to have it minutes before. She levered the
headset into place.

"Lace...the shop that has everything you need for that
special evening. And we have a special evening going here.
It's eleven—" Rori glanced at the huge black and white
clock on the wall "—actually, it's eleven-eleven right here
in the Big Easy. The temperature's seventy-nine, which is
cool compared to what we've been having. If you're going
out, though, be sure to take a cleaver with you. You're going
to have to hack your way through the humidity. Speaking of
humidity, there's a rumor floating around that we may actually get rain tomorrow. So dust off that umbrella...if you

can remember where you put it...and get ready for some of that wet stuff. C'mon, rain,'' she breathed, her voice a beckoning beacon in the night, ''and c'mon, listeners. Give me a call. I'll play a song for you...or we'll just talk...just you and me as we make our way toward midnight.''

The incoming call light flashed.

''Night Spice. You're on the air.''

''Rori?''

The single word wrapped around her like the warmest of woolen blankets, stifling her breath until it seemed to stop altogether. It was the voice of the man she'd been trying to forget all week. In that moment it struck her how foolish she'd been to try to block him out of her mind. How did you block something out of your mind when that something, that someone, filled it so completely?

As though his voice triggered the memory, she realized that she'd dreamed of him again last night...maybe the night before, as well...the same gentle kiss that devastated her senses. Even now the thought of its tenderness sent a desperate longing through her. God, how she needed the healing it promised. Out of the corner of her eye, she saw the technical engineer looking at her. She cut her gaze to his and saw the question on his face. Only then did she realize how odd her prolonged silence must seem.

''Yes, uh, this is Rori Kelsey,'' she managed to get out. She noted that her hand—the one unnecessarily still depressing the telephone button—was trembling. Unlike last week, the trembling was not out of fear. The fact alone was frightening.

''I'd like you to play a song for—'' he hesitated ''—for someone special,'' the familiar voice said. ''I haven't seen her in awhile. I've missed her.''

Rori felt her throat constrict. The feeling reminded her of his fingers moving up and down her neck before tightening, to capture the pulse at the base of her throat. The momentary fear that his caress had aroused had instantly been supplanted by warm, melting sensations of an entirely different nature—feelings revived now by the vivid memory. She felt weak.

"W-what song?"

"Do you have 'I'll Be Watching You' by the Police?"

His request gutted her chest of what little breath she'd managed to hang on to. She heard the soft swishing sound escaping over the airwaves.

"Rori?" the familiar voice said.

"Yes . . . yes, I . . . I think I have it here somewhere."

"Thanks. Remember, it's for someone special." He didn't give Rori time to disconnect, halting the call himself instead. Rori was left with the dial tone buzzing in her ear.

Glancing up, she saw the engineer still watching her. Throwing the program into an unscheduled commercial, she fought to regain her composure. Easy, she told herself as she removed the headset and stepped into the hallway. She had to appear normal . . . even if her heart was beating madly. She searched quickly through the shelves of past hits. Within seconds, she closed her trembling fingers around the cart she wanted. She had started into the control booth when the engineer called to her.

"Hey, Rori, everything all right?"

"Yeah," she answered, overbrightly, brandishing the cartridge in her hand as though it was the source of her peculiar behavior. "I hate it when they want something that isn't current." She closed the door and seated herself at the console.

In seconds, in a deceptively normal voice, she was introducing the song . . . along with its dedication. As the music played, she tried not to think of those dark, intense eyes that hinted at a hauntedness. But the more she tried not to think of them, the clearer they became. She tried, too, to ignore the snippets of conversation running through her head.

"I know lots of things about you, Rori Kelsey. I know you work for KKIX, that you host Night Spice, that you have the sexiest damned voice I've ever heard. I also know that you have a skimpy little teddy that drives me wild."

Rori shut her eyes, but more bits of conversation closed in around her.

"What do you want from me?"

"The same thing you want from me."

"I ... I don't know what you mean."

"Sure you do ... sure you do ... sure you do ..."

Somehow she got through the song, just as she somehow got through the remainder of the show. Declining the engineer's offer of a ride, as she had the two previous evenings, she exchanged her high heels for tennis shoes and started for her apartment. She'd been determined to resume her nightly walk home, despite the threats. Tonight she needed the exercise to clear her head. She wished he hadn't called. She wished he wasn't watching her. She wished he had just stayed comfortably, safely, outside her life.

Plunging through the muggy night, ignoring the shadows and eerie sounds she hadn't noticed until the week before, she arrived at the apartment house at twenty after twelve. Passing the row of hallway mailboxes, she made her way to the antiquated, grill fronted elevator and went into the car. After pushing the button for the third floor, she waited impatiently for the car to lumber up amid the groan of grinding gears. She opened the grill doors to the accompaniment of a loud grating noise, then stepped out of the car. She hesitated, listening, looking in a way she never had before the threats. Finally, she made her way down the deserted hallway.

From a few feet away, she saw the single rose lying in front of her door. Her heart began to thump...with what emotion she wasn't at all sure. Stooping, she picked up the red flower. Its sweet fragrance was like a gentle assault. Drawing it slowly to her nose, she inhaled. Though she wished he hadn't called, wished he wasn't watching her, wished he'd stayed outside her life, she had to admit that it felt nice to know she wasn't alone. In the world. In the city. In the night.

Chapter Four

Damn!'' Blade muttered, propping his elbow on the worn typewriter and thrusting his fingers through his hair.

The maid, a tall, bulky woman with cropped black hair and close-set black eyes, glanced up from her dusting but said nothing. She picked up the brass lamp, making it appear as light as a feather, and drew the dust rag across the console's glass-topped surface.

When she'd arrived that Friday morning, Alice Yearwood had found her new employer at the dining-room table. She often found him at the smaller kitchen table, but it was no wonder he'd had to change locations. One could hardly cut a walking path through the ankle-deep balls of paper strew around the kitchen. Intermingled with the wadded-up paper were candy wrappers in every variety known to junk-food fans. It had taken her a good ten minutes to pick up the trash, and by the time she had, he'd already started scattering a whole new batch around the dining-room floor.

As if on cue, Blade ripped a sheet of paper from the machine and crushed it in his fist. Tossing it to the floor wasn't enough to vent his frustration, so he threw it against the wall. He shoved the chair back and padded to the kitchen on bare feet—as always, he'd kicked off his shoes to work. Yanking open the refrigerator door, he snatched up a can of beer and popped it open. He emptied half the contents before coming up for air.

"Would you like a sandwich to go with that?" Mrs. Yearwood asked from the doorway.

Blade looked at his watch. It was straight-up noon, but he couldn't have been less hungry. More to the point, he wasn't hungry for food. He *was* hungry, desperately hungry, for a break in his writer's block; he was hungry, again with something akin to desperation, for the sight of the woman next door; he was hungry for the rain that had been promised yesterday but had fizzled out, leaving only taunting gray skies. Food didn't interest him.

"No," he said, remembering at the last minute to add, "thank you."

Mrs. Yearwood nodded, then disappeared into the dining room.

Momentarily, Blade heard the roar of the vacuum cleaner. He sighed. Why in hell hadn't he gone into domestic work? A housekeeper didn't have to wait for the creative urge to strike before she could vacuum and dust. A housekeeper didn't have to rely on undisciplined magic to make a bed, run a dishwasher or fold a load of clothes. A housekeeper's sanity wasn't in the hands of an always fickle, sometimes contrary muse.

Sanity.

Blade wondered if his was slowly slipping away. He still wasn't sleeping well, and when he did manage to doze off, his peace was fractured by the nightmare. Awake, he was riddled with guilt. It was a hell of a choice. Or, more aptly, no choice at all. He seemed to have no will in the matter, just as he didn't seem capable of moving the novel—the one due in three short months!—beyond the first sentence. He felt cornered, trapped.

In a symbolic gesture of escape, he opened the sliding glass door and stepped onto the balcony. Ignoring the heavy heat that surrounded him, he searched out the balcony beyond. It was vacant. He hadn't seen her since Sunday, hadn't talked to her since Wednesday night—if calling the station could be considered talking to her. Still, he listened to her show every night and waited each evening for her lights to go on—and thought about her. Whatever was between them remained. Why else did thoughts of her heat him to the boiling point? Why else was she avoiding him?

As if to drag himself back to the moment and the pressing need to produce some typewritten pages, he drew his hand across his face. *Think. Think!* He replayed the opening sentence in his head as he had a thousand times. *She sounded like an angel, but there was something evil in the sticky sweetness of her voice.* Great, Cavannaugh! Now, what goes with it? Suddenly the ever-teasing muse cracked open a door, and an idea occurred to Blade. Emptying the beer into the roses out of habit, Blade entered the apartment and made his way to the typewriter. Flopping into the chair, he rolled in a sheet of paper and began to pound the keys. At one point the furiously returned carriage toppled an empty beer can, sending it rolling across the table. Blade barely noticed.

One hour and six pages later, he ran out of steam. Plowing his fingers through his hair, he read over what he'd just written. With each page, a leaden heaviness settled more surely in his heart. By the time he'd reached the sheet still in the typewriter, he knew. What he'd written was garbage. Not even good garage. There were more things wrong with it than he could count, but principally there was no focus. Just as there had ceased to be a focus in his life. Unless, of course, you counted guilt. For the first time in a long while, he felt like crying. But society decreed that strong men didn't cry—not over six useless pages. The same judgmental society would have permitted him to cry at his wife's death, at her funeral—but, perversely, no tears would come then. Nor had they since.

Tearing the sheet out of the typewriter, Blade ripped it and its five compatriots into shreds and finally did what he should have done weeks before: he conceded defeat. He wasn't going to have this book finished in three months. In three years. And he may as well stop kidding himself. He owed it to his editor to level with him. Thad would go into a panic, but Blade had no option. The truth was, he should have told him already.

Stalking to the phone, he punched in the New York number, wedged the receiver between his head and shoulder and jammed his hands on his lean hips. As he waited for the phone to ring, he wondered if he was getting an ulcer. The burning in his stomach suggested he might be. If so, it would be an ulcer well-earned...

Blade frowned.

Why wasn't the phone ringing? He hit the dial button once, twice, three times. Nothing. The phone was dead. As dead as his career. The only thing that seemed to be alive was his anger. And it was not only alive but thriving.

"Damn!" he swore, slamming the phone down.

Mrs. Yearwood looked up sharply, as though unaccustomed to the harsh tone and profane word.

"You'd think I hadn't paid the bill," Blade mumbled as he crossed the room, grabbed the sneakers still under the table and rammed his feet into them. Squatting, he tied the laces with such force that they threatened to snap. He wished they would. It would help to fuel the anger that was already rising sky-high. It was an anger he wanted to nourish...simply because it felt good. Damned good! "Mrs. Yearwood!" he called, then, realizing she was in the same room, he lowered his voice. "The phone's out again. I'm going to report it. Just lock up when you finish." The implication was that he wouldn't be coming straight back and that, since she usually left at midafternoon, she'd be gone before his return.

"Yes, sir," she said, effortlessly moving a chair to vacuum beneath it. A dozen times Blade had offered to move the heavier pieces of furniture, a dozen times he'd been rebuffed. He fought the urge to offer once more. It was easier than usual, consumed as he was with his own misery.

Minutes later, at ten after one, he stopped by the office apartment of the building's live-in caretaker. Donald Weiss, a retired heavyweight boxer whose claim to fame was that he'd once been KO'd by Muhammed Ali, was, in essence, the premises' troubleshooter. He acted in the same capacity for the nearby house. Blade asked to use his phone, called the phone company and vented some of his anger. The phone company apologized profusely, promising to send someone out immediately. Blade, none too nicely, suggested sooner.

After asking the caretaker to let the repairman in with the passkey, Blade hit the streets for a marathon walk. He began by cutting through the courtyard to the adjacent building, intending to exit through its front door. It was a path he'd chosen lately to avoid some street construction that no one seemed in any hurry to complete.

As always, he looked around to see if, perchance, Rori was in the hallway. As always, she wasn't. He did, however, nod at the mailman who was distributing the daily mail into the neat row of mailboxes in the building's foyer. The mailman nodded as Blade disappeared out the door.

Blade no had idea how long he'd walked before his anger began to cool. He knew only that at some point his strong, steady heartbeat began to match his long, even steps. Chartres Street. He was on Chartres Street with its two Napoleon Houses, one of which was the site of a plot to rescue Napoleon from St. Helena. The Beauregard-Keyes House, once the home of a wealthy New Orleans auctioneer, also stood on the street, near the Old Ursuline Convent, where the Ursuline Sisters, for a long time the only teachers and nurses in the city, lived. There was an art studio nearby.

From out of nowhere came memories of another art gallery in New Orleans. Suddenly it was a winter-chilled February, the crowd wild with Mardi Gras celebration. Suddenly it was six years before. He was in the city to report on the Mardi Gras, an assignment he'd considered beneath his investigative reporting skills, but a job a well-known magazine was paying him top dollar for. Never having felt much one way or the other about art, he'd never understood why he'd gone into that particular gallery at that particular hour on that particular day. He couldn't remember ever going into a gallery before. But he had gone into this one... and, in so doing, had changed two lives.

Even now, as he walked in a sweltering maze of heat, he could feel the gallery's interior coolness; he could hear its reverent hush and the gauche fall of his footsteps on the old wooden-planked floor; he could smell the subtle fragrance of paint and oil and acrylic. He could see Anna Marie.

She had been... different. With her snow-colored hair, lavender eyes and a complexion so pale he'd at first suspected she used white powder, she was physically different in a fragile, tangible way from other women he'd known. She was also different emotionally. There was something ethereal about her, a spiritual otherworldliness. She had been an artist—the gallery had been displaying some of her paintings—and he had put her difference down to the sensitive artist's temperament he'd heard about. He'd wondered then, and still did, if part of his attraction to her had been that she'd appealed to his investigative personality. Perhaps he'd been intrigued by the question, what makes this woman tick? Or maybe she'd just appealed to his masculine strength. He'd sensed from the beginning that she needed protecting. It had only been later that he'd realized the person she most needed protecting from was herself.

In the eight months that followed their meeting, they wrote to each other and talked on the phone regularly. Three times he went to New Orleans. On the third visit, she'd asked him to marry her. Just like that! Without a hint of warning! Her forwardness, so atypical for her usually shy disposition, had surprised him. He'd also found it intriguing—another bizarre piece of her personality puzzle. Because he was in love with her, he'd said yes. They had been married a week later. A week after that, they'd gone to his home in Phoenix.

Thus began their agony and ecstasy.

Looking back, he guessed he could see his complicity. Her psychiatrist had referred to him as an enabler. He'd resented the label, possibly because he'd recognized its truth. The psychiatrist had also spoken of benign neglect—which he had assured Blade everyone needed a bit of to remain emotionally healthy, to develop a sense of self. Even Anna Marie needed to be left alone sometimes, although she gave the impression of needing constant attention. It was an attention Blade had given because he hadn't dared not to. He sensed that without it, she, like a rare hothouse flower, would wither and die—which began to happen anyway, the moment his writing career catapulted him into the limelight. He hadn't intended to be a novelist, much less a successful one, but it was the role fate had cast him in.

Possessive of her husband, Anna Marie had rebelled in her own neurotic way. With each step he took up the ladder of success, she became more convinced that he was unfaithful to her. He hadn't a clue where she'd gotten the idea. Discovering she couldn't have children had only made things worse. Horribly worse. She began to threaten suicide. The psychiatrist believed she was making idle threats in an attempt to chain Blade to her. The psychiatrist told Blade to give her space, to exercise a little benign neglect, forcing Anna Marie to confront her emotional insecurities so she could grow. The psychiatrist assured him that she wouldn't take her own life.

But she had.

One night, out of the clear blue, she had come into his bedroom and initiated lovemaking, which she'd never done—she didn't even like sex. Then she'd walked to her bedroom and hanged herself. He'd found her the next morning dangling from the rafter, her body eerily still, motionlessly suspended in space, void of all life.

From that second on, Blade hadn't taken a step without guilt striding beside him. And since then he'd felt pure anger. He was angry at Anna Marie for taking her life, for exiling him to hell—she'd left a note holding Blade responsible for her death. He was angry with the psychiatrist for misjudging Anna Marie's threats, and for advising him to quit jumping at her every neurotic request. He was angry with himself because he knew, deep inside, that despite the psychiatrist's advice, he'd already, of his own accord, begun to withdraw from his wife. And it hadn't been for her emotional well-being. It had been for his own. Slowly his feelings for her had altered as he'd lost patience with her neurosis. Slowly he'd realized that love couldn't live side by side with doubt.

Her mistrust of him hurt—more deeply than he'd been able to express. But undeniably and always, the bottom line was that he'd betrayed her. If only he'd believed her threats. If only he'd told her that one hundred and first time that he hadn't been unfaithful. The psychiatrist, the one who'd been dead wrong about her killing herself, expounded the theory that Blade couldn't write because of his guilt. Metaphorically, he had killed her with his writing career, and because of that he wouldn't allow himself to write again—to kill again. This time the psychiatrist might actually be right. Blade sighed, fighting the urge to bargain with some higher authority over the way things had turned out. If he could go back and replay that part of his life, he'd promise not to make such a mess of things. He'd promise— Something dampened his cheek, and for a moment Blade thought he finally was releasing those long-held tears. He realized, instead, that it was raining. And obviously had been for some time, because he was drenched. A vaporous steam rose ghostlike from the hot concrete, as if the city was offering up thankful praise. Blade angled his head skyward, allowing the warm, soft drops to drizzle down upon him. He felt suddenly tired—bone tired. Tired of anger, tired of guilt, tired of being trapped in an uncreative, unproductive world. The only thing he wasn't tired of was Rori Kelsey. Rori Kelsey of the sweet, satin voice. Rori Kelsey of the deep blue eyes and golden hair.

Golden hair.

He glanced ahead. Several working girls were getting an early start on the evening. They stood in front of a night-club called the Happiest Hour, beneath a pink-and-white-striped canvas awning. Obviously they, too, were enjoying the rain. One of them was blond. Even as he watched, the blonde turned to her companion, said something and they both laughed...a pretty sound that defied the ugly way they made a living.

The investigative reporter in him instantly posed a round of questions. How did prostitutes feel working in a city where three among them had been slain? Had these women known the victims? Was the blond woman afraid? Or did she assume, as was human nature, that nothing would happen to her? The investigative reporter acknowledged that there was a story in what was happening in the city. He'd known it the moment he'd read of the first murder, but he couldn't tap into it. His brain had seemed incapable of tapping into anything. But he wouldn't call Thad, after all. As fanciful as it was, now that his anger was spent, he allowed himself to believe there was promise in the rain, the promise that he'd soon find his way into the book—in time to save his ass and Thaddeus T. Abrams's cheek.

Rori brushed the rose blusher onto the high curve of one cheek, dusted the opposite cheekbone in a like manner, then surveyed her makeup efforts in the vanity table's beveled mirror. She shrugged her shoulders, which were bare except for the satin straps of a pure white teddy. It would have to do, she thought, swiveling her long, silk-encased legs from beneath the floral skirted table. The skirt, like an old-fashioned dress, was drawn upward and tied with small pink bows. Beige eyelets wickedly peeked through the gap, as a lacy undergarment might. The rest of the bedroom, decorated in pink, beige and teal, made the same statement regarding Victorian style and ageless femininity.

Rori went to the half-canopied bed, lifted the black piqué skirt from it and stepped into its slimness. She donned a white, puff-sleeved piqué top, cinched her waist in a black patent-leather belt and slid her feet into black patent-leather heels. She checked her watch. It read two thirty-one. Just time to run and get the mail before calling a cab for work.

Grabbing her key ring and exiting the apartment, she locked the door behind her and started down the hallway. A navy and burgundy runner on the oaken floors absorbed her footsteps. This time of day the building was almost deserted, since most of the people living in it were professionals with weekday jobs. She knew the same to be true of the adjoining building. She knew the two residences housed doctors, lawyers, an accountant, a banker, a couple of legal secretaries, a writer...

A writer.

She'd tried to erase Blade Cavannaugh from her mind, but the exercise was futile. Especially since his call to the station. She'd given up trying and indulged herself in thoughts of him as whim dictated. Like now, as the elevator creaked and groaned its way to the first floor. By the time it shuddered to a stop and the iron grate was pulled aside, Rori had arrived at the same quandary she always faced. He had stated bluntly that she was attracted to him. Was it true? She hadn't denied it. That much she remembered. Vividly remembered.

Yes, she admitted, she was attracted to this dark-haired, haunted-eyed stranger. Yes, she had responded to his touch. Dwayne had accused her of being cold and unresponsive, but it wasn't true. She had responded to her husband... at least in the beginning. But something always happened after the lovemaking began. She felt the sexual tension building, spiraling ever upward in search of a release. It was just that the release never came. Whatever it took to trigger it, whatever happened in other women to produce it, didn't happen to her. She was always left on the edge of an explosion, but never in its cleansing, cataclysmic midst. She was always left in sexual agony, indescribably frustrated and feeling less than a woman. She'd thought about consulting a therapist, but she'd been filled with too much shame. How did you tell a total stranger that you were inorgasmic? Particularly when your husband made it perfectly clear that it was all your fault?

The memory of the afternoon she'd caught him in bed—their bed!—with another woman came slamming back with a vengeance. The sick feeling clenched her stomach as it had then, the same this-can't-be-happening feeling.

"What are you doing?" she'd asked, stupidly as if it weren't obvious what her husband, the man who'd promised to love and cherish her, was doing.

He'd rolled from the woman, the strange, embarrassed woman, with an arrogant cockiness, a hurtful flippancy, that Rori wouldn't forget until her dying day.

"Ah, c'mon," he had said, slipping off the condom and laying it on the antique dish he'd given Rori for her birthday the month before, "you can't be surprised. A man can take only so much coldness. Cindy knows how to appreciate a man."

He'd said it as though it confirmed his virility, leaving Rori, in clearer moments, to wonder if he'd been so sure all along that the problem had been hers. On the one hand, some spiteful part of her had been glad he'd been worried, while on the other hand he'd proven beyond a doubt that the lack was Rori's . . . and hers alone. After all, Cindy with the sheet pulled tight to her throat, Cindy who looked horrified beyond words, hadn't had a problem.

"Let's be civilized about this, okay?" Dwayne had said.

Rori had said nothing. She'd turned and walked quietly from the room...and their marriage. The next day, when he was at work, she'd packed her things. She'd smashed the antique dish against the wall.

Rori swallowed the hurt, the bitterness, forcing the past to a spot that was tolerable, if not comfortable. Unbidden came an image of Blade—protector, comforter, a man who'd kissed her in her dreams and healed her pain. Even as thoughts of him swirled in her head, she heard the faint opening of a door. She glanced up quickly and saw the form of a man exiting the building for the one beyond. Someone had crossed through the lobby only seconds before her arrival—someone who'd reminded her of Blade. But then, every male tended to do that these days.

Banishing the subject of her neighbor, she walked to the foyer and the mailboxes. She inserted the key into her box and removed a handful of letters, then locked the box and started to her apartment.

An advertisement, a bill for a vase she'd seen and couldn't resist, her Visa bill, the electric bill—which would be exorbitantly high with all the hot weather they'd been having—she thumbed through her mail as the elevator bumped and crawled upward. As she exited it, her feet automatically started over the navy and burgundy carpet. She continued through the mail—a letter from a charity, probably asking for a donation, a catalog, a letter from her parents in Oklahoma. The latter brought a smile to her lips.

Suddenly the smile died. She stopped dead in her tracks.

The last envelope looked ordinary enough. It was white, legal-sized, and bore her typewritten address, as several of the other letters in her hand did. Yes, it appeared quite ordinary, yet something about it started Rori's heart pounding. It took her a second to figure out why. The letter had no stamp. It had not been marked by the post office. Someone had slid it directly into her mailbox.

She told herself there could be a dozen plausible explanations for the letter. Unfortunately, she didn't believe one of them. In some inexplicable way, she knew the letter was from whoever had sent the other three. A sense of unreality spread through her as she tore open the envelope. Slowly she removed the sheet of typewriter paper and unfolded it. At the top of the page, perfectly centered, was a single word.

Soon.

A numb coldness, like a northern blizzard, sleeted across her, chilling her flesh and bones. The sense of unreality intensified. This couldn't be happening. Ah, but it could, the reasoning part of her brain pointed out. And it was. And now the man, this stranger who meant her harm, had taken his threats a step further. He had insinuated himself into her private world, invading the foyer of her apartment building. Maybe he'd even stalked its halls and stood before her door.

Glancing around the deserted hallway, which suddenly seemed more empty than before, Rori rushed toward her apartment. Though she forbade herself to run, in the end, she ended up doing exactly that. She jammed the key at the lock with fingers that trembled so badly she had to try a second time before she could insert it. Turning her wrist sharply, she opened the lock, hastened inside and locked the dead bolt behind her. She leaned against the door, her heart thumping.

What should she do?

Calm down, she told herself. Just calm down. On the heels of that thought came another thought—call the police. *Dammit!* she thought as she started for the phone. Maybe she should have touched the letter more carefully. Maybe she'd messed up possible fingerprints. Then again, she couldn't be faulted for making a few mistakes. After all, she thought sarcastically, she wasn't exactly accustomed to people making threats on her life.

In minutes Detective Pinchera came on the line. In a voice that surprised her with its steadiness, she told him about the letter. She could tell by his momentary silence that he, too, perceived the subtle shift in the man's tactics . . . and that he viewed it with the same ominous feeling that she did.

"I'll come pick it up," the detective said in a brusque but kind voice. Rori had noted before that his tone always seemed clipped, as though he had no patience for the world's wrongdoings.

"I have to be at work at three," Rori said, checking her watch. It was two-forty-five.

"Surely it won't hurt if you're a few minutes late," the officer said. "I'll drive you if that'll help."

Rori assured him that it would.

"Ms. Kelsey," he said before hanging up, "we'll get whoever's doing this. You can take that to the bank."

Rori hung onto that thought in the minutes that followed. As comforting as the words had been, however, the letter still lay on the coffee table with a menacing presence, and perversely she kept reminding herself that, good though she imagined the police department's intentions were concerning the unsolved murders that had the city in a panic, the murderer was still walking the streets. This thought seemed to shrink the size of her usually serene apartment. Suddenly anything, even being smothered in heat, seemed preferable to being enclosed within four walls. In an attempt to escape, she stepped onto the balcony.

Rain was still falling, a slow, steady drizzle that had lowered the heat by degrees but increased the humidity until breathing was a chore. Even so, Rori relished the freedom. Freedom. She glanced across the courtyard. Blade's balcony was empty. A vast disappointment swept through her, and she realized, in some crazy way she couldn't explain, that she needed him. She needed the reassurance that seeing him offered.

But she didn't want to need it, she thought, closing her eyes. In her self-imposed darkness, she listened to the faint rumbling of thunder, to the peppering of the rain as it struck the wide leaves of the banana tree in the courtyard below, to the almost palpable sound of steam hissing off the rooftops. She willed her mind to go blank. She could not, however, will her emotions to cease. She felt fear—dank and sinister. She felt anger—flaming and all-consuming. She felt . . . him.

Opening her eyes, her gaze flew to Blade's balcony. He had stepped onto it, and his hand remained on the handle of the sliding glass door. Obviously he hadn't been expecting her . . . which was logical, considering she'd avoided the balcony all week. Now, however, his gaze drank as hungrily of her as hers did of him.

He'd been caught in the rain, she noted. There was no other explanation for the wet clothes he wore, or the way his hair was slicked back. It crossed her mind to wonder if he had been the man she'd seen exiting the lobby minutes before. The thought was fleeting, because her attention was drawn to his shirt, cotton and short-sleeved, which hung open. Both it and his jeans clung to him like skin. Jeans. Her eyes took in every denim detail—the way the fabric smoothed over his tight rear end, the way it molded his firm thighs . . .

Suddenly Rori found it even harder to breathe, and she knew the problem had nothing to do with the harsh humidity. While the rain had definitely cooled some things off, it certainly had not cooled the mysterious something going on between her and this man. In fact, the rain, or possibly the high emotions already running rampant through her, seemed only to have heightened her feelings.

She needed him. It was that plain. That simple. If it walked like a duck, if it quacked like a duck... Yes, she needed him. She needed the safety of his arms, the shelter of his body. She needed him to shield her from the unknown menace that was threatening her. That she needed him in other more primal ways she found as frightening as that unknown menace. Maybe even more frightening. Turning on her heels, she hurried into the refuge of her apartment.

Helplessly, Blade watched Rori disappear through her sliding glass doors. He had arrived home, checked his phone and found it working, then stepped onto his balcony—and had been stunned to see her. He'd been stunned, as he always was, at the sheer magnificence of her beauty, stunned by whatever he'd seen in her eyes. He'd seen the wanting, the longing, that he'd seen there before. But he'd seen something else. Something was wrong. That he would stake his life on. He turned on his heel and entered his apartment.

When Rori's telephone rang, she jumped. She checked her watch. It was ten minutes after three o'clock. Maybe it was Detective Pinchera telling her he was going to be late. Maybe it was Stony wondering why she wasn't at work. She should have called him. But she'd forgotten. She had too much on her mind.

"Hello?" Her voice sounded breathless to her own ears.

"What's wrong?"

Rori felt as if Blade's voice were a beacon seen across roiling, troubled seas. She closed her eyes and wallowed in the comfort it offered.

"Rori? What's the matter?"

No, don't! she warned herself. It would be so easy to get involved with this man. Too easy. Because she was so needy at the moment. She needed someone to hold her and tell her that everything would be all right, that some faceless maniac wouldn't harm her. She needed someone to erase the hurtful memories her husband had left her with. But no one, not even Blade Cavannaugh, could guarantee her safety. It was even less likely that he could erase her hurtful past. In all probability, he would only add to the pain.

"Blade, don't," she whispered. "Please just leave me alone. I can't cope with you and everything else."

Blade heard desperation in her voice, felt it in the marrow of his bones and wondered at its source. He also wondered at her cryptic remark—what everything else?

"Is that really what you want?" he asked hoarsely. When Rori didn't respond, he asked again. "Is that what you want, Rori?" When she still didn't answer, he said roughly, "Say it. Or you'll never make me believe it." Silence. "Rori—"

Suddenly, with a flagrant finality, she broke the connection. An empty quiet lingered.

Blade did what the situation called for. He speared his fingers through his damp hair and swore.

Chapter Five

Rori was glad it was still raining. It gave her the perfect excuse not to walk home after the show. Not that she'd needed to give an excuse to anyone other than herself. In light of what had occurred that afternoon, Stony had made it perfectly clear that he was prepared to hang around all evening, or until hell froze over, to drive her home if she wouldn't promise to take a cab. He made her swear she would on the most reverent thing they could find—the latest listing of their ratings, which once more ranked Night Spice the most-listened-to show in the area.

As the wipers rhythmically stroked the windshield, Rori laid her head against the seat of the cab and wondered if the audience had sensed she'd been rattled. No one around the station had said anything. No one had looked at her strangely, as if she'd misdedicated any of the songs or played a commercial out of its slot. But, then, would she have heard anyone who had said anything to her? Would she have noticed anyone looking at her strangely? The truth was, she'd been absorbed in her own little world all evening. It was a world of fraying nerves, suspicious shadows and hating herself for allowing herself to be so spooked.

Soon.

The word, like a sour vapor, seemed to fill the cab until it threatened the sweet air inside. Willfully, Rori pushed the image of the latest letter from her mind, allowing room for the memory of Detective Pinchera telling her that forensic experts were examining the message. He'd also assured her that a policeman could be at her door within three minutes of her phoning the police station. Even more reassuring had been his agreement that maybe the perpetrator of the letters intended no action beyond sending them. She overlooked the fact that she'd practically backed him into a corner and forced him to agree with her on the last point. The way she overlooked the way she'd lied to her mother.

During one of the show's segments in which several songs followed without interruption, Rori had called her parents in Oklahoma. She had needed to hear their familiar, loving voices. Her mother, ever attuned to her only child, had asked if anything was the matter. Rori, not wanting to worry her parents, had said no.

"What's the matter?"

This time she remembered the question being asked by a bold, deeply masculine voice. A voice that had sent, then and now, tremors of unnamed feelings chasing across her.

"Please just leave me alone," she had begged him.

"Is that really what you want?"

She hadn't responded... because she couldn't. One part of her undeniably did want him to leave her alone. Yet another part wanted him to... To what? That she carefully left unanswered.

"Ma'am?"

Rori jerked her head from the seat. Raindrops splattered the windshield, the wipers fanning them aside. The cab was no longer moving. It had stopped in front of her apartment building, and the driver was looking at her expectantly.

"Sorry," she muttered, reaching for her purse and the price of the fare.

Restless, Blade grabbed his walking shoes and laced his feet into them. It was late. After midnight. But he felt too unsettled to remain indoors. Ordinarily, he watched for Rori's return, but tonight he couldn't muster the patience to wait. He had to get out, had to mindlessly place one foot in front of the other. He had to think.

If he hadn't been certain that afternoon that something was bothering her, he would have been after listening to her show. Though perhaps discernible only to his ears, the strain in her voice, the repeated hesitations as if she'd had to focus her thoughts, the occasional false brightness sent Blade a clear message of distress. For that matter, she'd practically admitted on the phone that afternoon that something was wrong.

"I can't cope with you and everything else."

Everything else. What was this cryptic "everything else?" And did she really want him out of the picture? She had said she did, she'd begged him to leave her alone, yet when nailed to the wall for an answer, she had hung up.

Frustration tramped through him. Maybe he should do her a favor and bow out of her life before he bowed in. Maybe he should do himself a similar favor. Maybe they'd stared across the courtyard until they both had gone a little nuts. Then again, maybe what he ought to do was march over to her apartment, pound on the door and, when she answered it, pull her into his arms—a scenario that perhaps proved the nuts theory.

Ah, hell, he thought, yanking open the door of his apartment, he needed a breath of fresh air...and quickly. He needed a long walk in the warm rain.

Despite the umbrella shielding her and the short distance from the cab to the wide front steps, the rain managed to dampen Rori's clothes. She also managed to step squarely into a puddle, splashing drops of water against the stockinged calf of her leg. She moaned a protest to the rivulets running toward her ankle as she heard the cab pull from the drive behind her and onto the street. She turned and watched it depart, its bright red taillights disappearing in the mist. Instantly she felt alone. Uncomfortably alone.

Flanked by old-fashioned gaslights, the mansion sat amid huge, lacy-leafed oak and elm trees more than a hundred years old. A thicket of waist-high shrubs crouched animal-like against the building's front, creating a feeling of enclosure and shadowed darkness. Suddenly the night had eyes. Was the source of the anonymous threats lurking somewhere? Was he watching her as she was straining for a glimpse of him? Ignoring the skittering of her heart, Rori hastened up the steps.

In the hallway, she collapsed the umbrella, one of several courteously provided by the management of the building, and left it in the umbrella stand. Then she dried the soles of her patent-leather shoes on the heart-shaped greeting rug. As she passed the mailboxes, she couldn't help but cast her eyes in the direction of the box bearing her name. She wasn't certain what she expected to find—another troubling letter?—but the box was empty. Thankfully. Still, her heart was beating as though the box had been full of threatening messages. The fact that he'd stood right where she was standing that very day was more than upsetting.

What had he thought?

What had he felt?

What kind of person would do what he was doing?

Rori hurried toward the elevator. Her muted footsteps sounded unnaturally loud as her heels dug into the rug. She was uncomfortably aware of the moans and groans of the antebellum house. Overhead, the chandelier tinkled a one-note melody that sounded macabre in the silence, and the floor creaked as if unseen feet tiptoed across it. Even the stairway, which everyone avoided because it was too steep, creaked and popped. Rori thought she heard the faint opening of a door, but when she whirled, she saw no one.

Get hold of yourself, she chastised, trying to believe that the sudden goose bumps on her arms were nothing more than the result of the air-conditioning on her rain-splashed skin. She pushed the elevator button. The elevator car was on the third floor—her floor—and crept slowly down. So slowly that Rori thought she'd scream. She had almost convinced herself to take the steep stairs when the elevator finally bumped to a stop. She reached for the grate, but paused. A horrible thought crossed her mind. What if whoever was sending the letters was waiting for her in the elevator? What if he rushed forward, stifling her scream? What if—

She forced herself to open the filigreed grate. The rustic wooden doors, inset with amber and blue stained glass, rested behind the grill, and were sliding open. Slowly...to reveal...nothing. The elevator was empty. Relief burst through Rori, and she couldn't help but feel a little foolish. The first and only smile of the day tweaking her lips, she stepped into the elevator, pushed the button for the third floor and leaned against the wall. The elevator started up.

It had been a long night, a long day, but everything was going to be all right now. In less than a minute she'd be safely barricaded in her own apartment. Behind a state-of-the-art dead bolt. Behind—

The elevator lurched to a sudden stop, jostling Rori. Automatically she threw out a hand to brace herself. Before she could question what was happening, the elevator ground upward a few more inches, hurling her against the wall, then creaked to a jarring, decisive halt somewhere between the second and third floors. The overhead light flickered like a firefly.

Rori stood rooted to the spot. Her mind worked feverishly, trying to make sense of what was happening, while her heart, not interested in rationalization, thudded in reaction. Nothing to get upset about, she assured herself. Everyone in the building joked that the primitive elevator was seeing its last days. It was just her luck to get caught at its demise. She would act calmly, reasonably, rationally. She would . . . what? Push a button. Yes, she'd just push a button. Maybe she'd get the dying beast to move again. She jabbed one button, then another, then the entire panel of buttons, which included the one marked Alarm. Nothing happened. Absolutely nothing. With a fist, she pounded on the door until the stained glass rattled. That, too, produced no motion. Nor did it bring any response from outside the car.

There was only one course of action left, she thought, opening her mouth to call for help. It was then that she heard the noise. It was so faint that she was uncertain at first she'd even heard it. She cocked her head, listening, scavenging the silence for any sound. High overhead, in the workings of the elevator, she heard it again—a thunking noise, a clunking noise, the unmistakable sound of someone tampering with the elevator.

The lights flickered again.

Rori fought the copper taste of fear.

Trapped. She was trapped! What did she do now? Once more she stabbed at the alarm button. Again and again she pounded it . . . punching it until her fingernail broke. Nothing. The elevator was dead. As dead as someone wanted her? She willed herself to be still and listen, though she barely could hear anything above the hammering of her heart. Straining, she trained her attention upward. She didn't hear the sound again. Good. Though maybe it wasn't good. Maybe whoever had stopped the elevator was on his way to collect his prey.

Rori fought to keep her breathing even.

The lights blinked again, then went out. The elevator was plunged into midnight-black darkness.

No longer able to stop herself, Rori cried out, "Help! Somebody please help me!"

Time was measured only by stillness, darkness and heartbeats that staggered and stumbled. Rori waited. For what, for whom, she wasn't certain. She started to cry out once more, but the cry died in her throat at the menacing sound of approaching footsteps. As they drew nearer, ever nearer, she cowered against the wall of the elevator.

Abruptly the footsteps stopped. Silence, heavy with dread, swirled around her. Then she heard the grill being opened . . . slowly, gratingly, like skeletal fingers drawn across a wire fence. That noise was followed by the jarring sound of the doors being pried open. In seconds a crack appeared. A pale shaft of light shot into the small cubicle. It was enough, however, to blur the image of the man—she was certain it was a man—behind it. Rori squinted and tried to inch closer to the wall.

"Give me your hand," the man commanded.

The voice was familiar, wasn't it? Or did she just desperately long for it to be?

"C'mon, Rori, give me your hand!"

"Blade?" she asked tentatively, disbelieving but hoping beyond hope.

The man was more preoccupied with getting her out than with identifying himself. Laying aside what Rori thought must be a small flashlight, he positioned himself on his stomach and thrust an arm into the cavernous hole.

"Grab hold," he said, bracing his other hand against the elevator door.

Rori stepped forward, reached up and took the hand. It was large and warm and callused. It fought to secure a firm grip. It couldn't. The man tried again. "Grab hold of my arm with both hands," he ordered. "No, farther up," he added, positioning her fingers around his upper arm. He leaned forward and clenched his fist around the belt at her waist. "Hang on," he said as he gave a yank.

Rori felt her feet swing from the floor, and she was dangling in midair. She heard the man suck in a gulp of air. Slowly, almost hearing him grit his teeth, Rori began to rise. The biceps beneath her hands bulged mercilessly, and she thought it would surely burst. How could anyone be so strong? She was having trouble hanging on. Suddenly one of her hands slipped. Twirling like a circus performer, she cried out, her hand flailing at thin air. She grabbed at anything she could find. The man groaned as Rori's fingernails bit into the tender flesh of his neck. He gave one final jerk on her belt, an action that practically cut her in two. He tumbled onto the third floor. Rori fell into his arms.

Their harsh breathing rasped into the silence. Neither tried to speak, for neither could. Blade leaned his head against the wall. His hand was still holding Rori's belt, as though it had been frozen into a cramped fist, which he now couldn't release. Rori could feel the dampness of his rain-sprinkled jeans. She could feel his chest heaving. It was a wide, massive chest. A safe chest. A chest she tried to burrow into. Closing her eyes, she fastened both arms around his neck and rooted her cheek against his shoulder.

Slowly Blade's breath began to return, and he became fully aware of the woman in his arms. She was drawn across his lap, her long legs curled beneath her. Her skirt had ridden to midthigh, leaving the feel of smooth skin and silk stockings against one of his hands. The other hand, which, like his arm, still shook from the physical exertion he'd put it through, he unclenched from her belt. Without thinking, he did with it what felt natural and right. He brought it to the crown of Rori's head, protectively cradling her to him. Beneath his trembling fingers, he felt a tangle of hair. Ringlets curled like corkscrews, tumbling wildly over her shoulders and down her back. Because there was nothing in the world he wanted more, he plunged his fingers into the satiny mane.

"It's all right," he soothed, feeling her heart pounding against the hard wall of his chest, her plush breasts flush against him. It was a good feeling . . . as was the warmth of her breath fluttering against the hollow of his throat.

His words, his touch, consoled Rori, though not enough to make her forget what had just happened. One last surge of fear raced through her, and a tremor ran through her body.

"It's all right," he repeated, folding his arms around her and drawing her even closer.

They might have remained that way forever—neither seemed inclined to move—but voices from the stairway drew their attention. Donald Weiss, the building's super, appeared at the head of the stairwell, the accountant close on his heels.

"What the hell?" the super began.

"That damned elevator needs replacing," Blade said calmly, allowing Rori to move from his arms and rearrange her skirt.

Donald glanced at Rori. Her cheeks were flushed, her eyes bright. There was a wide run in one of her stockings. "Are you okay, Ms. Kelsey?"

"Y-yes," she answered, but when she tried to stand, she found that she was still shaky. She willingly accepted Blade's help. He leaned her against the wall while he bent to pick up his key ring. On it was a small flashlight. He also picked up her purse, which had been dropped at the elevator's entrance.

Taking Rori by the arm, he directed her toward her apartment. Neither spoke, and slowly the voices of Donald and the accountant grew fainter. They appeared to be pounding on the elevator doors and banging on buttons—all to no avail.

"Give me your key," Blade said seconds later.

Rori searched through her purse and finally came up with the item in question. When she handed it to him, their eyes met . . . and held . . . for a meaningful fraction of a second. Blade's look said, "I'm seeing you in, so don't argue with me if you know what's good for you."

Rori didn't argue. In fact, it seemed the furthest thing from her mind. Blade opened the door, let her in then closed the door behind them. Rori, on her way to the wet bar, turned on a lamp . . . and listened for the sound of the dead bolt being thrown. When she heard it, she breathed a little more easily. Without asking Blade if he wanted a drink, she tossed her purse aside and poured herself a good stiff belt of brandy, downing it in one burning gulp. She felt her trembling insides settle somewhat, though she wondered if her life would ever truly be settled again.

Blade laid her key on the bar. Rori's line of vision took the normal pathway—the key, his tanned hand, his muscled arm, his face with its watchful expression. Abruptly, carelessly, she raked her fingers through her hair, drawing it from her face.

"Do you make a habit of rescuing damsels in distress?" she asked.

Blade shrugged, thinking of his wife. "Not on purpose. The suit of armor just seems to fit. My lance, however, is sometimes rusty." His tone was sarcastic as he once more thought of his wife. His dead wife.

Despite her preoccupation, Rori heard the bitter note in his voice and wondered at it. Could it have anything to do with the haunted look in his eyes?

"Actually," Blade added, flinging the hurtful past aside, "I was on my way out to walk. I cut through your building to avoid the construction in front of mine. I heard you cry out."

It wasn't necessary to mention that he'd instantly recognized her voice. Just as it wasn't necessary to mention how his heart had jumped into his throat. He was still trying to make sense out of the intensity of his reaction.

Rori tipped the cut-crystal decanter and poured herself another drink. She raised the glass in salute. "To knights in shining armor who take midnight walks." She started to bring the glass to her lips. Blade, however, stopped her by manacling her wrist with his big hand. Her gaze flew to his in surprise. His eyes were a dark, intent, soul-piercing gray.

"What's going on?" he asked. Not giving her time to answer, he added, "It was obvious this afternoon that something was wrong. Then tonight you get stuck in an elevator and, while I'll grant you that it's nothing to take lightly, you were petrified. You still are petrified, for that matter."

The pulse in her wrist tapped a rhythm that proved his point.

"What's going on?" he repeated.

"Nothing much," she said flippantly. "Someone just tried to kill me tonight."

Blade was stunned. Some unfathomable emotion flickered in his eyes. He loosened his hold on her wrist. Rori took the opportunity to complete the glass's journey to her lips. She contented herself with a swallow of brandy before setting the glass on the mahogany counter. As though hearing the words for the first time, she gave a laugh that wasn't far from hysterical and again threaded her fingers through her hair.

"My God, it sounds so melodramatic, doesn't it?" she said, looking at him. He still said nothing. "I think this is the part where you ask me if I'm sure that someone tried to kill me... phrased, of course, in such a way that you don't imply that I've just imagined it, or that I should be locked up in the bonkers ward of some institution." When he remained silent, Rori shoved the rest of her drink toward him. "Here, it helps a little."

Blade reached for the glass and downed the brandy in one swallow, much as Rori had done minutes before. As he did so, Rori stepped to the sliding glass door of the living room and stared out at the rainy night... and at the apartment across the way. The apartment was dark. But, unlike the hundreds of other times she'd stared at the dark apartment, she knew tonight what its occupant was doing and where he was. He was in her apartment, after having rescued her from God only knew what... or whom. She remembered the relief she'd felt at hearing Blade's voice; she could still feel the safety of his arms. And she needed those arms, some part of her acknowledged, to fight the chill of fear rustling over her.

Blade watched Rori as she stood at the door. Silhouetted as she was, she was more than shadow, less than form. He could see her clearly enough, however, to observe that she wrapped her arms around herself as though she was cold—as though she was trying to hold herself together. He remembered the feel of those arms wrapped around his neck, with her so close that her heart beat against his chest. He wanted to feel her that close again. He didn't analyze the why of it anymore than he'd analyzed the why of his attraction to her. He simply knew he wanted to feel her close to him. Just the way he wanted to reject what she'd just said.

"What makes you think someone tried to kill you?"

Rori angled her head until her gaze meshed with Blade's. "Because someone implied that they would . . . and soon."

"What does that mean?"

"It means I've been getting threatening letters. Four, as a matter of fact. The last one arrived this afternoon. The first three were mailed to the radio station, but this one was dropped in my mailbox. Whoever the creep is, he was in this apartment building today. He was also here tonight."

"Did you see—"

"No," Rori interrupted, "but I heard someone fooling around with the elevator."

Blade looked as though he'd been poleaxed. "Are you certain? I mean, about hearing someone at the elevator?"

Rori smiled. "Why, Mr. Cavannaugh, it sounds as though you're asking me if I imagined it. Next thing I know you'll be asking me if I belong on the bonkers ward of some institution."

Blade exploded. He crossed the room in an angry stride that placed him before her, his eyes a smoky gray. "Dammit, that isn't what I said!"

"But it's what you thought!" she retaliated, uncertain why she was shouting at him. There seemed a surplus of emotion inside her...and, inexplicably, it was important to her that Blade believe her. In fact, she wasn't certain when anything had ever meant quite so much.

"Don't tell me what I think," he ordered. "I'm quite capable of figuring that out for myself. And, for your information, what I was thinking was that if you were certain someone had fooled with the elevator, that someone might still be on the premises. Which means it might not be a bad idea if I looked around."

"No!" Rori cried, surprising herself at the power she put behind the one word. That she was clutching Blade's arm also surprised her, a fact she realized as she followed his gaze to where her fingers were nearly cutting off his circulation. Embarrassed, she released her hold. "No," she repeated, this time more calmly, "I won't let you take that kind of chance." What she didn't say but felt strongly was that she didn't want to be alone.

"Then let's call the police," he said, hearing the unspoken words as clearly as if she'd said them. A sudden thought occurred to him. "You have notified the police about the threats, haven't you?"

Rori nodded.

"Then they should know this...now."

Without asking her permission, Blade took charge of the situation. He crossed to the phone, and related what had just happened. He was assured an officer would be there in minutes. Actually, it took ten minutes, not the three Detective Pinchera had originally promised, but Rori assumed the officers were looking around. During the wait, Blade asked Rori a thousand questions about the letters, about what the police were doing and about the precautions she was taking. It seemed strange to have someone to share the threats with, someone who seemed genuinely interested. Rori felt comforted. When the doorbell rang, she stepped to answer it. Before she could, however, Blade called out.

"Rori?"

She turned. Though he was buried in the room's shadows, her gaze unerringly found his.

"I don't think you should be in the bonkers ward of some institution," he said.

Something warm and sweet melted inside Rori, oozing over her lonely heart. She clung tightly to this warm, sweet feeling during the next few minutes as she told the police what had happened that night. Curiously, when the two young officers left after taking her brief statement—they had found no one suspicious on the premises—she felt keyed up again. Reliving the event had triggered the bleak, black emotions, the fear. As Blade let the officers out, Rori found herself standing once more before the sliding door, watching the rain thrash against the glass. She realized she was trembling.

She felt, more than heard or saw, Blade standing beside her. Silently, he handed her a drink of brandy. This one was only a swallow, in deference to what she'd already consumed. She downed it and handed the glass to him. She studied her hand—clinically, as though it belonged to someone else.

"I'm shaking," she said with a strange calmness, an abnormal detachment.

Blade set the glass down, then laced his fingers with hers. She could feel his steadiness. Her weakness seemed to merge with his strength. Slowly her gaze traveled the distance of his chest, his throat, his face. She found his eyes. They were just as steady as his hand.

"I'm afraid," she said, her voice little more than a whisper. "I've tried not to be—I hate myself for being—but I'm afraid."

"I'd say that's a pretty normal reaction to someone trying to kill you," he said, threading the fingers of their free hands just the way their other hands were joined. A grin—actually, a fraction of one—nipped his mouth. "If you weren't scared, I'd say you belonged on the bonkers ward of some institution."

Despite the seriousness of the topic, Rori's lips danced at the corners. Then, because she couldn't forget the subject's grimness, the smile died. So did Blade's. They continued to stare at each other. Then, with a naturalness that neither questioned, Blade drew her to him, directing her hands behind him, where he abandoned them in order to fold his arms around her. He pulled her body flush to his. Her hands splayed wide across his back.

"You're safe with me," he said fervently, as though making a pledge he'd rather die than break.

For a reason she couldn't begin to fathom, Rori believed him. Days before, she'd found herself wondering if she shouldn't have mentioned him when the police had questioned her about people in her life, but the idea that he was a perverted maniac had seemed ridiculous then. Now, standing in his arms, feeling her tensed muscles relax for the first time that day, for the first time in weeks, the idea seemed more than ridiculous. It seemed ludicrously ridiculous. She sighed softly as she nuzzled her cheek to his chest.

Her sigh flowed gently across Blade, like the waters of a peaceful river. In some strange way, her peace brought a similar peace to his chaotic life. Maybe it was just that, for a moment, he was thinking of someone other than himself and his own misery. The fear he'd heard in her voice earlier had torn at his gut. Now all he could do was try to absorb some of that fear into himself. As always when dealing with her, he didn't ask why it was important to do so. He just *felt* that it was.

"You're safe," he repeated, trailing his hands up her back, then down in a massaging, consoling way. As his hands connected with her hair, he entwined his fingers in the velvet softness, as though captivated by the bobbing curls.

Rori felt the weight of his fingers, their sweet, seductive motion, and something deep inside her deemed that she liked what she felt. Without thinking, she responded by turning her other cheek to his chest, placing her face toward him rather than away from him, placing her mouth at the hollow of his throat.

"Nothing's going to happen to you," he said roughly. He nudged aside the hair at her temple. "I swear it."

His breath brushed across the sensitive skin, and she felt a shiver of some emotion she thought she'd forgotten how to feel—pleasure at a man's touch. She'd once felt pleasure at her husband's touch, but the agony that had always followed had eventually programmed her to feel nothing. Except anxiety. It was good to feel pleasure again, she thought, nuzzling her head against Blade. It was good to feel safe...protected...shielded from harm.

Blade's cheek skimmed across hers, his feathery breath warm against her flesh. His nose nudged her earlobe, her cheek, her jaw—angling her face toward his by slow, almost infinite degrees. Nature, thousands of years before, had dictated what he was searching for.

"You're safe," he said once more. This time his voice was more breath than sound. His nose tilted and tipped until her mouth lay just beneath his. He hesitated for a fraction of a second, as though giving each of them time to think better of what was about to happen. But thinking had long ago been abandoned, sacrificed to hot, starry nights spent staring across lonely balconies. Nothing was left but feeling, need.

Nothing was left but the claiming of her mouth with his.

Chapter Six

The kiss wasn't a stranger's. Just as it wasn't a kiss that easily lent itself to description. It was gentle, as gentle as her dream had prepared her that it would be, but it was also intimate. Demandingly intimate.

Blade's lips didn't tease, didn't coax, didn't waste time introducing themselves. They simply smothered hers with an immediate tenderness—and sensuality. Warm and wet, they stroked hers, rocked gently, parted and changed angles slightly before sliding possessively to capture hers once more. His tongue flitted forward in a faint, airy flight, then brazenly entered the sweet haven of her mouth, embedding itself deeply and erotically. His tongue sought hers, curling and dancing with it, doing blatantly provocative things that normally only long-standing lovers engaged in. It was as though both their bodies understood that all that time spent staring back and forth had elevated their relationship to a plateau of familiarity.

Blade had to keep reminding himself that this was the first time he'd held this woman in passion, the first time he'd kissed her. He was vaguely aware—as aware as he could be of anything at the moment—that she felt far better than she had in his daydreams, his wide-awake night dreams. Though he had no idea how that was even remotely possible. She was soft—so soft she felt draped across his arms. And her lips were so sweet they seemed to drip honey.

Gliding his hands down the length of her back and onto the swell of her hips, he drew her against him. He remembered doing the same thing once with Anna Marie, pulling her into the heat of him, only to have her withdraw as though disgusted with the primitive nature of his action and appalled that he needed something as base as sex. What physical contact they had shared had been brief and infrequent and had always left him feeling as though he'd defiled his wife. But this woman wasn't withdrawing. Instead, she was moaning...and molding herself to him. And she didn't feel fragile in his arms, the way Anna Marie had. This woman felt strong...and soft...and deliciously sweet. She filled him with a need he'd never felt before, a need that was more than a little frightening because he felt laid bare by it.

Rori could hardly believe the sensations swarming through her. They were sensations she'd believed she would never feel again. Yet, though the kiss was heady, though the sensations were unbelievably forceful, she knew, too, that her reaction was unwarranted. While it was all right to feel tingly and giddy, it was not all right to feel as though the world had just been turned upside down. It was not all right to feel as though she'd never been kissed before—as though she'd never felt *anything* before this moment. But that was how all-consuming his kiss was, how potent his masculine nearness was.

Beneath the gentle intimacy, she sensed a thinly disguised, a pleading-to-be-released power. This man was capable of reactions, possessed of needs she'd never been exposed to before. Her ex-husband, for all that he liked to think himself the consummate lover, was nothing compared to Blade Cavannaugh. *And if she couldn't please her husband,* she heard the demon in her ask, *how could she entertain the notion of pleasing this man?*

"No," she whispered, wrenching her lips from those that were exquisitely devouring hers. She couldn't risk seeing the look in this man's eyes she'd so often seen in Dwayne's. The look of disappointment—even contempt.

But Blade's expression seemed only to say that he'd warned her before of their attraction to each other. It also seemed to acknowledge that he couldn't explain the intensity that existed between them any more than she could. His breathing as serrated as hers, he dropped his gaze to her lips, lips still wet from his kiss. His gentle kiss. His intimate kiss. This look said that, given another half second his mouth would be on hers. At the sensations this tender threat inspired, feelings that left her already weak legs even more limp, Rori pulled from him.

Blade let her go. And watched as she moved to stand once more in front of the sliding door. Heedless of the prints she was leaving, she flattened her palms against the pane of glass. Blade thought it looked like a beseeching gesture. But what was she pleading for? For him to leave her alone?

In one blindingly clear revelation, Blade knew what a mistake it was for him to be there. Rori wanted him, as badly as he wanted her, but she was in no condition to deal with that desire. What had happened tonight, the threat upon her life, had left her too shaken. Right now she was as vulnerable as a child. He couldn't, wouldn't, take advantage of her vulnerability. He conveniently overlooked the fact that he was feeling a little vulnerable himself. The intensity of his need for this woman was something he wasn't accustomed to.

Rori heard his footsteps as he turned and quickly, determinedly walked toward the front door. She had only seconds to assimilate what he was doing and to consider the repercussions of his action. If he walked out that door, she'd be alone...and, after the frightening night she'd had, being alone was the last thing she wanted. Furthermore, something deep within her told her that it was this man she wanted to be *un-alone* with.

"Don't leave!" she said, her voice a harsh whisper.

She didn't turn, but continued to stare out the door, her hands still braced against it. She heard Blade's footsteps halt and wondered if he could hear her heart beating from where he stood. Surely he could, for her heartbeats, uneven, unsure, seemed to be ricocheting around the room. Those heartbeats went wild when she heard him walking toward her—and wilder yet when he turned off the single light glowing in the room. The apartment was dark except for the dim light from the courtyard below, a faint golden glow. Rain, falling with a constant force, struck the glass door. New Orleans was hot and thirsty and drinking in every drop of the bountiful moisture.

When Blade stepped behind her, Rori realized that she felt a similar thirst for Blade's soothing nearness. Leaning into her, he placed his hands atop hers, creating a cage with his muscled arms. His hands were large and warm and hid hers beneath them. A wide leather band of a watch circled his left wrist, dark spirals of hair curling at its edges. His chest, hidden beneath a cotton shirt that still carried a hint of the rain's moisture, molded itself to Rori's back. His thighs, taut and firm, pressed against hers, just as his stomach nudged her hips. He made no pretense of hiding the arousal that lay behind the metal teeth of his jeans zipper.

Rori closed her eyes.

"If I stay," he whispered, his breath stirring the back of her hair, "we both know what's going to happen." It wasn't a question; it was a statement of hard, cold fact—of hard, *hot* fact.

Air seeped from Rori's lips, as though in silent supplication. Of what she wasn't certain. Was she begging him to stay? To go? Not to make her decide? But his next question proved that he wasn't going to be obliging.

"Do you still want me to stay?"

Rori dropped her head forward. Her hair fell around her like a sun-colored, silken drape. Blade had sworn to himself that he wouldn't try to influence her decision, yet he couldn't stop himself from rooting aside her hair and brushing his lips against the fragrant-smelling skin of her neck.

Delicate sensations shuddered through Rori, and she sucked her bottom lip between her teeth, biting gently at the tender flesh. Only once before could she remember sensations being anywhere near this potent, and that was in the days when she and Dwayne had been engaged in their whirlwind courtship. The same emotions, however, had betrayed her once they'd married. Surely she could never trust those emotions again. Could she?

"Answer me, Rori," Blade commanded, the tip of his tongue teasing the lobe of her ear.

Rori moaned and angled her head, giving his mouth anything of her neck it wanted. It obviously wanted more than it presently had, because his lips trailed soft, gingerbread-sweet kisses from behind her ear to the bent nape of her neck.

"Rori?" he urged with mounting impatience. His kisses were growing more demanding...more persuasive... more irresistible.

Rori couldn't remember whether it was she who turned in his arms or whether he turned her, but suddenly she found herself face to face with him, his hands still wedged against the sliding glass door, her hands flat against his chest. His eyes smoldered with the gray fire of yearning. Her body pulsed with a need, a want, so great that she hurt from the top of her head to the bottom of her feet with their red-lacquered toenails. Some ray of hope, borne out of sheer desperation, burst to life inside her. Surely this time would be different. Surely this man would be different. Surely her body would not betray her so traitorously a second time. Only marginally aware of her intent—that she would *make* this time different—she reached upward to answer his question. She did so by crushing his mouth with hers.

She took him by surprise. That much was evidenced by his momentarily delayed reaction. It took him but a second to recover. When he did, he groaned and, without removing his hands from the glass, began to work his mouth over hers in a frenzy. They kissed hotly, painfully, with a savage urgency that startled them both. Grinding, slashing, seeking a new angle to try to appease their raw hunger, they both worked to deepen the kiss.

Growling at the frustration he felt—he couldn't absorb the feel of her into him quickly enough—Blade pulled his hands from the glass door and, plunging his fingers into her hair, held her head still so he could ravish her mouth in a purely selfish way. He thrust his tongue forward, seeking her sweetness in a wild, thorough sweep. Rori grabbed a fistful of his shirt and held on.

At last he jerked his mouth from hers, and arching her neck by tugging gently at her hair, he placed his lips at the hollow of her throat.

"Tell me to stay," he demanded. His need to hear the words surprised him. He supposed that too many nights, too many times, he'd felt regret at having initiated lovemaking with his wife. Too many times her passiveness had scorned him, leaving him hollow, making him feel like a heel because he dared to have sexual needs.

"Stay," Rori whispered. "God, yes, stay!"

Blade's mouth closed over hers for a slow, hard kiss. At the kiss's end, he muttered, "I've wanted this for so long that it's seemed like forever." His breath was hot and thick and so sexy that Rori thought she'd instantly burn to cinders. If he didn't ask where the bedroom was soon, she'd never make it there under her own power. As it turned out the bedroom wasn't necessary.

One searing kiss led to another until they both felt the need for more... much more. Blade's hungry hand slid between them, molding the mound of her breast. She arched into his palm, moaning at the exquisiteness of his touch. The image of her standing before the balcony, clad only in a scanty teddy, raced through Blade's memory, gutting his senses and leaving only one question in his mind. What was she presently wearing beneath this very proper suit? He released one button, then another. His fingers fumbled with the belt he'd used to haul her from the elevator, then it, too, fell victim to his purposefulness. Boldly, brazenly, he drew the suit jacket from her shoulders, letting it drop to the floor. At the sight before him, both his hands and his heart stopped.

Slim straps of a pristine-white teddy slid over her alabaster-shaded shoulders. The tips of her breasts thrust against, but were not visible through, the garment's rich silk and lace. The swell of her full breasts, however, was clearly defined beneath the thin opaque fabric. The only thing thinner than the clingy fabric was Blade's breathing.

Lowering his head, Blade kissed the outline of one breast, feeling its weight shift oh, so subtly, oh, so sexily at his touch. He whispered his hot breath against the raised nipple. It peaked. Rori moaned. Blade rushed his open mouth to hers as he slid both hands to capture her need-swollen breasts. One of the teddy's straps fell, and his palm connected with bare skin. The caress destroyed Blade's senses.

The next few minutes were a montage of moans, of his shirt grabbed for by her but shed by him because she wasn't removing it fast enough, of her skirt slithering to the floor, of his jeans following. Somehow Rori and Blade ended up on the floor, on their knees, he kissing by turns her breasts, both of which were now exposed, the teddy hanging at her waist. Rori her neck arched, clung to his bare, hair-dusted chest for support.

When had anything seemed as important as this moment? Rori thought dimly. How had all the feeling in the world become transfixed into one need? Wouldn't she surely die if something didn't ease the tension soon? She could never remember feeling this intensity with Dwayne—or in any other aspect of her life. Her body had never been so wantonly preoccupied with satisfaction.

Rori made a sound of pleading, a low, guttural noise that further inflamed Blade. He called her name once, perhaps in disbelief at the tension chasing through him, as he lowered her to the carpet. Then, in economical movements of pulling and tugging, they shed their remaining clothes.

He stopped…looked at her…and thought her the most beautiful woman he'd ever seen. And the sexiest. He also thought what they were about to do was possessed of a wondrous rightness.

She stopped . . . looked up at him . . . and thought him the most handsome man she'd ever seen. And the sexiest. She knew that what was about to happen between them had been ordained from the first time she'd spotted him on his balcony.

Tentatively, yet with a curious familiarity, he touched her hair . . . her cheek . . . the crest of her breast.

Shyly, yet boldly, she touched his chin . . . his chest—and his heart when she whimpered as his knuckles grazed her breast's sensitive peak.

Wordlessly, his eyes fixed on hers, he stretched out atop her.

And then, as though choreographed, legs shifted, hips thrust, hardness sought its soft counterbalance.

His filling of her brought such pleasure that Rori thought she'd faint. Gasping, she arched her back and clawed her fists into the flesh of his buttocks. At the same time she pressed her hips into his. When he inched deeper, she cried out and wrapped her legs around him.

At her cry, Blade glanced at her with passion-hazed eyes. The ecstasy on her face, the wet heaven into which he'd buried himself, were almost more than he could bear. Gritting his teeth against a pleasure that was painful, he urged his hips into a slow, sensual rhythm, tempering his strokes, praying he could make them last for more than a few seconds in the face of his long abstinence.

Fire. Sheets of flame. Desire burning through her, scorching the edges of her body and soul. It had never been like this before. It had never been even close to this before. Surely this time, with this man, the ending would be different.

But it wasn't.

When Rori realized that history was going to repeat itself, she turned as cold as mountain-stream water. At least her senses turned cold. Her body remained a towering inferno of feeling. It was the way it had always been, only this time it was a thousand times worse. She felt raw with the need to let go of the tension coiled inside her feminine body. She felt perched on the edge of the climactic precipice. She felt trapped... unable to go forward... unable to go back. Tears formed behind her closed eyelids. Just as humiliation welled in her heart.

Why?

Why couldn't she respond like other women?

Why had something so simple, so elemental, been denied her?

And how, sweet God, could she keep her defect hidden from this man?

In the end, she thanked Blade for making it easy for her. When he was lost in his sudden, shattering climax, Rori faked a similar one.

Blade's breath beat against her ear while his body lay heavily across hers. She could still feel the occasional shudder, one last, delayed ripple of pleasure, scurry through him. Even with the misery engulfing her, maybe because of it, she marveled at the intensity of his release... and at the pure beauty of it. It had been so natural, so honest, so... so unlike the barrenness of her own capabilities. She fought the urge to hold him to her, to pull the very essence of him into her and, thereby, somehow make his release her own. She refused to indulge her desire to draw her hands the length of his sweat-dampened back. Something in her, something she'd never felt with her husband, made her long to soothe Blade's passion-depleted body. But doing so would be a kind of bonding. And she must not bond with this man. She must not bond with any man.

In a sudden unexpected motion, Blade rolled from her and to her side. He lay on his back, not the least self-conscious about his nakedness, his arm thrown casually across his closed eyes. Rori took the moment to flee. Grabbing her clothes, she held them to her as one might a shield, and escaped, via her bedroom, into the bathroom. Blade let her go. In fact, he didn't move an inch. He didn't even open an eye to watch her departure.

Inside the rose and teal bathroom, Rori leaned against the closed door. Disappointment, humiliation, disbelief in her utter and complete stupidity, raced through her. How could she have been so stupid as to think she could make something different just because she wanted it to be? The tears that had sprung to life earlier now mushroomed. One jumped from the corner of her eye and coursed down her cheek. Disgusted with the display of weakness, she swiped it away with the heel of her trembling hand. Emotions, jagged and piercing, still ran rampant through her passion-soaked body. She felt as though, with the right provocation, she might well explode into a million unfulfilled fragments—even, perhaps, with no provocation whatsoever. Curiously, the wanting, the needing, as sharp and severe as it was, had blended into a numbness that seethed beneath the surface of her being.

Crossing the bathroom, she stepped into the bathtub, and drawing the plastic curtain, turned on the shower. Cold water struck her, kneading her fevered skin with its icy fingers. Rori gasped...but forced herself to stand still. Chilled streams cascaded over sensitive breasts, down a belly quivering with desire, across hot, fevered thighs. By the time she stepped from the shower, she felt marginally better. She also knew what she had to do. She had to get rid of Blade Cavannaugh. She had to find a way to tell him that he wouldn't be staying the night—a tactful lie that had nothing to do with the truth.

Sliding her arms into a white terry robe, Rori opened the door and stepped into the bedroom. She stopped. Like the living room, the bedroom had been left in darkness. The only light illuminating it came from the bathroom. It was enough light, however, to easily discern her lover standing at the window, staring out. At the sound of the door opening, Blade turned. Rori realized two things simultaneously: he wore nothing but jeans and he was angry. She was uncertain which of the two was the more powerful realization.

"Why did you do it?" he asked, the question ripe with accusation.

Thrown by the harshness in his eyes and his voice, Rori was uncertain what he meant. At the same time she was certain that no man had ever looked so damned appealing! His chest was bare except for a mouth-watering amount of hair, while his jeans, which he hadn't bothered to snap, hung breathlessly low on his lean hips. His hands perched casually, haughtily, at his waist.

"What do you mean?" she asked, dragging her eyes from his supremely masculine body. She ignored the resurgence of desire that tripped through her. It was a desire that had not entirely dissipated.

"Let me spell it out for you, so you'll know exactly what I mean. Why did you fake an orgasm?"

On one plane of thought, Rori acknowledged that she wasn't surprised he'd seen through her deception. She didn't know how he had, but she wasn't surprised at his sensitivity. On another plane, she admitted that what she heard herself answering didn't in any way address the question.

"I see you made yourself at home," she snapped, referring to the fact that he'd arrogantly made his uninvited way into her bedroom. Then again, maybe he figured if he'd made love to a woman on her living room floor, he had an unspoken right to her bedroom.

When she would have plowed by him, he grabbed her arm, insisting, "Why?"

His eyes burned into hers. His touch branded her skin. She lifted her chin in defiance. "What makes you so sure—"

"Because I'm an expert on faked orgasms!" he interrupted. "I had a wife who knew all about them!"

The word *wife* sleeted through Rori. It was made tolerable only by the word *had*. Why had she never questioned this man's marital status? What else didn't she know about him? The truth was that she knew only one thing about him for certain. She had just been intimate with him.

Abruptly Blade released Rori's arm and restlessly, wearily shoved his fingers through his hair. His sigh whispered into the room. "I'm sorry. It wasn't your fault. If I hadn't rushed you like a sixteen-year-old in the backseat of a car..." He stopped. "I'm sorry," he repeated. "I hadn't been with a woman in a while. Nine months is a long time. I'd forgotten how—" his eyes found hers "—how good it could feel."

He could have added that he never remembered a woman feeling that good, Blade thought. For that matter, he couldn't remember anything feeling that good. That was why he'd died of pain, a pain he'd translated into anger, when he'd realized it hadn't been as good for her.

Rori remembered only too well how good his lovemaking had felt—how hot his kiss had been upon her lips, how gentle his caress of her breasts, how sure and strong the stroking of his body within hers. She remembered because, unlike him, desire had not been drained from her. No shower, however cold, could accomplish that.

"It...it wasn't your fault," she said, unwilling to let him take the blame for something she was responsible for. In some far corner of her mind, she wondered why he'd abstained from sex for nine months. Rather than ask, however, she turned to the window and repeated, "It wasn't your fault. It was mine."

He stepped beside her. "Even if I hadn't rushed you, you can hardly be blamed after what happened to you tonight. A threat upon your life isn't conducive to sexual abandonment. Our timing was just wrong...off."

Suddenly Rori was filled with an overwhelming frustration at her lot in life. She responded with a sarcastic laugh. "Tonight. Tomorrow night. Six months worth of nights. It wouldn't make a difference. The end would still be the same. And the end would still be my fault. Trust me, I have this on good authority."

Blade frowned. "I don't understand."

"Actually, it's quite simple. Just ask my husband whose fault it is. Pardon me," she added, "my ex-husband."

Blade's frown deepened. "What are you talking about?"

Sorry she'd said anything, Rori heaved a sigh and dragged her fingers through her love-tangled hair. "Nothing."

"Don't give me that. What did you mean?"

"Look, just forget what I said. Just forget tonight ever happened."

Silence stalked the room. In it, Rori could hear the rebirth of his anger. "Just pull up my pants and go home?" he sneered.

The image that flashed into Rori's mind, an image of tight denim and lean hips, whittled her breath. Her words came out sounding like a rush of river reeds blowing in a breeze. "Something like that."

Blade whirled her around. "The hell I will. The hell I will forget tonight!" If he was honest with himself he wasn't certain he could forget tonight if he wanted to. The feel of her hair wrapped around his eager fingers, her lips trembling beneath his, her body arching to meet his had pretty well eliminated forgetting as an option. "Now," he added, making it sound as though he wasn't going to ask again, "what did you mean?"

"It means, dammit, that you weren't the only one with an imperfect marriage! You weren't the only one married to an iceberg." Rori laughed without mirth. "You and Dwayne really ought to get together over drinks. You have a lot in common—particularly after tonight. You can tell him how I faked it with you. And he can tell you how I never even came close enough to fake it with him. You might even get him to tell you about my finding him in our bed with another woman—and how this woman didn't have to fake anything."

A picture—an ugly picture—was forming in Blade's mind. Rori held the lapels of the terry robe as if she was suddenly chilled to the bone, but Blade needed her to confirm what he was thinking. "Say it straight out," he demanded.

Rori looked as though she'd just been slugged on the chin. "Don't make me—"

"Say it straight out," he repeated, giving her no quarter.

Slowly—regally, he thought—she raised her chin. "Okay. Straight out. I'm inorgasmic. That's a fancy clinical word for can't get it off. I don't do that thing that other women not only do, but many do multiple times. You'd think nature in all fairness would have given me one of some other woman's multiple. Just one lousy one," she added, her voice rich in sarcasm. The sarcasm drained away, however, and she sounded vulnerable. "One would have done me just fine."

Rori turned from Blade and back toward the window. The rain had stopped. She felt as if her heart had stopped with it. "I honestly thought it would be different with y— I honestly thought it would be different tonight."

Blade heard what she'd almost said, that she'd thought it would be different with him. He wanted to pursue it, but he sensed that now wasn't the time. There was something more important to do, anyway—like somehow ease her pain.

"Rori—" he said softly, touching her arm.

She pulled away. The action stabbed him in the heart. "Just leave. Please."

"Rori, listen to me," he said, trying again, "we blew it. Both of us. I rushed you . . . you were in no emotional condition to be making love, anyway . . . and so you do have a problem—"

Rori turned and faced him coldly. "You still don't get it, do you, Cavannaugh? I don't respond. I'm cold, frigid, like the proverbial ice maid—"

Rori never got the opportunity to finish the word *maiden*. In one powerful, fluid movement, Blade hauled her to him, grinding his manhood into the cradle of her femininity as his lips crushed hers. His tongue instantly delved into the startled openness of her mouth, taking lover's liberties.

Rori was aware of the overwhelming strength in his arms. He could have snapped her in two had he chosen to! That thought fled, blending into the sudden, thick feelings his touch elicited. She felt fire blazing along her nerve endings, a fire that defied the cold shower she'd taken. Defied it. Mocked it. Laughed in its chilled, impotent face. Rori gripped Blade's strong arms, anchoring herself in the midst of the white-hot fire storm. But then, counteracting that move and casting herself adrift, she unknowingly molded her body to his—seeking, searching, sensually pleading for the fulfillment this man promised. She moaned low and deep.

Blade wrenched his mouth from hers, peering into her passion-soft eyes. "Whatever your problem," he rasped, as though supremely satisfied to have proven his point, "it isn't unresponsiveness. Not only aren't you cold, lady, you're hotter than hell!"

Desire was so ravaging her body that Rori could hardly think, much less speak. Even so, she could hardly have denied the logic of his statement. She certainly didn't feel cold. She pulled from him, desperately needing to escape into her own space. She laid her hand on the back of a chair for support . . . and tried to steady her erratic breathing.

Blade saw her sensual agony. And cursed himself for his insensitivity. Why hadn't he realized the misery she must be going through? The misery she must have gone through a hundred times before? Why hadn't he realized she was dealing with pent-up emotions that had no release valve? It gave a whole new meaning to the shower he'd heard running moments after she'd left the living room. A cold shower, he now suspected.

"Come here," he said tenderly, reaching for her to offer what solace he could.

She shrugged off his touch. "Leave," she said, adding, "please."

"I can't do that," he countered gently but firmly.

She turned on him, her eyes snapping with fury. "Dammit, I'm not some charity case in need of your pity!"

"I never said you were. Right now all I'm saying is that you—both of us—need a good night's sleep. We'll talk about everything in the morning."

Before Rori could offer further protest, he scooped her into his arms and started for the bed. She was so stunned it took her a moment to react. When she did, her response was violent.

"Let me down! And you're not staying! I—"

Blade yanked the covers, tossed Rori onto the bed and followed her down, his body pinning her struggling one.

"Don't!" she cried, pushing against him with both hands. They were hands he immediately, and easily, manacled with his own. His leg thrown across her thighs subdued her trashing. "Leave me alone, Blade! I don't want... I don't want..."

Oh, God, she thought, she didn't want what she could feel coming. She didn't want to cry. Not now. Not in front of this man. Despite what she wanted, however, she could feel the tears rushing to her eyes. Suddenly, they spilled forth. Her body heaved with their deliverance. And then her usual steel nerves shattered, and she didn't care how she might be disgracing herself. Nothing mattered except the shedding of tears so long denied. She cried because someone was trying to kill her. She cried because her body still ached with desire. She cried because it somehow felt like the right thing to do in this man's arms.

Blade said nothing. He offered no meaningless words in the face of her suffering. Instead, he pulled her into the shelter of his body and held her. Guiding her hands to his chest, he released them, then drew his own along the curve of her back. He tucked her head beneath his chin.

Rori had no idea how long she cried. A minute? Five? Ten? At last the tears stopped, leaving her depleted and world-weary. She stirred.

"Blade—"

"Shh. Go to sleep," he whispered, envying her the cleansing tears she'd shed.

Sighing softly, she nuzzled her tear-damp cheek to his chest and whispered something she didn't realize she was saying. "Stay," she said.

Blade heard the tiny thread of sound. It touched his heart as nothing ever had. Not trusting himself to speak, he tightened his hold on her.

Then, because she could not stop herself, Rori did as he'd bade. She drifted off to sleep. Her last coherent thought was that, for the first time in a long while, she felt safe. And if her body still remained frustrated, her soul was not, for inexplicably she'd shared something with this man that was far more intimate than the joining of two bodies.

Chapter Seven

When the phone rang, Rori jerked her head up, clipping Blade squarely beneath his beard-roughened chin. He moaned, the sound mingling with the crisp peal of the telephone. Still dazed with sleep, Rori stared at the man sharing her bed, the man in whose arms she'd been lying only seconds before. And lying peacefully, if the relaxed state of her body meant anything. Sometime during the night, Blade had slipped from his jeans, and his bare legs were warmly entwined with hers. Or were hers entwined with his? Both, she decided. The truth was, they were warmly, intimately entwined together.

Blade gazed into Rori's eyes, realizing that for the first time in he didn't know how long, he had slept the entire night without the dream's nightmarish intrusion.

"The phone," he said at last, nodding toward the still ringing instrument on the bedside table. "By the way, did anyone ever tell you that you have a hard head?'' He raised one hand to his chin and flexed his jaw.

Rori mumbled an apology, untangled her legs from his and pushed her hair from her face, then reached for the phone.

''Hello?'' she said, leaning against the headboard. She noted that Blade raised up on one elbow...and that the cover slid down his chest, crumpling at his waist. She withdrew her gaze, but couldn't banish the memory of her cheek against the strength of his chest. His sexy chest. His hair-dusted chest. His—

''Ms. Kelsey?'' The tone of the voice suggested that the caller had repeated her name.

Rori forced herself to focus her attention. ''Yes?''

''This is Detective Pinchera.''

''Yes, Detective.''

''I understand you had some trouble last night.''

The statement reminded Rori of being trapped in the elevator. Once more she felt fear, the jackhammering of her heart, the relief that had flooded her when Blade pulled her from the stifling cubicle and into his arms. Unable to stop herself, she looked at him. He was watching her. Intently. Even as she watched him watch her, he lowered his eyes. Hers followed suit. Her terry robe had fallen open, not entirely, but enough to reveal the generous swell of her breasts. Self-consciously, she drew the lapels together, fighting a blush.

''I spoke with the officers who answered your call last night and read their report—'' Rori's concentration returned to what Detective Pinchera was saying ''—but I'd like to speak with you myself. This morning, if that's convenient for you.''

''Certainly.''

''In an hour?''

Rori glanced at the antique-gold bedside clock. "Ten o'clock would be fine."

"See you then," the policeman said and hung up.

Rori cradled the receiver. "That, uh, that was Detective Pinchera," she told Blade, adding, "he wants to come by at ten. He wants to talk about what happened last night." Throughout her announcement her eyes never met Blade's— which she could feel boring into her. She hugged her robe to her, as though trying to hide in its depths.

Blade said nothing.

She shot him a quick look.

He was still propped on his elbow. Nonchalantly. As though he couldn't be more relaxed.

It suddenly dawned on Rori that she had no experience whatsoever in handling the morning after. Did you play it demurely, shyly? Or did you play the sophisticate extraordinaire and bat your lashes in an I-do-this-all-the-time attitude? She realized dismally that, whatever protocol was usually acceptable, none of it presently applied. Last night had hardly been a typical romantic liaison. In truth, it had been nothing but an embarrassing fiasco.

"I, uh, I better get dressed," she said, starting to slip from the bed.

Blade's hand shot out and captured her wrist. In one lithe, seemingly effortless motion, he hauled her back onto the mattress and imprisoned her body beneath his. As her gaze traveled up his chest to his face, she realized that this was a position she was finding herself in often of late. She also realized that he was naked, and only a sheet separated their bodies, since her robe had traitorously fallen open.

"Is that your idea of a proper good morning?" he asked.

Rori took in his sleep-tumbled hair, his suggestively slumberous eyes, his chin and jaws thick with a stubble of bristly shadows. It was the same jaw she'd whammed the dickens out of earlier. If her hand had been cut from her the following moment, she couldn't have stopped what she did next. Reaching out, she drew her fingertips across his chin.

"I'm sorry," she whispered. "Did I hurt you?"

"Yeah," he said, "I'm in excruciating pain." The huskiness of his response hinted at a pain that had nothing to do with the blow she'd given him, but rather with the state of another part of his body.

Gently, he nipped at her fingers with his teeth. Crazy fire shot through Rori, but she had only seconds to acknowledge the sensation before he lowered his head, his mouth targeting hers. A panic seized her.

"No," she whispered, rolling her head to the side.

Blade captured her chin in his unrelenting grasp and forced her mouth to his. She could feel the feathery sound of his voice against her lips when he said simply, unequivocally, "Yes."

His kiss was warm. Sweet and warm. Wet and warm. And it was all Rori could do not to respond to it. But she forced herself not to. It wasn't fair to him or to her. It wasn't fair to a relationship that was going nowhere—because there was nowhere for it to go. A relationship demanded both a man and a woman. Theirs was noticeably, hurtfully lacking the latter. Yet, despite herself, she could not help one response. At the healing quality of his kiss, filled with all the gentleness she'd dreamed of, her eyes misted with tears.

At her willed passivity, Blade didn't push. He withdrew his mouth and began to trace the outline of her lips with his nimble tongue. He heard the garbled moan she choked off in her throat. His tongue provocatively penetrated the seam of her lips, dipping ever so fleetingly, ever so teasingly inside. Blade knew he wasn't playing fair, and he didn't give a royal, not even a plebeian, damn. When Rori's moan turned to a gasp, Blade pushed home his advantage. Applying a light but insistent pressure to her jaw with his finger and thumb, he forced her mouth open like the petals of a flower. He eased his tongue inside, sipping at the honeyed nectar as though he were taking a cool, slow drink after a long, hot walk.

This time Rori couldn't hold back the deep-throated moan. Nor could she hold back the response he demanded—not if her life had depended on it. Her mouth parted beneath his, greedily taking what he was offering, offering in return a gift that he hungrily accepted. Her arms ached to slide along the curve of his bare back, her hands to spill through the thickness of his mussed hair, but these luxuries she would not allow herself, because if she indulged in them, forgetting this man would be more difficult. Instead, her fingers knotted themselves into the sheet. Tightly. Painfully. Pleadingly.

When her breathlessness rasped against the sunny-morning silence he pulled his mouth from hers—slowly, leaving his lower lip to cling momentarily to hers. His eyes drifted open to meet hers. Hers still held unshed tears.

Blade frowned. But something in her look pleaded for him not to ask why the tears were there.

Rori knew she couldn't explain the dreams about gentle, healing kisses. Nor could she explain the fresh tears that welled up when Blade lowered his head and kissed the corner of her dewy eye.

"Good morning," Blade whispered. When Rori didn't reciprocate, he added, "I think it's your turn."

"G-good morning."

Blade groaned, a deep, rich, masculine sound, as he trailed his knuckles down the ivory column of her throat. "Damn, but I love your voice! It's pure, unadulterated, gold-plated sexy."

At the word *sexy*, a streak of pain, humiliation and embarrassment coursed through Rori, and she turned her face from his.

"Look at me," he ordered. When she didn't, he forced her eyes to his. "You do know how sexy you are, don't you?"

"Blade, please—" she began in a tormented whisper.

"Obviously you don't, so I'll rephrase it. You do know how sexy *I* think you are, don't you?"

His eyes shone steady and strong, and if she hadn't known better, she almost would have believed he did think she was sexy. But how could he? Surely a man wanted a woman who was whole, who could enjoy lovemaking to the fullest. He'd already said enough to let her know that he'd once had less than whole. He didn't strike her as a man who'd compromise a second time.

"I was right," he said, "you are hardheaded."

Despite the seriousness of their discussion and the knot in her stomach that she feared stemmed more from his nearness than from the awkwardness of the morning after, Rori's lips twitched. Blade's joined in, though she thought his smile never quite reached his eyes. His haunted eyes.

Blade's smile faded. "We have to talk about last night."

"No," Rori pleaded, closing her eyes.

"Rori, it isn't going to go away."

Her lashes, the color of spun gold, raised to reveal eyes streaked with pain. "No, it isn't," she agreed. "But you can."

"I told you last night that I can't."

"Blade, please," she begged. "Just leave me alone."

"I asked you before, and you hung up the phone rather than lie to me. I'm going to ask you again, Rori. Is that really what you want? Do you really want me to walk out that door and keep walking?"

It was unlike her—downright foreign to her—not to know what she wanted. She'd wanted a career in radio communications, and she'd worked her rear off to get it. Night and day, because her small-town, small-farm parents hadn't been able to help with her college expenses. Then Dwayne Rogers had come along, and swept her off her feet. She'd wanted him, too. Their marriage had turned out badly, but she could never say that in the beginning she hadn't known what she'd wanted. But now? What did she want now? God help her, she knew the answer. She wanted to be normal...and to pursue this relationship with this man, wherever it might lead. But it was an option denied her. She wasn't normal.

"Dammit, Rori, answer me!"

"Yes!" she cried. "I want you to walk out that door and keep walking!"

Blade glared at Rori, still sprawled beneath him. Her hair spread around her in tantalizing disarray, while her aquamarine eyes tugged at his senses like the unrelenting pull of the sea's undercurrent. He wanted to shake her senseless, then pull her into his arms and kiss her into the same mindless state. Instead he spoke a single word with accusation. "Liar."

He rolled from her and slid from the bed. The sheet fell away to reveal a lean expanse of backside, tan except for the white outline of underwear. Obviously brief underwear. Just as obviously Blade felt no inhibition as he strolled around the bed, retrieved his jeans from the floor and thrust his legs into them. His back to her, he hauled them over his hips.

Her heart slamming out a heavy-metal beat even as her breath slowed to a three-quarter waltz, Rori watched him. One second seemed to merge with another. Suddenly, as though coming to herself, she threw her legs over the side of the bed, drew the robe around her and headed for the bathroom. She had just reached the door when Blade called out.

"Rori?"

She turned...her eyes drawn as if mesmerized to the open v at the front of his jeans. The night before he hadn't bothered to snap them. This time he hadn't even zipped them. She was very much aware of the wedge of skin and the intimate fringe of dark hair, matching that on his chest, that peeked out. Rori's gaze hurried upward. Blade's eyes seemed to be waiting patiently for hers to join them.

"Don't ever fake another orgasm," he said softly, but with an unmistakable sternness.

For all the powerful effect the words had on Rori, what he implied was far stronger, far more potent. Silently, he'd said that he was not walking out of her life despite what she said she wanted...and that they would again be lovers.

A tingly feeling spread through Rori's body, making speech an impossibility. Pulling her gaze from Blade's, she stepped into the bathroom and closed the door behind her. She started to offer up a prayer, but hadn't the foggiest idea what to pray for. That he'd be gone by the time she dressed? Or that he wouldn't? Or simply that she'd be able to decide which to pray for?

Twenty minutes later, the smell of freshly brewed coffee told her that not only hadn't Blade gone, but that he'd also made himself at home. Neither fact surprised her. What did surprise her was her reaction. She felt a flash of something that, though she didn't allow herself to analyze it, almost resembled relief.

As she crossed the living room, Blade's shoes and socks and shirt caught her eye. They were still on the floor where they'd been hastily abandoned the night before. The memory of their abandonment burned brightly within her. As did the disappointment that followed—and the embarrassment. And the fact that Blade had held her as she'd cried her eyes dry and her heart empty. Dwayne had never comforted her. He'd only blamed, accused, made her feel like the total failure she was.

As though she was the guest, Rori hesitated in the kitchen doorway. Blade leaned against the counter, one bare foot crossed over the other at the ankle. He gripped a mug in one hand. His other hand held a folded newspaper, and he seemed to be devouring an article.

Suddenly sensing Rori's presence, Blade glanced up from the newspaper, letting his eyes laze over her long legs, which were sheathed in starched jeans. From there he took in the red knit top, the absence of all but the most basic of makeup and the unstyled sweep of her hair, which suggested she'd done no more than rush a brush through it, allowing the willful curls to fall at their capricious whim.

At last he pushed from the cabinet and set down the paper, which he'd collected from the hallway. He poured a mug of coffee.

"Cream? Sugar?" he asked.

Rori forced her attention from Blade's chest. Though she'd been forewarned that he wasn't wearing a shirt, she nevertheless hadn't been prepared for the sight of him seminude. Nor for the roguish appeal his unshaved appearance gave him. She was grateful that he'd at least zipped and snapped his jeans.

"No," she said in answer to his query. "Just black."

He handed her the mug. Careful not to touch him, she took it, pulled a chair at the table and sat.

"If you want anything more for breakfast, you're on your own," Blade said. "I've just gone through my repertoire of culinary skills. Although I do pull a mean tab on a can of beer."

Rori dabbled with a grin. It felt good to ease the tension if only for a bit. "I don't eat breakfast."

Blade pulled out the chair opposite hers and sat. "Me, either. And if I do, it's likely to be at noon. Dinner's just as likely to be at midnight. And both are likely to be junk food. My eating habits drive Mrs. Yearwood—Dave's house-keeper—crazy."

Rori brought the mug of coffee to her lips and sipped. "Dave is the friend you sublease the apartment from?"

Blade nodded. "Yeah. He's in Europe for the summer... on an investigative reporting assignment."

Remembering that Blade had told her he was a writer and that he'd seemed vague when she asked what he wrote, she said, "Are you a reporter, too?"

The mug destined for Blade's lips hesitated, then completed its journey. "I was. Actually, I guess I still am. I think being an investigative reporter has more to do with personality than vocation. Some people are just curious by nature."

"But you write something else now?"

Again, there was a hesitation, which Rori noted. "Fiction. I write a little fiction." Before she could comment, he added, "Actually, it was during my days as a reporter that I began my odd eating habits. You go with a story no matter the hour."

Rori sensed he'd avoided her question, but she didn't push the issue. "Well, that's the nice thing about living alone. You can eat what you want, when you want."

"How long have you been divorced?"

The question came suddenly, catching Rori completely off guard. "Eighteen months." Even as the words spilled out, she thought that Blade Cavannaugh must be one heck of an investigator.

"And?"

"And what?"

"No 'three days, eighteen hours, three minutes and thirty seconds... but who's counting'?"

No, Rori amended, he was a dynamite investigator. He knew just the right question to ask. "I did my counting waiting for the divorce to become final."

"You were that eager?"

"I was that eager," she said, unable to keep the bitterness from her voice.

"Does he have a name?"

Rori stood and went to the coffeepot to freshen coffee that didn't need freshening. "Dwayne...Dwayne Rogers."

Blade frowned. "Why does that name sound familiar?"

"He does the weekend sports on Channel Four."

"*That* Dwayne Rogers? The Robert Redford look-alike?"

Rori gave a mirthless laugh at an image of her ex-husband standing before the mirror, comb in hand, his eye peeled for any imperfection, any—God forbid—sign of middle age. "Believe me, for that comment, he'd probably put you in his will."

"He sounds like a river that doesn't run too deep," Blade said bluntly, not even trying to like the guy.

Rori assessed the statement. Sadly, she had to agree with it. In the beginning Dwayne's aggressiveness, his workaholic fervor, so much like her own, had appealed to her. She had grown, however, to see that his aggressiveness and his fervor were based on insecurity. Beyond the insecurity, there was a shallowness, a reverence for surface rather than substance. Yet he could be charming. How else had he managed so quickly, so thoroughly, to talk her into being his wife? Rori shrugged. "He had his moments. He was good to kids and dogs."

"Unfortunately, he wasn't good to his wife," Blade said, watching the instant hurt that leaped into Rori's eyes. He would have liked to slam-dunk Dwayne Rogers for the sheer pleasure of feeling his fist smash into the other man's pretty-boy face. Let the jerk report that on the evening sports news!

Suddenly the hurt was too much for Rori to cope with, especially on a morning when everything seemed confusing. "What about you?" she asked, directing the conversation away from her.

"What about me?"

"You're divorced, too, right?"

"No."

The single word was like the slash of a knife. It took a moment for the throbbing ache to begin. Rori didn't analyze the ache's intensity. "But I thought—"

"My wife's dead." The blandness of his tone said far more than any emotion could have. Despite Blade's obvious pain, Rori couldn't help but feel relieved. Nor could she help the guilt she felt at her response. But it didn't change the fact that, inexplicably, she didn't want this man tied to another woman.

"I haven't been with a woman in a while. Nine months is a long time. I'd forgotten how good it could feel."

The words came back to Rori, bringing with them a feeling of triumph. It was a small thing, but it was more than she was accustomed to. She'd felt good to this man. Albeit she hadn't been perfect, and maybe he'd been desperate, but still he'd said that she felt good. It was more than she'd gotten from her husband. "Your wife died nine months ago?" she asked.

"Yeah," Blade confirmed. He rose to fill a mug that was far from empty. The two stood at the counter—side by side, thigh to thigh.

Suddenly Rori wanted to ask a thousand questions. How had she died? Had it been unexpected? And was he still crazy in love with her?

"Was she ill?" Rori heard herself asking.

"No...yes..." he said, raking his fingers through his hair. "Look, could we just forget it?"

His sudden curtness stung. "Sure," Rori said, her voice clipped with hurt.

To hide the emotion, she glanced at the paper and started to read. A quarter of the page, the article Blade must have been reading, dealt with a psychologist's interpretation of why the strangler was selecting only blond-haired women.

"The killer unquestionably has ambivalent feelings regarding blond-haired women," Dr. Bernard Haven was quoted as saying. "While on the one hand, a blond-haired woman has probably been the object of his love, this same woman has disappointed him—angered him, hurt him, betrayed him—and now he can no longer distinguish between that blond-haired woman and all blond-haired women. Without doubt the killer is fascinated by blond hair..."

"I'm sorry." Blade's apology cut through Rori's halfhearted attempt to read the article. Her eyes rested on the newspaper without seeing a word of print. Cupping her cheek in his palm, Blade drew her gaze to his. "I'm sorry," he repeated. "It's just that my wife's death is an ugly story."

"My divorce isn't exactly a remake of Cinderella," Rori pointed out.

"We've both been hurt," he said, his voice low and gravelly. "Couldn't we make a truce and try not to add to each other's pain?"

As Blade asked the question, the hand at her cheek came into contact with renegade curls. They played about his fingers, teasing like silent sexy sirens. Immersing his fingers in the tangle of wayward swirls, he threaded the hair from her face, then slowly, like a worshiper at a blond altar, drew his fingers the length of the ribbonlike skeins.

"God, your hair's beautiful," he whispered, watching his fingers slide through the tawny mane. Carefully grasping a fistful, he brought the shiny gold to his face. He buried his nose in its apricot-clean smell and nuzzled his hair-roughened cheek in its satin softness.

Rori's breath splintered at the pure sensuality of the act.

Blade's breath fractured as a wave of hot desire washed over him.

She stared at him with hazy blue-green eyes.

He stared at her with eyes of heated gray.

Time stood still.

The sudden sound of the doorbell shattered the moment.

Reluctantly, as though it were the last thing he wanted to do, Blade released her hair. "I'll be in the shower," he said thickly, then turned and walked from the room.

As Rori watched his bare back and lean hips, the doorbell rang again. It rang a third time before she answered it.

Detective Anthony Pinchera stood four years away from retirement and one inch above the department's height requirement. He was thin and impressively wiry. A black cap of hair waved across his head, and royal-blue eyes peered from beneath thick, angular eyebrows. A full mustache, as dark as a winter night, slashed across his upper lip.

"How are you?" the officer asked, his concern genuine. Rori led him into the living room, at the last moment worried that Blade's clothes might be scattered around. She breathed a sigh of relief when she realized he had picked them up. Then she heard the shower running.

She shrugged, settling comfortably on the sofa. "All right, I guess. To be honest, I'm not too sure how I'm supposed to be."

"Scared, angry, wishing to hell the police would do their job."

A grin nipped Rori's lips. "Then I guess I'm feeling normal."

"Believe me, Ms. Kelsey, I know it looks like we aren't doing much, but we're doing everything we can with what we have to work with."

"Which isn't much, right?"

"It isn't a lot, but it's not totally negligible, either." With that, he reached into a folder he'd brought with him and removed a sheet of paper. He moved to sit beside her on the sofa. "The lab has finished with the letters you received."

Rori glanced at the paper in his hand. The four short letters had been photocopied onto one page. "Did they find anything?" she asked eagerly.

"There were no fingerprints—"

"I knew it!" Rori interjected.

"But," Detective Pinchera said, snagging Rori's attention immediately, "we did identify the typewriter."

"That's good, isn't it?" she asked, trying to recall every crime show she'd seen.

"It's something," Tony Pinchera acknowledged, "and at this point, I'll settle for anything."

So would she, Rori thought, vaguely aware that the shower had stopped running.

"It's a manual typewriter. The make is Underwood, the model one that was discontinued in 1963. The interesting thing is," he said, indicating with his lean finger, "that it has a faulty *o* key. See, it doesn't quite close at the top." He slid his finger to several *o*'s to prove his point.

Rori noted that, indeed, in each case, there was a slight gap at the top. As pleased as she was to have something to go on, she was nevertheless disappointed. "This isn't exactly going to lead us to his door, is it?"

"No," the detective admitted, "but it'll help us to nail the door shut on him."

Rori refrained from pointing out that they had to find him first. As though she could no longer sit still, she rose and walked to the sliding glass door, which admitted bright sunshine. The temperatures were swelling to sweltering proportions. Or maybe she was picking up some of the left-over heat from the passion the room had witnessed the night before.

"By the way," Tony Pinchera added, and something in his tone warned Rori she wasn't going to like what he was about to say, "the official report on last night's elevator incident reads that there were insufficient grounds to deem it an attempt on your life. An elevator maintenance crew was here today. They crawled all over the system and could find nothing wrong—other than that the elevator is old."

Rori stared in disbelief. Anger, a seed planted in frustration, sprouted and bloomed. "It wasn't an accident! I heard someone, Detective. I'd stake my life on it." She laughed harshly as she pushed her hair from her face. "In fact, that's exactly what I did. Last night."

"Isn't it possible that someone wedged something between the cable and the drum and came back later and removed it?" a third voice suggested.

Startled, Rori glanced toward the door. Blade was advancing into the room as though he owned it and the world. He was dressed in his jeans and thankfully, this time he'd added the shirt, though he'd left it hanging outside.

"Blade Cavannaugh." He introduced himself, extending his hand to the police officer, who stood at Blade's approach.

"Detective Pinchera," the man replied.

"Mr. Cavannaugh...Blade...is my neighbor," Rori explained. With his shower-damp hair, unshaven face and casual familiarity, it was obvious he was more. She wished to heaven she knew exactly what that more was.

"To answer your question," Tony Pinchera said, "that's possible, of course. Personally, I find it highly suspicious that there was nothing wrong this morning with an elevator that had stopped altogether last night."

"I can assure you that it was dead in the water around midnight," Blade said.

"Blade is the one who found me," Rori added, her eyes grazing his. She couldn't keep her cheeks from heating as she remembered the hours that had followed.

The detective nodded. "Someone could have come back and removed a wedge without anyone being the wiser," he admitted. "Last night my men checked the premises for someone who shouldn't be here."

"What about someone who should?" Blade asked.

"You mean, what if whoever is sending the threatening letters is someone in the building or someone in the neighborhood?"

"Exactly," Blade answered.

As the two men discussed that chilling possibility, Rori listened with grim fascination. It wasn't anything she hadn't thought of before, but hearing it spoken aloud gave the idea a whole new, frightening meaning. Frightening also was what the two men didn't say. By deliberate design, Rori concluded, neither man suggested what everyone in the room was thinking. Was there a possibility that the threats were tied in with the prostitute killings plaguing the city?

Minutes later, however, Rori received some idea of just how serious Detective Pinchera thought the matter was. "Oh, by the way," he said as he was leaving, "I've made arrangements for a car to swing by and pick you up—both going to and coming from the station."

"Is that necessary?" Rori asked, uncomfortable with the thought of an escort but equally uncomfortable, after last night, with the thought of not having one.

"I think it's time to exercise caution," the officer said.

"I'll see that she gets to and from work," Blade said.

Rori turned, her eyes finding those of the man who'd made the offer. Blade was watching intently, waiting for her approval. Both knew he was asking for more than the right to escort her. He was asking for entrance into her life on a more intimate plane. Earlier he'd made it clear that he wasn't walking out of her life. Now he wanted some assurance that she wasn't going to run from him, that she, too, recognized that something was happening between them.

Later, Rori marveled at how easy the decision had been. She hadn't expected that. She'd expected to feel the same confusion she always felt with this man. But what she saw when she looked into his eyes was a plea. A plea to trust him and to believe that he'd protect her. A plea to give the two of them a chance.

"A police escort won't be necessary," she said softly.

Some emotion passed across Blade's eyes. For a moment, Rori might well have believed that her trusting him had been the single most important thing in the world.

Chapter Eight

That, my nighttime friends," Rori said, her bedroom voice gliding onto the airwaves as though it was slipping between satin sheets, "was Steve Winwood and his current hit. Yes, Steve, we hear the night music playing. And we hear it right here on KKIX. That's ninety-six point seven on your listening dial. And guess what, night owls. I know, I know, I can't believe it's time to go, either, but the midnight hour is upon us—drawing us into its sweet embrace, brushing us with its dark kiss, whispering its alluring promise." Rori spoke the last in a tone that pledged something unbelievably seductive to each listener. "Join us again tomorrow night, and until then, be healthy, be happy, be in love."

The station ceased broadcasting and Rori, sighing with fatigue, pulled the headset off and laid it on the console. She was making a concerted effort, as she had all evening, not to think of the man who'd driven her to work that afternoon, the man who'd promised to be waiting for her at the end of the show, the man who should be waiting for her at this very moment.

Blade.

Her heart skipped a beat despite her resolve. She'd seen little of him over the weekend. He'd phoned twice on Saturday, three times on Sunday, quick calls to make certain she was all right. She'd half expected—no, wholly expected—him to try to see her at least one night. But he hadn't. It was as though he sensed he should give her the time and space that unquestionably she had needed. She'd been working to reconcile two seemingly irreconcilable facts. One, she didn't want a relationship with him, she had nothing to offer him, she was only setting herself up for another humiliating fall; and two, knowing all that, she could not turn away from him. Nor could she help but miss him. The latter had led her to wonder if maybe his giving her privacy had been a sly maneuver on his part to show her just how much she did want him.

Gathering her things, she left the control booth and headed for the door that would take her out of the building. "G'night," she called to the engineer.

"Night," he called. "Hey, you sure you got a ride?"

"Yeah. Thanks, though."

The summer night, no longer impressed with the cooling rain of days before, was hot and humid. When she opened the door, the ebony darkness hurled itself at her, impaling her with its sticky, stifling breath. She glanced toward the alleyway, where cars parked in lieu of a proper parking lot, but she saw only the engineer's van. She hesitated on the verge of re-entering the building. She told herself it only made sense to await Blade in air-conditioned comfort, but the truth was that she didn't want to wait outside alone.

Someone stepped from the shadows. Rori's heart turned over until she recognized Blade's broad shoulders, lean hips and loose-limbed gait. Both hands were casually tucked into the front pockets of his jeans. His snug jeans.

"Hi," he said, ambling toward her.

"Hi," she answered, suddenly more breathless than the hot night warranted. "I, uh, I didn't see your car."

"I thought you liked to walk home after the show."

She vaguely remembered telling him that in one of the brief weekend phone calls. "Yeah, I do, but I didn't mean—"

"Can you make it in those things?" he interrupted, looking at her heels.

A giddy exhilaration rushed through Rori at the prospect of returning to her schedule. It would be the first time she'd walked since Wednesday. Her eyes bright, she said, "Let me get my walking shoes."

She'd already turned for the door when Blade said, "Give me your purse and notebook."

He took them before she could pass them to him. In the process their hands brushed. Rori's eyes hurried to Blade's, then lowered, as though ordained by some primitive, savage authority, to his lips. She hadn't kissed him, or been kissed by him, since Saturday morning. Right now it seemed an eternity ago. Would his kiss still be so gentle it brought tears to her eyes?

"You gonna get your shoes?" the lips she was staring at asked.

"W-what?"

"Your shoes," Blade repeated, hauling Rori to her senses.

In less than a minute, she returned with a pair of tennis shoes that obviously had made the journey more than once. Sitting on the brick border that surrounded a huge palm tree, starlight skipping through its stiletto-like fronds, Rori slipped quickly out of her heels and laced on the walking shoes. Standing, she bent to retrieve the heels.

Blade's gaze lowered to her slim, shapely rear end. An image of that same anatomical part unclothed flashed through his mind...and through his body, leaving him aching with an exquisite pain. Had it been only that weekend he'd pinned her beneath him, his hands cupping the sweetness he was presently looking at? Had it been only that weekend he'd mindlessly lost himself in a way he never had before?

"What?" he asked, realizing she'd spoken.

"I said, are you ready?"

"Yeah. Sure. Let's go."

They started off side by side, Blade matching his stride to Rori's. Though she was tall, he was a good head and shoulders taller. Occasionally his shoulder brushed hers or hers brushed his. Each time she was left feeling safe and secure. Even so, she peered at every suspicious shadow, turned at every unexpected sound. She thought she sensed a wariness in Blade as well, though he said nothing. She said little. The silence that swelled between them was strangely comfortable, oddly familiar, as though they'd often communicated without the encumbrance of words. Which was true enough, Rori decided. They'd spoken to each other for weeks with nothing more than gazes, glances and stares.

As they crossed an intersection after pausing at a stop sign, Blade, like a schoolboy carrying his girl's books, shifted her purse and notebook to his other hand.

"What me to take them?" Rori asked.

"Uh-uh. They're fine. Want me to take those?"

Rori looked at the shoes she dangled by their heels from one hand. "No, they're fine."

"How was work?" Blade asked.

"Kinda hectic. There were a lot of call-in requests."

"I know."

She glanced at him, wondering if he always listened to the show. She didn't ask, though. Instead, she said, "How was your day?"

"Fair."

"Do writers write every day?"

Blade thought of the hailstorm of paper on his kitchen floor. "Most would like to, but it doesn't always work out. Sometimes the muse goes on vacation." He added, with noticeable sarcasm, "Mine seems to have taken a slow boat to China."

Rori noted the frustration in his voice and wondered if this was the writer's block she'd heard about. Emboldened by the fact that he was at least talking about the writing, which was more than he usually seemed willing to do, she said, "You said you write fiction. What kind?"

Blade slanted his gaze, dreading the questions he knew would follow, yet wanting to get them over with. They were inevitable, unavoidable questions. "Novels."

The interest he knew he would see, the interest he'd seen a thousand times in other eyes, sparked in Rori's. "Novels? What kind?"

It was coming, but he could delay it. "Murder and crime, blood and gore—all that stuff readers shell out money for."

"Yeah?" Rori asked, now clearly fascinated. "Have you published any?"

"A few."

"I don't read much murder and crime, but my dad does. I'll have to see about getting them for him. Maybe you could autograph them for him?" she asked hopefully.

The time had come. There was no avoiding it. "I, uh, I don't write under my own name. I use a pseudonym." He paused, then said, "B. J. Nichols."

Rori halted in midstep, her eyes rushing to the man beside her, taking him in as though she'd never seen him until that moment. She started to speak, obviously had trouble forming a sentence, then, on a second try, blurted out, "You're B. J. Nichols?"

Blade had little choice but to stop walking, too. Either that or leave her behind. "No," he said, knowing he was splitting hairs, but saying it anyway, "I'm Blade Jefferson Cavannaugh. I just write as B. J. Nichols."

Rori raked her fingers through her hair. "I can't believe it," she said. "You're B. J. Nichols."

Blade didn't feel like splitting hairs again, so he said wearily, "It's no big deal."

"No big deal? My God, you and Tom Clancy and Robert Ludlum and Stephen King have the best-seller list wrapped up."

"It's no big deal."

"I bought your book for my father for Christmas! *Murder in a Minor Key*. It was the only one he hadn't read. Even Dwayne read—"

"Dammit, Rori, it's no big deal!"

His vehemence and anger startled Rori even as they confused her. They also hurt a bit. Maybe a lot.

Blade saw her confusion and hurt and loathed himself for inflicting his pain and insecurities on the woman beside him. "I'm sorry," he said, sighing heavily into the muggy night. "It's just that my wife didn't handle it well."

He didn't define *it*, but Rori surmised that he meant his success.

"Look, it's no big deal, okay?" he asked, his voice soft. Rori thought it held a note of pleading, the same pleading she'd seen in his eyes Saturday morning as he'd waited to see if she was going to grant him access to her life. Though she didn't clearly know in what way, she knew this man had been hurt. Badly. By his wife. Just as she had been hurt by

Dwayne. How odd that two broken spirits should find each other.

"Okay?" he repeated.

Rori nodded. "Okay."

The rest of the walk passed in silence, as did the elevator ride to her floor. As the ancient cubicle jostled its way up, Blade glanced at her, lending support for what had to be a difficult ride following her experience Friday night. She sought his gaze as though needing that support. Opening the grill gate, Blade wordlessly motioned for Rori to precede him. She did, just as wordlessly asking him to pass her her purse. When he did, she fished inside for the key to the apartment, wondering if he would come in. Should she invite him? Should she offer him a nightcap?

My, God, he was B. J. Nichols!

Perhaps, a part of her argued, but it was going to be hard to think of him as anyone other than the stranger on the nearby balcony, the man who grew beautiful roses with beer and neglect, the man who'd rescued her Friday night—the man who knew how to kiss her breathless, until her knees trembled.

She unlocked the door, stepped inside and turned on a lamp. Before she could make any offer, Blade followed her in, depositing her notebook on the thin-legged Victorian commode that held a vase of perky pink roses. He then proceeded, wordlessly, to check out each room of the apartment. He walked to the door, from which Rori had not roamed. She watched his approach, wondering if she wanted him to say or to leave. It seemed to be the question she was always asking herself.

"Bolt the door after me," he said, making his intentions obvious. Once more Rori was uncertain how she felt, though she could have sworn a part of her was disappointed.

"Thanks. For walking me home."

Blade's eyes found hers, lingered, then lowered to her lips. Rori felt her insides tighten. Before she could ponder whether she wanted him to kiss her, he angled his head and, sliding his palm along her cheek, placed his mouth over hers.

His kiss was warm, gentle, undemanding. The moment his lips connected with hers, she realized with a perfect clarity that she had wanted this kiss. Maybe more than she'd ever wanted anything. Certainly more than she'd wanted anything in a long while. She splayed her hand against the broad wall of his chest and sighed, a soft, throaty sound that Blade heard and was helpless not to respond to.

Reaching with his other hand, he laid it along her other cheek, holding her face toward him. His lips quickened, burying themselves in hers with an ardent intent. For seconds, his mouth worked against hers, hard, fast, boldly taking the pleasure and sustenance he needed, giving in return what he sensed she, too, needed. Then, as quickly as his kiss had burst into a searing blaze, it died to a teasing flame. Slowly, he pulled his mouth from hers. His hands still cradling her cheeks, his lips still only a whisper from hers, he spoke.

"Bolt the door behind me."

She nodded her head, unwittingly brushing her lips against his. He moaned as fire danced in his veins. Giving her one last quick kiss, he left . . . as though if he didn't go now, he might stay. As he stepped into the hallway, Rori called out.

"Blade?"

He turned.

"About you're being B. J. Nichols," she said quietly, sincerely. "It's no big deal."

"It's no big deal."

The words echoed in Blade's mind the next afternoon as he drove from the radio station, where he'd delivered Rori, to the public library. He had felt like a million bucks since she'd uttered the parting words the night before. But then, what had he expected her to say and do when she learned what he did for a living, when she learned how successful he'd been at doing it?

The truth was, he hadn't known what to expect. It was just that when you'd been burned once, you were leery of all fire. Anna Marie's insecurity had conditioned him to expect everyone to respond that way. At least every woman. But Rori wasn't Anna Marie. His fame and success didn't mean anything to her; they didn't cause her to think less of herself. Probably because she had fame and success—hell, he'd passed two billboards on the way to the library with her gorgeous face plastered all over them in advertisement of the station! No, Rori wasn't insecure. She was sure and confident. Except in one area of her life. And that he intended to do something about ... if there was any way he could.

He parked the car and jogged the short distance to the library, taking the stairs in leaps of two and three. He found the card catalog, then the shelf bearing books on sexual dysfunction. Unloading the entire shelf, he located an empty table and amassed the books around him like skyscrapers. He began to read.

Six hours later, around nine o'clock, he was ready for a break. He also was ready to assimilate some of what he had learned. Standing, avoiding the curious look of the prim librarian who had noticed the subject matter of the mountain of books surrounding him, he walked to the water fountain and took a long swig of cold water. Certain conclusions were taking shape. Sexual dysfunction problems ranged in severity. A woman who had never had an orgasm presented a different challenge from a woman who was unable to achieve one under a certain set of circumstances...or with a certain partner. One fact he read in text after text—the one quality that had to be present for a woman to abandon herself to a climax was trust in her partner.

Trust.

No one knew the importance of that more than he did. No one had suffered more from its absence than he had. Was it possible that Rori had suffered, too?

"How did you meet Dwayne Rogers?" Blade asked that night as he and Rori walked from the radio station to her apartment. The question had interrupted a long stretch of silence.

Rori glanced at him. She hadn't been expecting that question. "Actually, he bought me."

Blade arched an eyebrow.

"It was a charity auction. He'd just moved here from Kentucky to work at Channel Four."

"How much did you go for?" Blade asked, curiosity getting the better of him. He wanted to know what the going rate was for the sexiest woman he'd ever seen.

Rori looked embarrassed. "You have to understand that he didn't spend his own money. Channel Four, for publicity purposes, picked up the tab."

"How much?" Blade repeated.

"Twenty-five hundred," she said in a small voice that she hoped he didn't hear.

He whistled. "Twenty-five hundred? Did anyone go for more?"

She shook her head again. "But it wasn't his money," she hastened to point out again.

Blade's mouth quirked into a grin. He suddenly realized that of late he'd started grinning again, sometimes even when he was alone. It felt good. "At those prices, I certainly hope you validated parking."

Rori smiled. Of late, Blade had been smiling more. She liked it. A lot. "I didn't, but the restaurant I took him to did."

The grin disappeared slowly, replaced by a look that curled her toes. "Frankly, I think he got you for a steal."

Her curled toes curled more tightly.

"So," he asked, tossing out another question, "How long before you married him?"

"Two weeks—I know," she said, her voice filled with self-reproach, "I thought it happened only in the movies, too. And you're right, I should have known better. But, honest to goodness, he was so charming. So damned charming! Believe me, there's nothing worse than a charming man."

"Did you sleep with him before you got married?" Even though Rori knew quite well that Blade could be blunt, she wasn't expecting him to be this blunt. Her startled look evidently said as much because he added, "I'm just trying to find out if the problem came before or after."

Rori felt her face coloring. "After."

"Meaning?"

"Meaning?" she repeated.

"Meaning, did it come afterward because you were able to climax before you married him, or did it come afterward because you didn't sleep with him before the wedding?"

"You are an investigative reporter, aren't you?" she asked. "Ten to one, you were tops in the profession."

Blade thought of the two prestigious awards he'd won, but didn't mention them. At the moment he cared about only one thing. "Did you sleep with him before the wedding?"

"No!" She sighed. "No," she said softly.

"Have you ever climaxed?"

"Blade—" she pleaded.

"With any man? Alone?"

She groaned.

Blade grabbed her wrist. They had stopped in the middle of a residential street. Overhead, a sliver of new moon hung like a scythe in the black sky.

"I have a right to know," he said gruffly.

Even in the dark, she could see his eyes, could feel their power charging through her. He did have a right. She knew that, *felt* that. He'd had a right since the first time their eyes had connected over the lacy filigree of balcony railings. She had no idea what intangible thing bound them, but he did have a right.

"Once," she whispered so faintly that it sounded like the muted buzzing of a nocturnal insect. "A long time ago with my high school sweetheart. I, uh, I didn't date much in college," she added, feeling the need to explain her almost celibate life. "I was too busy trying to work and go to school. Then, afterward, I was too busy trying to get established in a job. Actually, I never stayed too long in one place before New Orleans. Moving around is part of the business. At least in the beginning. You're always moving up to something better."

"But you did climax once?"

"Yes, Blade, yes!"

"Good. Excellent." At her questioning look, he explained, "It tells me that your body can. It's just chosen not to."

"Chosen not to?"

"Wrong word. A better word is conditioned. You've become conditioned not to climax. The female orgasm can be conditioned easily and is subject to inhibition. For whatever reason, there was a time when you consciously held back a response. After several repetitions of this voluntary inhibition of the orgasmic reflex, the inhibition seems to become automatic, something you no longer can control.''

Rori stared. ''You sound like a textbook.''

An image of the dozens of books he'd read at the library flashed through his mind. ''Close enough. One other question.'' At her look of oh-please-not-again, he said, ''This one's easy. At least easier. Were you and Dwayne competitive? Professionally, I mean?''

Rori gave a mirthless laugh. ''You're right. That one *is* easy. The answer is yes. He resented it every time Night Spice climbed higher on the charts. I could never figure out why,'' she said, her voice revealing her genuine perplexity...and her hurt. ''I was so pleased every time something good happened to him. But no matter what success he had, it never seemed to be enough.''

Blade longed to comfort her. His hand, the one that had grasped her wrist, slid into her hand, their fingers locking together. ''Success,'' he said, ''is always hardest on those who don't have it.''

Rori could feel his pain. She longed to comfort him, and the feeling made her brave. ''Your wife couldn't handle yours, could she?'' The question caused him to withdraw. He tried to pull his hand from hers, but she held on. ''I have a right to know,'' she said, using his words.

She did. Blade knew that. He also knew that he wanted to share his pain with her. He wanted to tell her everything, every sordid thing, about his marriage, but he couldn't. Not yet. He couldn't tell her of his guilt, because he feared that she would think him guilty...and that he would see the accusation in her beautiful blue-green eyes. That, he couldn't stand. There was one thing he had to share, though, because the weight of it was crushing him.

"She, uh..." He swallowed, searching for the best words. There were no good words, however, for what he had to say. "Nine months ago she...she hanged herself." He made the announcement with no emotion whatsoever.

Hanged herself.

The words crept into Rori's senses like a nightmarish beast, leaving a horrid image of a woman dangling in thin air. Perhaps because she'd been so focused of late on strangulation, Rori's throat constricted as though a thick, hemp rope had been drawn around it, choking off all oxygen. She fought the urge to claw at the unseen, villainous cord; she fought at the swell of panic rising inside her. At last she felt it receding.

"I..." she started, but didn't know what to say. What did you say to a man whose wife hanged herself? What about the truth? "I'm sorry, Blade. So very sorry."

He made no response. He didn't react. He adopted a vacant look. They made the rest of the trip in silence, though their hands remained entwined. After they stepped into her apartment, he closed the door behind them and, leaning against it, he pulled her into his arms. Neither spoke. Each held and was held by the other. At last he pulled back and whispered a fleeting kiss upon her lips. Then he was gone, leaving her to feel that they'd shared something special, something forever worth remembering.

Wednesday passed much like the two days before it. Considering the mood in which they'd parted, Rori wondered what their next meeting would be like. The drive to the station was so short that it gave no hint of how Blade was feeling. For the first time since escorting her to work, however, as if he, too, felt that their relationship had taken a step forward, he leaned across the seat of the car and kissed her.

"See you later," he promised.

Because the kiss was unexpected, because it tingled like champagne bubbles on her lips, Rori nodded.

As usual, at midnight he was waiting for her. He wore shorts and a T-shirt that were only one notch away from being casually slouchy. He couldn't have looked better, Rori decided the moment she set eyes on him. But then, hadn't she been counting the minutes until she saw him again?

"Here," he said, holding open a small sack as they started their trek.

"What is it?" Rori asked, unable to see what he was offering.

"Pralines," he said, referring to the sweet confection made of brown sugar and pecans.

Rori groaned as she reached into the sack. "Do you know how many calories in one of these?"

"A million ten?"

"A million fifteen."

"The more the better. When a writer can't write, he consumes calories. Lots of them. Preferably sugar-coated."

"Well, I can assure you—" she moaned as the candy dissolved in her mouth "—this is the last thing I need. At the station we try to avoid that sedentary disease known as fanny spread."

"Let me reassure you," Blade said, his voice suddenly as dark as the night, as husky as the chafing heat, "that there's nothing wrong with your fanny."

The words seemed to knock the props from Rori's knees. The memory of his hands sliding over her derriere, her bare derriere, sculpting her body to his, danced through her mind. It was a heady, provocative memory, one of many she daily, nightly, tried to keep at bay. She looked away before his smoldering gaze set her body blazing.

Rori cleared her throat...and changed the subject. "I take it you're having trouble writing."

Blade gave a brittle, harsh laugh. "That's an understatement. More accurately, I'm not writing at all."

"Why?"

He glanced at her, his look saying he resented such a simple, logical question. "Sometimes the creativity just isn't there." He withdrew his eyes and crushed the empty sack in his hands. He threw it into a wire trash basket they were passing. "Sometimes the magic just isn't there."

"Why?" Rori repeated. "I mean, as a nonwriter I don't understand that. If you can write one day, why can't you the next?"

"My wife's psychiatrist says I can't write because I feel guilty," Blade said, surprising himself with the admission. He hadn't been going to get into this subject. Why was he doing it now? Why was he risking everything? Was it because he felt himself getting in over his head with this woman? Perhaps, if they had no future, he wanted to know it now.

"Do you feel guilty?"

Blade kept his eyes straight ahead, as though seeing specters in the night. "Yes," he said hoarsely. "If I'd paid her more attention, if I'd taken her death threats seriously, if..." He sighed. "Damn, I hate that word!"

"Do you think your wife would want you to? Feel guilty, I mean."

"Oh, yeah," he said, the admission, as sharp as a new knife, coming without a second's hesitation. "She'd be delighted."

Rori had been so certain of his negative response, so certain she'd scored a victory, that his reply left her all but speechless. She'd sensed that his marriage, like her own, had been troubled, but she'd never realized how morbidly troubled. Suddenly she understood more clearly the haunted look in his eyes. What she didn't understand was the ache in *her* heart, caused by the desperate need to do or say something that would ease his pain.

"Then she'd be wrong," Rori said emphatically.

"How do you know?" Blade asked, something akin to anger bursting free. "You don't know a damned thing about me! Maybe I deserve to feel everything I'm feeling! Maybe I deserve a hundred times more!"

They had stopped beneath the spreading limbs of one of the elm trees outside the apartment. In the shadows, Blade stood as though ready for battle.

He had spoken the truth, Rori realized. She didn't know anything about him. Nothing tangible. Nothing she could swear to in court. Yet intuitively she knew a world of things about him. Heart things. Things that couldn't be explained. Things that couldn't be denied.

"I know that you could never hurt anyone deliberately. That I'd stake my life on."

Blade said nothing. He watched Rori, assessing the certainty in her eyes, the conviction in her voice. How amazing that this woman, whom he'd known such a short while, could have unlimited faith in him when his own wife... Groaning, Blade reached for Rori, yanking her into his arms and crushing her mouth with his. The high-heeled shoes she carried fell to the ground. He kissed her roughly, harshly, needing to drink in every ounce of her faith, needing to dine on the absolution she so unsparingly offered.

"You taste sweet," he murmured against her lips.

"Pralines," she whispered.

"No," he said, his mouth still eating at hers, "salvation. You taste like salvation."

Rori had no idea what he meant. She knew only that no one had kissed her as he was kissing her. No one had kissed her as though his sanity, his life, depended on it.

At two o'clock on Thursday afternoon, Rori's phone rang.

"Hello?"

"Walk over and I'll cut you some roses to take to work. I might even offer you a beer."

Rori recognized the caller instantly, and she smiled. She could tell Blade was in a good mood. She could hear the smile in his voice. A million times she'd thought of the conversation they'd had the night before. A million times she'd thought of the way he'd kissed her. And she'd wondered where the two of them, each wounded, were headed. A million times, she'd told herself she shouldn't be headed anywhere, yet she heard herself saying, "How can a woman refuse that kind of offer on a hot summer afternoon?"

"That's kinda what I thought," Blade said. "C'mon over," he added.

"Give me ten minutes."

"Five."

"I need to finish dressing."

"Not on my account," he answered huskily.

Rori closed her eyes as the sultriness of his voice feathered across her senses. Though he hadn't pushed, she knew he wanted to be intimate. She knew because it was what she wanted, too. Sometimes she thought she'd burst wide open from wanting it. Yet, regrettably, ironically, their joining would not ease her pain. It would only increase it.

"Five minutes," he repeated, then hung up before she could respond.

In less than ten minutes, but more than five, Rori, wearing a red and white sundress with a red bolero jacket and white strappy sandals with high heels, opened the door of her apartment en route to Blade's. At the sight that greeted her, a cry jumped to her throat and her hand went to her chest.

"I'm sorry, Ms. Kelsey," Donald Weiss apologized.

"That's all right," Rori said, reining in her runaway breath. "I just wasn't expecting you."

The building's troubleshooter stood well over six feet six inches, and despite the fact that he hadn't boxed in years, he looked as though he could hold his own with just about any man. The sleeves of his khaki shirt were rolled up to reveal bulging, blue-veined muscles, and his neck and shoulders were bulldog thick. A huge key ring, containing passkeys to all the apartments in both buildings, was clipped to a belt loop.

"I just stopped by to see if you were all right after the other night," he said, his accent, after more than two dozen years in the South, still bearing a trace of his New Jersey upbringing.

Rori knew he was referring to the elevator incident. As it always did, the memory brought a fearful feeling.

"Yes, I'm fine," she said.

"The police said something about you not thinking it was an accident. Said you thought you heard someone."

"Yes, I did."

"The police said that everything checked out, though. The elevator was working fine the next morning."

"Yes, I know."

"But you still think—"

"I know what I heard, Mr. Weiss," she insisted. She didn't mention the threatening letters she was receiving. The fewer people who knew, the better.

Donald Weiss looked thoroughly confused, as though he didn't know quite what to believe. "Well, if you ever need me, Ms. Kelsey, you just call. That's what I'm here for."

Rori smiled. "Thank you."

His key ring jingling, the ex-boxer walked down the hallway. Rori watched him. She guessed she'd never realized how tall and able-bodied the building superintendent was. Because he was balding, she always tended to think of him as an older man. He was probably in his early to mid-fifties. She frowned. Something Blade had said to Detective Pinchera came into her memory, something about maybe someone in the building or the neighborhood being responsible for tampering with the elevator. That perhaps that was why the police hadn't found anyone who shouldn't be in the building. Because whoever had been responsible had a right to be in the area. Surely Donald Weiss, who lived in the adjacent mansion, fell into that category.

Stop it! Rori thought. The paranoia was getting out of hand. She was being stupid, ridiculous, utterly...paranoid. She grabbed her purse, went out, closed the door behind her and started for Blade's apartment. She bypassed the elevator, opting for the impossible-to-negotiate stairs. She made no excuses, but accepted her action—she was afraid to take the elevator unless Blade was by her side. Which was the way that, more and more, she felt about life in general. How had this man so thoroughly stormed the bastion where she safeguarded her emotions?

She had her answer minutes later when he opened the door of his apartment. It lay somewhere in the irresistible way that rumpled brown hair spilled across his forehead, in the sensual way his pewter-gray eyes undressed her with a single heated look. It lay somewhere in the way his sexy, sultry voice drawled, "You're two minutes late."

Chapter Nine

I...I got tied up,'' Rori said, taking in the blinding contrast of bronze skin with white tennis shorts, white T-shirt and white sneakers. A wrinkle slashed across the tennis shorts; the shirt hung free and full with not even the slightest pretension of tidiness; the sneakers, one notch above grubby, hugged his sockless feet. If time was money, Blade had spent only cents dressing...and he'd ended up looking like a million bucks. Maybe two, the rhythm of Rori's heart beat out.

He stepped aside, wordlessly inviting her to enter. She did. She looked around at the shiny chrome and glass, the bright black and yellow. ''Nice,'' she said.

Blade shrugged. ''I guess so,'' he said. ''Sit down. I'll get us a beer.''

Rori started to ease into a black and white floral chair, but halted in midair as Blade snatched a couple of pieces of crumpled typing paper and two candy wrappers out of the way.

"Sorry about that," he said, also grabbing a shirt and a single dirty sock that lay sprawled on the carpet. "The housekeeper comes twice a week. The rest of the time I live like a slob," he explained as he shoved everything, including the typing paper and the candy wrappers, into a nearby closet.

Rori hid a smile... or tried to.

"I see that," Blade said with a smothered grin. "I can also see you don't know the real purpose of a closet."

"Obviously your creativity has more than one outlet," Rori teased. Teased? Yes, they were teasing each other, another facet of the relationship they were exploring.

"Actually," he said, "I can be creative in a lot of ways." The words, delivered in a rough-edged voice, were suggestive enough. Blade's gaze traveled from her eyes to her lips, then lowered to her legs, which she'd left bare of stockings in deference to the summer heat. His look only reinforced the message, leaving a trail of languid heat running through her.

Rori felt as naked as the day she was born. She squirmed in the chair and fought the urge to draw her legs beneath her.

Blade moved restlessly where he stood. He fought the urge to run his hands beneath the splashy red sundress, to... "I'll, uh, I'll get us a beer," he said gruffly.

Once he was out of the room and she could breathe again, Rori stood and walked aimlessly around, looking first at this, then at that. She wondered where he did his writing, when he did it, which, according to him, wasn't all that often of late. His writing, or inability to do so, brought the memory of their conversation the evening before. Guilt was eating him alive. How could any wife want the husband she'd left behind to live with that kind of pain? Not for the first time, she had a most uncharitable feeling regarding this mystery lady. She wondered what his wife had looked like, then caught herself. Blade—his wife, his past, his guilt—was none of her business.

"You don't happen to know if your housekeeper is looking for additional work, do you?" Rori called, forcing the thoughts from her mind.

"I don't know," Blade said from directly behind her.

She turned. Unnaturally aware of his nearness. For a split second, something inside her said she was wrong, that this man was very much her business. Whether she liked it or not.

"Why? Are you in the market for one?" he asked, holding a can of beer out to her.

"Maybe," she said, wrapping her hand around the chilled aluminum. "On a part-time basis."

"She works here a couple of days a week. Usually on Tuesdays and Fridays, although she called earlier to say that she'd be in on Saturday this week. Something about needing to see about her daughter."

"Does she have a young child?" Rori asked, taking a drink of the cold beer. It tasted good slipping down her dry throat.

Blade gulped a hefty swallow. "I think her daughter's a teenager. Although I'm not really sure. Mrs. Yearwood's a quiet, private person. She did say something once, though, about working at several other places." He brought the can to his lips. "Want me to ask her about working for you?"

"Would you?"

"Sure," he said, his voice dropping a couple of octaves. "I owe her a favor, anyway. She's the one who told me that the sexy voice on the radio belonged to the woman across the courtyard."

Something in the lazy way he spoke conjured up erotic images in Rori's mind.

"Did you?" she asked, wondering where she was getting the audacity to ask the question. She was unaware that her naturally sexy voice had grown sexier.

Blade was well aware of that fact. Just as he was aware that her question had come out of left field. "Did I what?"

"Did you really watch me undress?"

Suddenly the erotic images switched mental screens. They were now flashing across Blade's memory in provocatively slow motion. "Yes," he drawled, low and deep. "Until I was hotter than the night and ready to die of the ache."

His admission did the most curious thing to Rori. Suddenly she felt as hot as the heavy air blasting against the windows, but at the same time she felt soft. Womanly soft, as if a shower of sparkling fireworks was going off deep within her. The fireworks seemed to shimmer through her body in weakening shades of desire—pinks to mauves to bloody, bold reds. She fleetingly wondered what eventually happened to women who could never release this tension she was feeling. Did they explode the way she'd repeatedly felt she would? Did they melt into a sticky, warm puddle? Or were they destined to live in a frustrating, unending purgatory?

Blade moaned at the softening of Rori's eyes. "C'mon," he said, roughly, "I'll take you to work."

His words shattered the spell. Rori blinked, focusing on the man who was heading for the kitchen. "I'll get the roses. I've already got them cut," he added. In seconds, he'd returned with a bouquet of crimson roses wrapped in newspaper. "Sorry, but Dave apparently doesn't own a vase. I've looked everywhere."

"That's okay. I have one at the station." As she reached for the flowers, a thorn bit the plush flesh of her thumb. She gave a startled gasp.

Blade jerked his head up. "What is it?"

"I just pricked myself."

"Here, let me see," he said, relieving her of the beer can and the bouquet and negligently laying them aside.

"It's all right. It's only a prick."

"Let me see," he insisted, taking her thumb in his hand. A scarlet drop of blood oozed from the puncture. Without the slightest hesitation, he brought the fleshy pad to his mouth, where he sucked gently.

His provocative action sucked away Rori's sanity. Her eyes rushed to his as desire unfurled all along her body. In an act of self-preservation, she pulled her hand from the exquisite torture of his lips.

She stared.

He stared.

"It's . . . it's all right," she finally managed to say, removing her hand from his.

Blade released her, but reluctantly. Somehow touching her, being touched by her, involved more than mere sexuality. Something in her touch made him feel whole, which was something his shattered self hadn't felt in a long while.

"There's a Band-Aid in the bathroom off my bedroom," he said, his voice strained. "Get it while I put some more paper around the roses."

Glad for anything that would put a little distance between her and Blade, she sought out his bedroom. The bed, the bottom sheet twisted, the top sheet thrown back carelessly, looked as though it had been left exactly as Blade had crawled out of it. In a way she chose to ignore, it looked inviting. Sensually inviting.

She passed quickly into the bathroom, and with a minimum of searching, found the tin of Band-Aids. She applied one, returned the tin, shut the medicine cabinet and walked from the bathroom. It was then, as though a spotlight had suddenly been directed on it, that she saw the picture by the bedside. It was the picture of a woman. Rori's first thought came in the form of a question: how had she missed it when she'd entered the bedroom? Her second thought answered the question: possibly because she'd wanted to.

There was no ignoring it now, however, just as there was no question in her mind whom it was a picture of. Rori crossed the room, picked up the frame and cradled it in hands that were suddenly unsteady. She forced herself to look at the woman in the photograph. A dozen thoughts, one bleeding into the other like bright bolts of lightning, slashed through her mind. *He still keeps her photograph by the bed... she was beautiful... though she looks as though she might break if touched... she had blond hair... to my darling husband, Blade, with all my love—Anna Marie... her name had been Anna Marie... and she'd had blond hair... blond hair... blond hair...*

As if she had tunnelvision, Rori screened out all aspects of the photograph except the hair. The blond cloud of satin seemed to float around the woman's pretty face. The curls, not as many as Rori had, but curls nonetheless, meandered haphazardly. Even the shade of blond, that of toasted honey, matched her own. A chilled feeling, a sick, hurt feeling, crawled into the pit of Rori's stomach. It curled up there, as though bedding down for a long stay.

Sensing something in the doorway, Rori glanced up. Blade stood watching her. His eyes, his face, were totally unreadable. Seconds, years, two lifetimes passed. At length, with a composure she was far from feeling, Rori placed the frame on the bedside table. Her eyes, as blank as his, refused to make contact.

"I have to get to work," she said, starting toward the doorway, which his solid frame blocked.

"We have to talk."

Driven by the pain possessing her heart, she managed to push past him. He reached for her, but missed ... primarily because she'd begun to run toward the front door, the roses, even her purse, completely forgotten.

"Rori?" he called—in anger, in anguish, in a hundred emotions he couldn't have identified. "Wait!"

But she didn't.

"Rori!"

She yanked open the door of the apartment. From out of nowhere, a hand slammed it shut.

"Dammit, Rori, will you wait!"

Within the cage of his arms, she whirled. Unshed tears glistened in her turquoise eyes. "Is that all I am? A substitute? Do I just remind you of her? Were you pretending it was her when you made love to me?"

God, she thought somewhere deep inside her, *I didn't know it was possible to hurt like this!*

"No!" he roared. "God dammit, no!"

The power of his reply brought on a stunned silence. For long seconds, his words bounded about the room, lacing themselves with Rori's battered breathing.

Blade was aware of every curve, every softness, every heartbeat of the woman in his arms. He was also aware of her pain, a pain that cut cruelly at him.

"No," he repeated, this time quietly, so quietly his voice sang like a muted song in the stillness, "a substitute is not all you are. You do not just remind me of her. And I was not pretending you were her when we made love."

"Then what about the hair?" Rori had to ask.

Lowering his arms, Blade sighed. He stepped back and tunneled his fingers through his hair. "In the beginning..." He stopped, searching for the truth and the words with which to speak it. "In the beginning, it *was* your hair that attracted me. But," he hastened to add, "is that so hard to understand? Is that so unforgivable?"

Rori didn't answer. She didn't know whether she understood. She didn't know whether she forgave.

"Hell, I'm not even certain what I mean by attraction!" he erupted. "Maybe I simply mean I noticed you first because of your hair. If you'd been a brunette, would I have noticed you then? I don't know. I'm trying to be honest. I don't know, Rori. But I do know," he said, taking a step toward her, "that you are not a substitute for Anna Marie. You couldn't be—" he took another step toward her and he was directly in front of her "—because you're nothing like her. Nothing," he repeated emphatically.

While Rori waited for him to finish the sentence, her heart seemed to stop beating. Now it slid into a sure cadence.

"She was insecure; you're not," he explained. "She was fragile; you're not. She was self-centered, selfish; you're not. She merely tolerated my touch; you"—his voice lowered "—beg for it...with every look, every breath...every...everything." He heaved a sigh, as though releasing a great burden. "She made me feel like slime for wanting to make love to her. After a while I didn't even want to anymore. It wasn't worth the guilt. And then I saw you on your balcony..." His gaze slid into hers, the way his body had once slid into the hollow depths of her body. "You wanted, you want, everything I do...just as hard, just as fast, just as much as I want it."

Rori closed her eyes to the searing feeling skipping through her.

"Don't you?" he whispered. "Tell me you do, Rori. I know it, but I have to hear you say it." When she didn't answer, he said, "Say it. Please!" The last was said as if his life depended on her obeying his request.

She opened her eyes, her gaze leveling with his. "Yes," she whispered, adding quickly, "but don't you see that I'm not whole? I'm not—"

"Shh," he ordered, laying his finger across her lips. "I'll find a way." He didn't have to explain what he'd find a way to do. Rori knew what he meant. She wanted to argue, to tell him that helping her might not be within his power, but when he uttered the next words, she was helpless not to believe.

"Trust me," he begged, removing his finger and replacing it with his lips.

Yes, she believed.

In the kiss they were sharing. In his statement that she wasn't a substitute for a lost wife. In the golden promise he made.

Blade made the decision Friday morning with a candy bar in one hand and the telephone in the other.

"Diamond Publishing," came the businesslike, feminine voice of the New York secretary.

"I'd like to speak with Thad Abrams, please."

Blade had awakened with an idea about the book that he wanted to talk over with his editor. He supposed the idea had been in the back of his mind for awhile. Something had told him that basing the book on the prostitute murders was an intriguing premise. What he'd decided he wanted to do was tell the book from both the murderer's and victims' points of view. Toward that end, he was going to try to find the blond-haired prostitute he'd seen the afternoon he was out walking. He would try to interview her. He was hoping to gain some perspective into what prostitutes in the city were feeling.

He knew two things. One, you obviously couldn't take the investigative reporter out of the man, and two, whatever was going on between him and Rori was responsible for this breakthrough in his attitude. He wasn't ready to start writing, but thinking about the book did have an exciting appeal that had been sadly lacking before. He knew, too, that Thad was going to die when he heard Blade hadn't even started the book. Seconds later, as Blade listened to the secretary announce that Thad was out of the office for the day, he acknowledged that fate had postponed the editor's demise—at least temporarily.

"Could you have him call Blade Cavannaugh? He has the number."

"Certainly, Mr. Cavannaugh," the secretary replied, not in the least aware that she was speaking to *the* B. J. Nichols. Otherwise, she'd be falling all over herself, Blade thought, and making him feel awkward as hell.

Dressing in his usual attire, jeans, Blade left the apartment in search of the prostitute. He went to the bar where he'd seen her the afternoon it had rained. There he asked questions, pulling out a twenty-dollar bill with each, until he found her. It turned out that she lived and worked upstairs in a room cluttered with clothes and filled with the raw, stale smell of sex. Sleepy-eyed though it was almost eleven o'clock, the young lady of the evening agreed to talk to him if he'd buy her breakfast.

Thirty minutes later, at a nearby restaurant, the woman, who said her name was Savannah Brown, devoured ham and eggs and hotcakes, while Blade settled for a cup of strong coffee. Wearing skin-tight jeans and a red knit top that invitingly cupped her bare breasts, she was eager to answer Blade's questions. Yeah, she knew that prostitutes were getting knocked off in the city. Nah, she wasn't scared. She had a guy who took care of her. Blade didn't point out that he'd found her without her pimp being any the wiser, and that if he could find her, the murderer could, as well.

"Hey," Savannah said to Blade an hour and a half later as they were parting in front of the bar, "you wouldn't be interested in a freebie, would you?"

Blade, notebook in hand, looked at the commercially sexy woman who couldn't be more than twenty-two or twenty-three years old, a woman who'd seen too much, said too much and felt too little. He thought of another blonde, a woman with blue-green eyes and a whiskey voice, who was a hundred times sexier without even trying. Just the thought of Rori made his blood boil in a way that Savannah Brown's cultivated provocativeness couldn't hope to match.

Not wanting to hurt her feelings, he smiled. "Thanks. But it's a little too early in the day for me."

She shrugged, not entirely able to hide her disappointment. "You know where to find me," she said, turning. With a sway of her hips, she walked away.

Blade watched her go, suddenly feeling a soul-deep sadness, not so much at the tawdriness of her life as at the emptiness of it. It was an emptiness he could identify with.

"Savannah," he called, feeling a strange comradeship with this woman. When she turned, he said, "Take care."

That afternoon Blade took time from organizing his notes to drive Rori to work. He leaned across the seat and kissed her goodbye. He'd intended the kiss to be a simple, if thorough, gesture of parting, but once his mouth touched hers, his intentions traveled the proverbial path to Hades. Moaning, he deepened the kiss by entwining his tongue with hers. When hers reciprocated, he felt the world fall out from under him. Tearing his mouth from hers, he whispered, "Hold the thought."

The only trouble was, Blade held the thought, too. Or rather, the thought held him. He finished up his notes, then tried to work on the book, only to confirm that, although he'd made progress, he still wasn't ready to start writing...and maybe he never would be. This depressing thought after his first really optimistic day sent Blade once more to pounding the pavement in a marathon walk.

For the first time in weeks, Blade didn't listen to Rori's broadcast. He felt too restless, too tense, too...horny, he admitted, calling a spade a spade. Even the sound of her voice made him ache. The only consolation he had was that she was aching, too—he saw it in the pout of her lips, heard it in her soft sigh, felt it in the fevered brush of her tongue against his. If anything, she was hurting worse than he was. Which, as merciless as it sounded, was what he wanted her to do. He wanted her to hurt so badly that she'd be willing to risk failing again. He wanted her willing to play the game by his rules. He wanted her willing to take a chance on some of the therapeutic techniques he'd read about in the innumerable books he'd read. She had to trust him, though. She had to trust him enough to fail in front of him. Had she reached that point?

God, he hoped so, he thought as he let the cold spray of water sluice down his back as he turned in the shower. He prayed the prayer again as he stepped out of the tub, grabbed a fluffy towel and, dragging it through his wet hair, walked into the living room, where he flipped on the ten o'clock news. His hand stilled as the television newscaster reported the opening story: "It's the fourth killing of a blond-haired prostitute here in New Orleans this summer. The police, who are withholding the victim's identity until notification of family, believe that she was strangled sometime between four o'clock this afternoon and eight o'clock this evening. The first victim, Amy Covetington was killed

June 4; the second, killed just ten days later on June 14, was identified as . . .''

Faces of blond-haired women, like a grisly gallery, began to appear on the screen. Blade didn't pay them a fraction of attention—any more than he heeded the water puddling on the white carpet. The only thing he noted was the sick feeling of fear in the pit of his stomach.

What if there was a link between the murders and the threats Rori had received? What if next time he turned on the television it was Rori's death they were reporting?

Rori knew something was wrong the minute she saw Blade. For one thing, he'd driven instead of walked. She could see the car parked in the alleyway. For another, instead of his usual casual attire, he wore a pair of pleated dress pants and a freshly ironed cotton shirt. What really convinced her, however, was his expression. It was as dark, as impenetrable as the sultry night. Fleetingly she wondered if his being out when she tried to call him at six o'clock had anything to do with whatever was wrong.

"What is it?" she asked without preamble.

"Get in the car," he said, throwing his arm around her shoulders in a gesture of protectiveness.

Rori felt a prickling of anxiety. She looked into his unfathomable face. "Blade?"

"C'mon," he said, opening the car door for her. She scooted in, the linen of her dress clinging to the velvet of the seat so that a slice of her stockinged thigh came into view.

Despite the seriousness of the moment, Blade couldn't help but be moved by the intimate sight. No more than he could help but notice the way the pale pink dress, with buttons running along its front, enhanced the rose color in her cheeks . . . or the way the white heels were perfectly coordinated with the white stockings that snuggled next to her shapely calves . . . or the way her hair, piled in a loose top-knot, fell alluringly around her temples and neck in here-and-there sprigs. Blade wanted to capture every one of them, but he closed his mind to the temptation as he closed the door, rounded the hood and climbed in beside her. He let his heart beat a time or two, then reached for her hand, unerringly finding it in the dark.

"There's been another murder."

It took Rori a second to process what he'd said. When she finally did, her fingers tightened. "Another prostitute?"

"Yes."

"A blonde?"

"Yes. She was strangled sometime between four this afternoon and eight this evening."

Rori closed her eyes to the horrid images springing to life—images of a bloodless face, a bruised neck, a woman fighting for her last breath. "My God," Rori whispered, "what a nightmare."

"I want you with me," Blade said. "Night and day. Until this creep is caught."

Rori opened her eyes and stared at the man silhouetted in shadows. Grim lines radiated from his hard-set mouth.

"I don't know," he continued, "whether these murders are related to your letters, but I'm not willing to risk it. I'm not willing to take the chance." His voice grew husky as he added, "You mean too much to me."

It was the closest thing to a declaration of feeling either had made. Rori drew the words around her as one draws memories of a warm summer day on a cold winter's eve. She didn't know what she felt for this man. She knew only that she felt something—something she couldn't put into words. Obviously he didn't expect a response, for he released her hand, straightened and started the motor.

"Where are we going?" she asked when he turned the car away from their apartments.

He glanced at her. "I've booked us into a hotel for the weekend." He looked at the road. "I think we both need to get away. By the way, I called Detective Pinchera and told him where we'd be." He thought, too, of the note he'd left for the housekeeper telling her where he could be reached should his editor try to return his call.

"But I'll need some things," Rori said.

Blade nodded toward the back; she followed his gaze. Two pieces of luggage sat on the seat. One of them was hers.

"I got the super to let me in," Blade explained. "I packed what I thought you'd need."

The thought of him rummaging through her personal belongings, her intimate apparel, did warm things to her body. It was nothing, however, compared to the heated feelings she experienced twenty minutes later as she stood by his side in the shiny marble lobby of one of New Orlean's most affluent hotels and watched him sign the register.

Mr. and Mrs. Blade Cavannaugh.

Her heart thumped, her mouth went dry—and she knew it had to do with more than the sharing of a room. It had to do with the sharing of his name. Laying the pen down, Blade looked at her. Something in his eyes said that he was feeling everything she was. Wordlessly, he slipped his arm around her waist and headed for the elevator.

They passed gleaming brass, sparkling crystal chandeliers and priceless antiques. Their room, located on the third floor and decorated in shades of moss green and apricot, overlooked a private courtyard where plants abounded, water flowed lyrically and moonlight splashed down as though this spot had been specially chosen by the gods. Rori, purposely keeping her eyes from the turned-down bed, walked to the wide window and peered out. She could hear Blade tipping the bellman for bringing up their bags.

"Enjoy your stay," she heard the bellman say, then heard the faint closing of the door as he left.

Alone. She and Blade were alone in a hotel room. Registered as man and wife. Rori gave an unsteady sigh and listened to the crazy dance of her heart.

Suddenly the lamplight died, leaving only moonlight to spill into the room. Rori heard Blade's muted footsteps as he crossed the short distance to stand behind her. She felt the weight of his hands, a gentle but firm pressure, on her upper arms.

"Are you all right?" he asked, the question as light as the moonbeams frolicking in the courtyard.

"I don't know," she whispered. "My heart's pounding."

He pulled her against him so that his heartbeat drummed into her senses. "So is mine, if that's any consolation."

Yes, Rori thought, it was some consolation. Instinctively, because it felt the right thing to do, she laid her head against his shoulder. "Oh, Blade, I'm scared."

"Of what?"

"Of you. Of me. Of us. Of where we're headed. I don't even know if I can go there."

"I'm only asking you to go where you want to. I'm only asking you to go where you can."

"And I'm scared about the murders. What if it's the same nut that's sending me the letters—the same nut that screwed up the elevator?"

"We don't know that."

"But what if it is?" she asked, her voice displaying her desperation.

Blade turned her in his arms. Even in the dark, their eyes met. "I won't let anything happen to you," he said. "I swear that."

Something in the way he said it, as though he'd fight every demon in hell twice over, made her believe him. A smile nipped at her mouth. "Ah, Cavannaugh, I think your shining armor's showing again."

He smiled, too, but then their smiles disappeared as his hands moved to cradle her heart-shaped face. His fingers brushed her throat. "I'd never let anyone hurt you," he vowed, his mouth lowering to hers.

His kiss was slow and gentle—so damned gentle that it brought an ache to her heart, and a tear sprang to her eye. It was so damned gentle that she didn't think she'd ever forgive him for it. As long as she lived, whatever road she traveled, she'd always remember this kiss. The kiss she'd first known, felt, in a dream.

With a sublime languor his tongue played at the seam of her lips, stroking, probing, before finally, lazily penetrating the sweet cavern of her mouth. She whimpered as the hot, velvet rapier filled her, searched for her tongue and dueled unhurriedly, as though it had eternity and more. Unable to stop herself any more than she had been when he'd kissed her goodbye that afternoon, she curled her tongue around his, meshing heat with heat, wet with wet. When he leisurely guided her tongue to his mouth, provocatively drawing on it in a sucking motion, Rori whimpered again.

Ending the kiss as slowly as he'd begun it, Blade buried her face in his shoulder, and for long moments he held her to him—shielding her, protecting her, making silent promises. At last his restless fingers began to tease the sprigs of hair coiling at her neck. Then, as though tasting her with his fingertips, he trailed his splayed hands over her shoulders, down her delicately curved back and over the flair of her hips. Slowly, sexily, he cupped the rounded cheeks and pulled her to him.

The steel-hard state of his body eloquently, undeniably proved his point when he said huskily, shakily, "I want you."

"I want you, too," she said, unable to deny either of them the truth. "Oh, God, Blade, I do want you. It's just—"

"Shh," he said. "I've got a new game plan."

She raised her head until their eyes met—blue and gray starlight caressing in the night.

"I've been reading up on your problem," he explained. "I know I'm not a psychologist," he said, heading off any objection she might make. "I don't pretend to be, but just listen to me, okay? Certain things I've read do make sense."

"Like what?"

"Like part of the problem may have been the professional competitiveness between you and Rogers. At least his competitiveness with you. Think about it. No matter what he did, you eclipsed him. It was you who had the name, not him. It was you with the billboards all over town. It was you people recognized when you were out. I can see where that could devastate an insecure personality. So much so," Blade added meaningfully, "that he wanted to punish you for it. Oh, not consciously, probably, but he wanted to punish you just the same."

Rori thought of the time she'd been approached for an autograph while she and Dwayne had been dining and how angry he'd been, ostensibly for the interruption. "Go on," she insisted, intrigued.

"Sometimes a lover unconsciously withholds the touches, the caresses that would please his partner. With your limited experience with sex, you wouldn't even know you were being denied. Add to it," Blade continued, "your certain intuition that you couldn't trust this man."

"An intuition that proved sound," Rori sneered.

"Exactly," Blade said, adding, "over and over I read that the single most important factor in the female orgasm is trust in her partner. You simply didn't trust this Rogers guy enough to let go, so what you did was force yourself not to climax."

"I conditioned myself?" Rori asked, remembering their conversation of earlier that week.

"Precisely."

"Then why can't I cli—" she stopped, not as comfortable with the candid terminology as Blade. "Then why can't I with someone else? Why couldn't I with you? I wanted to!"

Blade heard her frustration. "Because it isn't that simple. Remember what I said Tuesday or Wednesday—whenever we talked—about inhibitions becoming automatic and no longer being controlled voluntarily?"

She nodded. "I think so."

"Well, that's what's happened to you, I think. You told your body not to climax in the beginning...and it learned to do precisely what you told it to."

What he was saying made a sort of convoluted sense. Rori allowed herself a tiny ray of hope. "Can my body unlearn it?"

"Very possibly. The fact that you've had an orgasm before says that your body once knew how."

"So how do I unlearn it?"

By trusting me, Blade wanted to say. But trust wasn't something you asked for and got. Trust was something somebody gave you, bestowed like a precious gift.

"You start by putting no demands on yourself, by putting yourself in a no-fail situation. Right now you've become so obsessed with making yourself climax that it's all you focus on. An orgasm comes naturally out of feeling good, not by trying to make it happen."

Rori couldn't argue with what he was saying. With Dwayne, then with Blade, she had tried, as though her teeth were gritted, to bring about the climactic end she sought— to the exclusion of all else. She had forgotten, if she had ever known, what intimacy without anxiety was.

"What you need is an encounter—maybe several, maybe many—in which there's no way you can fail."

"I don't understand."

"We'll just touch each other, make each other feel good, with the understanding that you won't even try to reach a climax. In fact," he said, a grin on his lips, "you lose the game if you do."

He had expected her to smile, too. Instead, she pulled from him and faced the window. She wrapped her arms around herself.

"You don't know what you're asking of me. The tension... there's nowhere for it to go... I feel as though I'm going to come apart in a thousand pieces. And it's worse with you than it ever was with Dwayne." She hadn't intended to say this last, but it had tumbled out.

The words, like ribbons of gold, tied themselves around Blade's heart until he felt so humbled he hurt. His hands slid to her arms. "I'll play by the same rules," he said, his voice uneven. "Neither one of us can do anything more than make the other feel good. When it begins to hurt, we'll stop. Both of us."

She turned, her gaze finding his. "That isn't fair to you."

"Let me be the judge of what is and isn't fair to me. You pay me back by one day trying the real thing again... even if it means failing again...and again...and again...before we get it right."

"And what if we—I—never do?"

"*We* will," he said with deliberate emphasis. "Trust me."

Rori said nothing. She didn't know how to catalog what she was feeling. Blade's generous, unselfish offer was one her husband had never made. He'd never tried to find a solution. He'd only sought to ridicule. But what if she couldn't bring about what both she and Blade so desperately wanted? Could she stand to disappoint this man?

"Blade—" she began, uncertain what she was going to say.

"Shh," he said, tipping her chin up with a crooked finger and silencing her lips with his. She sighed.

"Does that feel good?" he whispered.

"Yes," she answered, her breath a fleeting wisp of air.

"And this?" he asked as he trailed a row of tiny kisses along the column of her neck.

Unknowingly, she arched her neck.

"Yes," she said, the sound a soft mewling.

"How about this?" he asked, dipping his tongue into the hollow of her throat.

Rori purred.

"Touch me," he whispered. "Touch me somewhere to make me feel good."

"Where?" she whispered, the word fluttering against the lips still at her throat.

"Anywhere," he said. "Anywhere you touch could only feel like heaven."

She hesitated, knowing that with compliance came commitment. What did she want to do? Did she want this man badly enough to take the risk? She knew he was waiting; she could feel the impatience coiled in his every muscle. Slowly, in answer to her question, in reply to his plea, her fingers threaded themselves through his thick hair. Just as slowly, she drew his mouth to hers. Her lips closed gently over his.

This time it was Blade who moaned, low and deep, as he felt washed onto the blissful shores of heaven.

Chapter Ten

It would forever remain one of the great mysteries of the universe, Rori thought dimly, how Blade could be so gentle yet release such violent emotions within her. His lips were softer than a kitten's cry, but she felt a raw, hungry need eating away at her body, making her lips tremble, making her hands tighten in his hair, making her moan in such a wanton way that she should have been embarrassed. Then again, perhaps she should have been more embarrassed by the fact that she wasn't embarrassed at all.

"Easy," Blade said raggedly, though his tone suggested that he was feeling everything she was. "There's no hurry," he whispered, pulling his mouth from hers, but just barely. His tongue licked across her lips before dipping into the corners of her mouth. He slid his tongue inside for the briefest of moments, then, like a hit-and-run driver, he was gone, departing the moist cavern for other destinations. He toyed with the curved lobe of her ear, planted kisses on cheek and chin, rained nips and tiny bites along her neck.

Molten desire bubbled in the pit of Rori's stomach, in the cradle of her thighs, making her feel all fevery and hot. She could never remember feeling this way, as though a roaring fire burned deep and relentlessly within her. Oh, God, how could she withstand the emotions that were building? Yet how could she stand it if he stopped this sweet torture?

"Easy," Blade repeated, but this time it was himself he cautioned. He could feel her need as it shuddered through her body and into his own—an honest need, a need far too potent for the beginning of their lovemaking, a need that made his body cruelly pulse with pain. He wrenched his mouth from her neck and held her to him, wondering if any woman had ever made him want her as much as this woman did. No, he thought, not even having to ponder the question. No woman had ever spoken to him in such a primitive way. "Do you know what you do to me?" he whispered, his breath stirring the wisps of hair trailing at her ear.

"Tell me," she whispered, wanting desperately to know what she did to him. All she'd ever done to Dwayne was frustrate him, anger him, drive him into the arms of another woman.

"You make me crazy. You make me a candidate for the bonkers ward of some institution. You make me hurt." This last he said as though he was, indeed, in pain.

"I know," she said. "Oh, God, I know."

He pulled back until his eyes—Rori thought they looked like liquid silver in the moonlight—found hers. "Do you want to stop?" he asked.

Did she? Did she want to stop the ache before it reached a more unbearable plateau? She should. She knew she should. Before she was ready to climb the walls. Before sleep was a thing she chased but couldn't catch.

"No," she breathed, helpless to say anything else, helpless to keep her lips from finding his square chin, his neck, the thumbprint indentation of his throat. She kissed him softly, slowly. Her kisses were like snippets of starlight.

He groaned, blindly burying his fingers in her hair. At the realization that it was pinned up, he groaned again, this time in disappointment. Rori searched through her hair, plucking out the few pins holding it in its casually upswept style. She let the pins fall to the floor, allowing her hair to tumble around her shoulders, the flaxen curls rushing forward like the white crests of a wild, raffish river.

Blade plunged his fingers into the silk at her temples, drawing his hands the length of the shiny mane. The sandy-colored tips sifted against the pads of his fingers, individual strands clinging like eager lovers.

"Damn, but your hair is beautiful!" he said.

The day before, Rori had worried that Blade had been attracted to her only because her hair reminded him of his dead wife, yet now, with his worshipful caress moving hotly over her, she knew as only a woman could that his mind was solely on her. She relished the feeling.

She reveled in the feel of his hands traveling across her shoulders and down her back. Lightly, he drew his knuckles over her ribs—up, up, until his thumbs encountered the plush fullness of her breasts. Rori moaned as his hands brazenly slid to cup each.

"Oh, Blade," she whimpered.

"I know," he said, his mouth seeking hers as his fingers sought the buttons of her dress. Slowly, as his mouth worked in sweet coordination, he released one button, then another. He released her belt and let it drop to the floor. He unfastened two more buttons before sliding his hands beneath the fabric at her shoulders and gliding it from her. The dress slithered the length of her tall frame and fell into a linen heap at her feet. Using his arms to balance her, she stepped out of it.

Blade felt he was losing his mind at the sight that greeted him. Even in the moonlight, he could tell that the silk teddy was a pale shade of pink. It was lacy, its bodice held together by only a slender ribbon. Lace-topped thigh-high stockings sheathed her long legs.

"Good, Lord, how many of these things do you have?" he whispered, touching the teddy.

"One of the show's advertisers is a lingerie shop," Rori said. "The owner keeps me supplied."

"Remind me to thank her," Blade said, running his hand over the frilly lace. "That is, if I can still talk." He fingered the thin straps, then lowered his head to kiss the crescent swell of one breast above the fabric.

Rori looked at the crown of his dark head. His lips were warm and wet against her skin, and she longed to feel his mouth close over this tender part of her. She desperately wanted to feel his mouth kneading, sipping, suckling—

She moaned at the ecstasy of the thought.

"Untie the ribbon," he demanded, his voice strong with passion yet as fragile as the lace blooming across the teddy's bodice.

"What?"

"Untie the ribbon."

He eased his head back just far enough to allow her hand to do as he'd bade. Slowly, her fingers made contact with the satin ribbon . . . and the edge of his lips; slowly her fingers pulled, diminishing the bow in small increments.

"All the way," he insisted when she left the ends dangling.

Rori closed her eyes as she used her index finger to open the bow. She felt the strap at her shoulder fall onto her arm. She felt, too, the front of the teddy shift. Instead of slipping downward, however, the silk snagged on the peak of her breast.

Her heart fluttered in anticipation as Blade's warm breath bled against her skin. Then she felt him whisper, "Pull it back. Show me what you want me to do."

It might have been an unusual request coming from someone else, but coming from a man whose wife had made him feel guilty for needing some form of intimacy, it made sense.

"I want you . . . to touch me," Rori whispered, her hand going once more to the teddy. "I want you to kiss me," she said, edging the diaphanous material aside. "I want—" She moaned as Blade's mouth closed over the rosy tip of her breast.

She was dying, Rori thought, and she didn't care at all if she did. Blade's mouth tugging at her breast, licking, laving, was quite a wonderful way to walk into eternity. He was right. Dwayne had denied her pleasure. She could never remember Dwayne doing anything but hastening her with his own need. He'd never tried to make her lose her mind by flicking his tongue across her nipple, by brushing the same nipple with his thumb, by using that thumb to ease the nipple into his mouth where he could suck—

Rori moaned and sagged against Blade. He swung her into his arms, crossed the room and set her on the bed. The mattress swayed beneath her. Watching her in the dim moonlight, he took in her tousled hair that spread about her like a dreamy cloud, the disheveled teddy that revealed far more than it concealed. With a maddening lack of haste, he slipped the high heels from her feet and pulled the stockings from her legs. Then he reached for the buttons of his shirt. In seconds, he loomed before her, bare chested.

"Touch me," he whispered, unable to hide his own need.

Rori stretched out her hands, her fingertips tracing the curves of his shoulders from his neck to his arms. His muscles rippled; his flesh trembled. In an unhurried pattern, she drew her fingers down his chest—over pectorals, across burning skin, through densely matted hair whose crisp texture spoke an exciting, sexy language. Blade moaned when she brushed the hard nubs of his nipples.

Languidly pushing herself up, the teddy gathered at her waist, her hands on his ribs, she kissed his chest softly, as though he was breakable. Kissing first here, then there, whispering something about his body being beautiful, she turned her head so her hair flowed with her every movement, each swish and sway driving Blade toward a more ecstatic insanity.

Finally, he could stand no more. Roping her hair around his fist, he pulled her mouth to his. As he kissed her thoroughly, with lips and teeth and tongue, she folded her arms around his back. He drew her to him, flattening her breasts against the hard width of his chest. Both were momentarily lost to the divine feelings.

"Damn, you feel good!" he whispered.

"Blade..." she started, but couldn't finish, primarily because she had no idea what she wanted to say. Did she want to tell him that nothing had ever felt so good, yet so awful? Did she want to tell him that there wasn't enough cold water in the city of New Orleans to end this ache? Did she want to tell him that her body might never be the same?

Dragging his mouth from hers, he pushed the love-tangled hair from her face as he eased her onto the mattress. "Do you want to stop?" he asked hoarsely.

Yes. No. Didn't he know that she didn't know what she wanted? In the end, it was her half-naked body that made the decision. Beneath his wrinkled slacks, Rori felt Blade hard and pulsating. She moved her hips in search of the swollen sweetness. Blade's breath hitched at the volatile contact. Cupping her derriere, he hauled her closer, candidly rubbing his body against hers.

At the gush of white-hot sensations that erupted in him, he said, his voice broken, "We should stop...tell me to stop."

"We...we...should stop," Rori whimpered. It was the closest she could come to obeying him, because the feelings consuming him were playing the same havoc with her.

"I want to touch you," he whispered, not needing to specify where. "I need to touch you. God, Rori, you're so sweet...so sweet..." As he spoke, he trailed one hand from her hip to her belly and downward, stopping as his fingers encountered a thatch of fleecy curls through her teddy.

Rori moaned, placed her hand on his and slid his hand to mound her intimately. She gasped...just as Blade's breath dribbled piecemeal into the stillness.

"You're so hot!" he whispered. "So hot and so..." Pulling the teddy aside, his fingers slid into the creamy folds of her femininity. She cried out, arching against him in an instinctive reaction, needing the frictional play of his fingers against her sensitive flesh. Pushing a finger deep inside her, he sought the delicate bead of her desire. When he found it, Rori cried out, a loud, harsh sound.

Immediately contrite for having allowed things to go so far, Blade pulled his hand from her and hugged her close, soothing her with touch and word.

"I'm sorry," he said. "So sorry...we'll stop...no more...I promise." Her body trembled; her heartbeat was wild against his bare chest. She clung to him as though she was afraid to let go. "C'mon," he said at last, pushing her from him, "let's go to bed."

As he spoke, he withdrew the filmy lingerie from her body, leaving her as physically naked as she felt emotionally naked. Pulling back the cover, he motioned for her to crawl in. She did. And watched as he unsnapped and unzipped his slacks. His knit underwear followed. She could clearly see that he was still very much aroused. Sliding in beside her, he tugged her to him, body to body, and brushed a kiss across her forehead.

"Go to sleep," he said thickly.

As her ability to think slowly returned, Rori was aware of the fine tremors scoring Blade's body. She felt, too, the thin layer of perspiration that had formed on his back. She knew what he wanted. What he needed. What any man would want and need under the circumstances. Once more she was consummately aware of her inadequacies, inadequacies that Blade was paying for as dearly as she.

She ran her hand down the furry planes of his chest, past his navel, onto his tight abdomen. And beyond.

"Let me ease your ache," she whispered, her hand heading for the throbbing fullness of him.

He gripped her wrist, stopping her before she could reach her target. "No!" he said emphatically, drawing her hand to his mouth where he kissed the palm. "We're in this together."

"Blade—"

"Together," he affirmed, skimming her lips with his and laying her hand flat against his chest. "Now, go to sleep."

She was asleep. At last. She had tossed and turned until she'd exhausted herself. Even now she twitched occasionally, telling him either that unsated desire still roamed her body or that she was dreaming—perhaps of fiery kisses, perhaps of murdered prostitutes. The miracle was that she could sleep at all. It was after two o'clock, and he hadn't even pretended to go to sleep. His body was still too intent on punishing him for unfinished business.

God, she was sweet!

God, she was sexy!

How had she repeatedly withstood this torment?

Rori turned, whimpered softly, drew her knee up until it almost brushed against that steel part of him that still ached. Carefully disengaging the arm beneath her neck and the leg entwined with hers, he slipped from the bed. He contemplated a cold shower, but dismissed it as a poor idea. He didn't want to risk awakening her. Instead, naked, he stepped to the window and stared out.

A thousand thoughts raced through his mind. Was Rori really in danger, or did someone, some jerk of a human being, want to frighten her? Was whoever was sending the letters the same person strangling the prostitutes? The possibility made him feel sick. He wouldn't let her out of his sight...not even if it meant his body had to ache twenty-four out of every twenty-four hours.

This reminded him of the dull pain in his loins. God, how could she think she wasn't sexy? Everything about her was sexy—the way she looked, the breathtaking silk teddies she chose to wear, the way she fell apart at his touch. He'd never known a sexier woman. Nor a woman who could make him feel more like a man. She was not at all like...

Anna Marie.

The name crept into his consciousness like a bad dream, and he realized, with a start, that it was the first time he'd thought of her in a while. Immediately, a wave of guilt washed over him. He wondered if there'd ever be a time when the name didn't scald his senses this way. He sighed, praying there would be, but not believing much in the prayer.

As fragile as the sound was, because she was not wholly committed to sleep, the sigh awakened Rori. She reached out for Blade, and finding him gone, she raised herself onto an elbow. Even in the shadowed room, she saw him standing at the window. She knew immediately that he was lost to the dark side of his nature, to the haunted side, to the murky corners of his soul. Quietly, she crawled from the bed, picked up his shirt and fitted her arms into it. She fastened only a couple of the buttons.

Stepping behind him, she banded her arms around his chest and laid her cheek on his back. He jerked in surprise.

"Sorry, I didn't mean to scare you."

"I thought you were asleep," he said as he placed his hands on hers, drawing her closer. He felt her breasts next to him. He liked the feeling. Immensely.

"I thought *you* were," she retaliated. She had known he was naked, but the warmth of his skin reminded her in a tactile way what sight had only marginally called to her attention. Before he could say anything she asked, "What're you thinking about?"

He could have lied, but then he'd never found a point to falsehood. The truth always managed to emerge, anyway. "Anna Marie," he answered, hoping to God Rori didn't pull from him, hoping to God she understood some of the demons that possessed him and cared enough to stand by him.

Rori had known what she would hear even before she heard it. She had steeled her heart for the name. Even so, she wished he had not spoken it, that she had not heard it. Instead of wallowing in the sudden pain she felt, however, she said, "Tell me about her." Blade's muscles tightened infinitesimally. Silence hung in the air. Finally, Rori prompted, "Where did you meet her?"

"Here in New Orleans," he heard himself say and wondered if he was really going to talk about the past—something he'd never done. "I met her at an art gallery. She was an artist. She..."

It was strange how easy it was to talk once he got started. He hadn't expected it to be easy. And once the words began to tumble out, there seemed to be no stopping them. None of them. He told her about Anna Marie's fragility, her disinterest in sex, her neurotic dependence on him. He told her of how his success had driven them apart, how she'd become obsessed that he was having affairs, how her inability to have children seemed only to worsen her suspicions. Then had come her suicide threats, followed by her suicide. He told of how she'd come into his room, initiated lovemaking for the first time in their marriage, then walked to her bedroom and killed herself. He told in graphic detail, that left him and Rori shuddering, how he'd found her the next morning.

A silence fell after he'd finished. Into it, Rori whispered, "I'm sorry." She walked around him and stepped into his arms. "I'm so sorry," she repeated, drawing her knuckles across his cheek. "We've both suffered from our success, haven't we?"

"Yeah," he said darkly.

"Blade, surely you know how emotionally ill she was?"

"Yeah," he repeated in the same tormented tone, "but it still doesn't ease the hurt, the guilt."

"I know, but—"

"You don't know how it hurts," he interrupted her, the words strained and hard to say, "to be accused of something you're innocent of... especially by someone who's supposed to love you." He swallowed, and Rori thought she saw a sheen of moisture glaze his eyes. He fought against the tears. "I wasn't unfaithful to her," he said, his voice barely audible. "I swear to God I wasn't."

"It never crossed my mind that you were," Rori said.

She'd done it again. She'd believed in him when his wife hadn't. This woman who knew so little about him had believed. He laid his hand on hers, pressing the goodness of her into his cheek as one would press balm into an infected wound.

"I did betray her, though," he said, as if he had to make the admission. "If I'd just told her one more time I hadn't been unfaithful, maybe I could have made her believe. If I hadn't believed that damned psychiatrist when he said her threats were idle!"

"You were paying for a professional judgment. You can't be blamed for taking the expert's advice. And are you so sure *you* were the betrayer? I think you might well have been the betrayed."

His glassy eyes looked deeply into hers as he tried to understand her remark.

"Love believes," Rori said simply, softly. "Don't you see that it was she, even though she was ill, who chose not to trust you? You didn't betray her, Blade. She betrayed *you*."

He said nothing. Nor did his moonlit eyes give away anything of what he was thinking, feeling. Rori did sense, though, that she was offering him an absolution he had not considered. Perhaps he was trying to decide if he deserved such a gift. Just one last time she would try to persuade him. Standing on tiptoe, she grazed his lips with hers and whispered, "Let go, Blade. Let go of a guilt you don't deserve."

A strangled cry escaped him as he reached for her in desperation and held her. She stepped deeper into his embrace. His breath came harsh and heavy, and she could feel his pain, a pain he'd lived with so long. It was a pain she would have given anything to ease, a pain she would have gladly taken unto herself. She felt, too, the pain of his arousal. Performing to nature's design, his body had responded to her nearness...or perhaps it, like her own body, had never completely let go of its earlier response.

Wanting, needing—God, when had she ever needed anything so badly?—to ease the part of his pain she could, she sought his mouth, savagely sipping at his lips. Startled, his body shivered with a spasm. Then he groaned, plunging his tongue deeply, hungrily within her. She drew her hands down his bare, perfect back, over the firm cheeks of his bare buttocks, one hand rounding his thigh to capture the silken heat of him.

She surprised him. His gasp told her that. His fingers clamped around her wrist. He wrenched her hand away, but not before she had circled him, stroked him.

"No!" he said raggedly, his eyes hot with passion, yet equally hot with restraint. "I don't have the strength to resist you again," he admitted. "Not twice in one night."

"Then don't resist me," she said, freeing her hand from his and returning it to where it had been. Her hand closed around him. He was hot, wet, thick with need.

"Rori, don't!" he ordered, but already he didn't have the willpower to stop her from doing what was feeling so wonderfully good. Instead, all he could do was tremble.

"Let me at least ease this pain," she whispered.

"I don't want you...to hurt," he said, his speech, his thoughts, already growing incoherent.

She *would* hurt. She knew that. For in making love to him, she would renew, reawaken her own need. But it was a hurt she would cherish. Any price was worth paying for bringing peace to Blade—even if all she could bring him was a physical peace. She didn't question the all-consuming need that drove her. She knew she had to *give* him something, even if there was nothing to take for herself.

Unbuttoning the shirt she wore, she slid it from her shoulders and let it fall to the floor. She pressed her naked body to his.

"Love me," she whispered.

"Rori—"

"Love me," she repeated, taking his hand and leading him to the bed.

"Rori, I—"

Her mouth covered his, halting the words. He moaned. When she eased onto the bed, he was helpless to do anything but follow. Down, down she sank—kissing lips and neck and chest—until she lay on her back, her hair scattered wildly. She drew his lips to hers.

He felt sweetness, hotness, an unbearable longing to join their bodies in a more intimate caress. He fought the urge, promising himself he'd indulge himself in this kiss, then try once more to explain... Oh, God, he thought as her long, beautiful legs shifted and parted in invitation. He couldn't hurt her, wouldn't hurt her. He... Oh, God, no please, no! he thought as he felt the tip of his manhood nudge the soft petals of her womanhood. Taking her hands, she opened herself to him, guiding him into the hollow of her woman's body. No! he thought, but when she arched against him the sentiment quickly changed to Yes! Yes!

As he slid into the moist warmth, a thousand bright sensations, like a kaleidoscope of feelings, burst to life, and he wanted only to tunnel as deeply into her as he could. To lose himself. To bury his pain—his physical pain, his emotional pain. Slipping his arms beneath her shoulders, nestling his face in the curve of her neck, he gave himself up to the beauty of what he was feeling. She had started a gentle thrusting of her hips. Suddenly there was no beginning, no end, to any of life, no yesterday, no tomorrow, nothing resembling reason. There was only a rhythm, a primitive, pagan rhythm that destroyed all in its path.

Rori felt Blade's tattered breath strike the skin of her neck, felt his fingers dig into her shoulders. She felt, too, the sensual abrading of his chest against her pleasure-swollen breasts. Perspiration had formed at the small of his back, and her hands slicked through it as she urged him closer. She gasped as he quickened the pace. Good! He felt so good! And she wanted only to feel him lose himself in her. Nothing else mattered. With that thought in mind, she gave herself up entirely to pleasure—his pleasure.

In-out...in-out... A tiny ripple of feeling purled through her. She moaned. Good...he felt so good...his breath...his sweat-damp hips...in-out... Another ripple danced through her...good...so good... His mouth found hers, his tongue moving...in-out... Another ripple burned through her belly...followed by another...and another...then...

The paroxysm came suddenly, out of nowhere, with a force that was stunning. Rori gasped, uncertain what had happened to her. Before she could consider it, another pulsation struck her, then another. She cried out against his mouth, her body bucking, writhing, to meet the ecstasy flowing through her.

Blade jerked his gaze to her. Her eyelids were half closed, her breath screaming through parted lips, her body moving unmistakably.

She was climaxing!

Hard.

And fast.

And over...and over...and over.

He'd never felt anything like the joy singing through him...or the pleasure—the pure, unadulterated, physical pleasure. When had her pleasure become his? Thrusting his hips to the rhythm she was setting, he felt himself joining her. Quickly. Completely. With a tender violence. He groaned as he emptied himself into her. Again and again. With her receiving him again and again. The moment lasted for one long, beautiful forever.

Finally, Blade rolled from her, dragging her with him until they lay on their sides. Her face was buried in his chest, her heart stampeding savagely. He held her as he waited for her body to calm. Cupping her hips, he gently thrust them against his. One last belated spasm, this one fainter but no less precious, claimed her. She whimpered and nuzzled her cheek against him. He drew her close.

After a while, she raised her head, her eyes finding his in the dark. Even so, he could see the tears in hers. When he brushed the hair from her face, a tear splattered onto the back of his hand.

Blade smiled. "Didn't I tell you we'd do it together?" Another tear fell. She sniffed. Obviously fighting off the barrage she could feel coming. When another tear fell, he cradled her head and nestled her face into his shoulder. "Cry," he whispered. "It's okay."

She did. For the beauty of what they'd shared. For the most victorious feeling she'd ever had. For the final easing of her body's misery.

Blade's eyes misted, too. For all of her reasons, and for one very personal reason, as well. She had brought peace to his body, but she'd also managed to do something he had begun to doubt would ever again be possible. She had brought peace to his battered soul.

Chapter Eleven

The following evening, Preservation Hall, a shabby old building on St. Peter Street, shook to its foundation with foot-tapping, body-swaying jazz. The discordant notes, which were the true heartbeat, the soulbeat of every New Orleanian, rained down on the undulating sea of listeners. With no luxuries like air-conditioning or drinks to relieve the sultry Saturday night, the audience, packed to overflowing, perspired en masse, sending a savagely alluring scent into the Southern air. Although there were a few pillows up front for patrons to sit on, and a couple of rows of benches just behind them, most people stood, not daring to leave for fear of losing their spots to one of the faces peering wistfully through the window.

"You okay?" Blade asked, his lips close to Rori's ear so he could be heard. They had arrived late—a little after ten o'clock—and had been lucky to find a place in the back of the room against the wall.

Rori nodded, sliding her arm beneath her hair and raising it off her damp neck. "Hot," she mouthed in answer.

The arm at her waist tightened, pulling her intimately against jean-sheathed thighs, while Blade's lips brushed the nape of her neck. "Yeah," he whispered provocatively, "tell me about it."

Her eyes found his. Their smoky-gray expression said what she already knew—that he hadn't been talking about the room's sweltering temperature, but rather about a sexual condition that had relentlessly plagued both of them since waking that day at noon. In each other's arms.

She had been frightened that what had happened to her body had been a fluke, that it wouldn't repeat itself, but Blade had gently, sensuously led her to the same climactic conclusion. Actually, he'd led her to far more than the same. This time he had sent her soaring so high into the heavens that she'd been uncertain she would ever land on earth. But it had been a trip she hadn't taken alone—which had made the journey all the sweeter.

Exhausted, they'd slept again, awakening in the middle of the afternoon. Sending for room service, they'd dined on thick, juicy hamburgers and candy bars from a vending machine. They'd taken a shower—together—during which Blade had once more proven Rori's new capabilities. As the water had washed over them, along with the fading ripples of passion, they had stared at each other—a little bewildered by the magnitude of what had happened between their bodies, of what was happening between their hearts. As though words were no longer trustworthy, as though neither knew quite what to say even if they had been, neither spoke. Blade, however, was infinitely aware that Rori had trusted him in the most basic, perhaps the most beautiful way. Rori was aware of just what that trust meant to a trust-starved Blade.

As she stood now in Preservation Hall, the floor throbbing with the syncopated music of clarinet, saxophone, trumpet and trombone, she saw that Blade's thoughts mirrored her own. Again, neither knew quite what to say...and so she leaned into him, angling her head against his shoulder. He tilted his head until his temple found hers.

Rori felt his arm at her waist, protectively snuggling her to him. *Why is it that this man, by his very nearness, can make me feel so safe, so secure?*

Blade felt the slight round of her belly, a belly his hand had touched only hours before. *Wonder what that belly would feel like filled with my child.* The thought came from nowhere, leaving him shocked that it had come at all— shocked, but strangely moved by the images that formed in his head.

Rori smelled his rich after-shave...and thought of how she, seated on the bathroom counter, had watched him shave...and what a sensual experience it had been... especially with his lips finding hers about as often as the razor found his jaw. *Where is our relationship headed?* The thought came out of nowhere, frightening her a little because she hadn't realized their relationship had progressed to the point of asking that question. It also frightened her because she didn't know what she wanted the answer to be.

Blade inhaled her perfume, a heady fragrance combining frangipani and jasmine. She smelled wonderful... womanly...wickedly wanton. *Where is this relationship going? Where do I want it to go?* Where he wanted to go this minute, he realized, his attention drawn to the sweat-moist swell of her breasts, breasts that he knew for a fact were bare beneath the red sundress he'd packed for her, was to bed. Again. Unbelievably.

Rori felt him stir against her, as though he was growing restless. Something in his movement, something in the way his thighs pressed into her hips, transmitted the restlessness to her. She realized with a start that it was a sexual restlessness. She wanted him! Again. Incredibly.

The band finished a swinging rendition of "When The Saints Go Marching In," then chose that moment to take a ten-minute break. The crowd burst into appreciative applause at the entertainers' outstanding performance. Many viewers began to flock toward the door, to seek the other treasures the French Quarter offered in such abundance. The French Quarter's crowdedness had been the reason Blade had been willing to venture from the hotel. He'd reasoned that, if Rori was indeed in danger, there was safety in numbers. That protective crowd, now alive with a personality of its own, seemed intent on shoving them apart . . . or possibly even trampling over them.

"Want to hang around for more music?" Blade asked, holding tightly to her as people shifted around them.

Rori's eyes boldly found his. "No."

"Want to go find a drink somewhere, then?"

"No."

"Want to walk some more of the Quart—"

"No."

The way she so decisively interrupted him, the way she was looking at him as if the rest of the world had ceased to be, started Blade to burning around the edges of his libido. "What do you want to do, then?" he asked, his voice husky.

"You," she mouthed.

Her unabashed aggression, something he was totally unaccustomed to, something he'd desperately wanted from his wife, proved the most powerful of aphrodisiacs. His breathing shallowed. His eyes darkened. He fought with the devil to keep from reaching for her right there.

"Race you back to the hotel, Cavannaugh," Rori said, her mouth twisting into a sassy grin. Before Blade knew what was happening, she'd pulled from him. In two steps, she was swallowed by the crowd.

As the people closed around her, Rori knew a moment of panic. She'd foolishly thought Blade would be right behind her. Now she realized they were separated by a middle-aged couple and a young couple with a child. Rori caught snippets of conversation in which the foursome were trying to decide whether or not to call it a night. Looking back, Rori's gaze connected with Blade's. He motioned for her to keep to the left.

She did, and in seconds the thick night air, cooler only by contrast to the sticky heat inside the building, poured over her like warm honey. The street was congested not only with people leaving and entering Preservation Hall, but also with Saturday-night revelers passing by en route to somewhere else. Loud, boisterous laughter punctuated a consistent din of conversation, and music spilled from nearby doorways, one of them a fun-filled night spot known as Pat O'Brien's, home of the famed rum-based Hurricane. Taxis and a smattering of cars cruised the street. Jostled by the crowd, and seeking a place out of the way, Rori headed for an old-fashioned lamppost.

Blade kept Rori in sight by training his eyes on her tawny-blond hair. "Excuse me," he said as he dodged the sightseers in front of him. They stepped aside . . . just in time to allow a passerby, one who'd obviously had one drink too many, to plunge full steam into Blade.

"Hey, man, I'm sorry," the young man slurred, grabbing Blade by the arms as if to steady him, when it was he who needed balancing.

"No problem," Blade said, extricating himself and glancing around. He looked at the spot where he'd last seen

Rori, but she wasn't there. He frowned. Where in heck was she?

When Rori felt the hand on her shoulder, for one split second she thought it was Blade. She could already feel the excitement beginning to flow at his nearness; she could feel herself turning to acknowledge his presence. Nipping both in the bud, however, was the fact that the hand at her shoulder inconceivably gave a sharp shove, causing her to lurch forward. She fell from the curb and into the street. She was vaguely aware of the crowd's startled gasp and the squealing tires of a car. The hood of the car, now curiously right beneath her palms, bounced up and down. Like the crack of a gun, the car door flew open.

"Hey, lady, what you be, crazy or something?" the cabdriver screamed in his Cajun dialect.

Rori saw the man, saw the frightened expression on his face, a fright he was translating into anger, for she could tell that he was hollering at her. She couldn't hear his words, however, because the blasting of her heartbeat in her ears blanked out all other sounds. Neither could she hear the racket around her.

"My God!" someone shouted.

"Rori?"

"Is she hurt?" an onlooker asked.

"Rori?" This time Blade shook her.

"She fell," another voice called out. "I saw her. She just fell off the curb!"

"Rori!" Blade cried, yanking her hands from the hood of the car and forcing her attention to him. She seemed surprised to see him.

"Blade?" she whispered.

"The lady, she need a keeper," the scared cabdriver yelled to Blade, who, as far as the dark-haired, dark-eyed Cajun was concerned, was obviously responsible for the woman standing in the middle of the street. "She be mad," he said touching his temple, then ended by saying that she needed to be locked away in an asylum, a *maison de fous*.

"Are you all right?" Blade asked, oblivious to the crowd and to the ranting cabdriver.

"I . . . I felt something at my shoulder . . . I thought it was you . . . then I felt a shove," Rori said, her gaze holding onto Blade's as though it was a lifeline.

It took Blade a second to compute her statement. When he did, he jerked his head toward the sidewalk, scanning the gawking crowd for . . . For what, whom, he wasn't at all certain. Did he expect someone to step forward and announce that it was he who had pushed her? The question became moot when Blade suddenly realized that Rori was trembling. Turning to the cabdriver, he asked, "Can you take us to our hotel?"

The man shook his head. "I'm off duty," he said, starting to climb inside the car.

"Fifty bucks!" Blade cried.

The man paused, considered, then motioned toward the backseat, mumbling something about getting the menace off the streets. Blade yanked open the car door, ushered Rori in and climbed in beside her. Putting his arm around her, he drew her shaking body to his. After Blade gave the address of their hotel, no one spoke for the duration of the short ride. Within minutes, Rori and Blade had entered the hotel and were taking the elevator up, still not speaking, Blade continuing to hold her within the secure embrace of his arms.

Once inside their room, as though she'd been saving the words for that moment when the two of them were alone, she said, "Maybe it was an accident. Maybe I overreacted. I mean, the street *was* crowded. Maybe someone bumped into me. Maybe they didn't even know they had. Maybe I just lost my balance." The bright look in her wide eyes said clearly that she wanted him to agree with her. "It's possible, isn't it?" she pleaded.

Considering the street's congestion, considering the drunk who had run into him, considering that he wanted to believe the theory as much as Rori, Blade said, "The street *was* wild."

This seemed all the encouragement Rori needed. Raking her fingers through her hair, she said, "No one in his right mind would try to harm someone with that many people around. No one would take that kind of risk."

Blade didn't point out that the operative phrase was *no one in his right mind*. Mainly because he was finding the premise more and more appealing. The thought of Rori in danger did sickening things to him. Gut-sickening things.

"A drunk did run into me," he pointed out.

"See!" Rori said triumphantly. "It was probably just a crazy coincidence that it happened to me. I mean, with the letters and all." She laughed, but the sound was brittle. "I just got excited." There was still an edge to her every word, her every move. "Yeah, I just got excited. I should have realized the street was just crowded. I should..." She stopped. Her eyes looked deeply, worriedly into his. "It *is* possible that it was just an accident, isn't it?"

Instead of answering her, Blade reached out and drew her tightly to him. She folded her arms around him, her hands gripping the fabric of his shirt in fierce fistfuls.

"I thought it was you," she whispered, the fractured quality of her voice indicating that she was reliving that moment at the curb. "When I felt something at my shoulder, I thought it was you. I thought—"

"Shh," he said, his lips searching for hers.

They kissed, neither trying to hide the desperation, neither trying to pretend the fright hadn't happened. Both were aware that Blade had never really answered her question.

Their lovemaking that night bordered on wild. Rori couldn't have said exactly why, except that it seemed important, as in the single most important thing in the world, to be lost in each other's arms. Their kisses burned with the heated brilliance of fire; their blistering sighs singed the silence. Their caresses, though, no matter how hard they tried, could not fill a void that each felt yawning deep within.

Blade tried to fill his emptiness by sheathing himself deeper and deeper within the haven of her body. Compliant, Rori urged him to find a deeper spot within her. At the moment of their simultaneous release, when time stood still and eternity trembled, Blade buried his face in the crook of Rori's shower-damp neck.

"I love you!" he groaned, surprised at what he was saying, yet more surprised that it had taken this long to say what he'd known in his heart from the beginning. He didn't want to have to explain what was inexplicable. How did you fall in love so quickly? How did you fall in love by staring across a balcony? But that was exactly what he had done . . . and that fact could not now, or ever, be undone.

Miraculously, Rori demanded no impossible explanation. "I love you," she whispered, thinking how right the words sounded, how right they felt. What had taken the two of them so long to say them?

Blade glanced at Rori, and she met his gaze.

Tears threatened Rori's eyes and she saw matching moisture well in his as they realized that the yawning void had just been filled.

* * *

The following day at noon, they reluctantly checked out of the hotel and entered the real world. On the way home, Rori forced Blade to stop at a bookstore so she could buy a copy of the latest B. J. Nichols novel. Embarrassed, he assured her that he could tell her the story and save her $19.95. She insisted on buying the book, threatening to reveal who he was to every bookstore patron if he didn't give her a quick kiss as they stood in the aisle between mystery and science fiction.

"Why, Ms. Kelsey, that sounds remarkably like extortion," he said, placing both hands on the bookshelf and intimately hemming her within the cage of his arms.

"Yes, I guess it does," she said, already breathless from the anticipation of his mouth on hers.

"Despite the threat, however, I don't think I can comply," he said gruffly. "With the quick part, that is. If I kiss you, I'll feel compelled to make it long and slow and wet." The last word practically dripped with moisture.

"Oh," she whimpered, feeling her knees buckle at his clever reversal of her extortion.

"'Course," he continued, "if that's the kind of kiss you want right here in the presence of Isaac Asimov and Robert Ludlum, I'll be happy to oblige. I mean, I guess I really have no choice if you insist on exposing me."

Her heart tripping in her chest, Rori said, "Maybe I was being rash. Maybe we should discuss this at a more private place. Do, uh, do you give rainchecks?"

"Oh, yeah," he said, his eyes dusky, his voice husky, "and a lot more." At the instant hazing of her sea-green eyes, at the sexy parting of her lips, Blade growled, "C'mon, let's get the hell out of here!"

Twenty-three minutes later—Blade counted each hellish one of them—he opened the door to Rori's apartment, let her pass in front of him, then, barely closing the door behind them, he pulled her into his arms. He made the kiss that followed long, slow and wet. Rori gave a low moan. At the kiss's end, Blade, as breathless as she, rested his forehead against hers.

"I love you," she whispered, the words as new as a Christmas present that had to be looked at again and again.

"I love you," he whispered, feeling the same magic, feeling the need for another kiss. This time it was Blade who moaned, adding, "I need to go to my apartment . . . and, if I don't go now, it might be a while before I do."

"Why?"

"Because I'm going to take you to bed if I stay."

Rori smiled. "No, I knew that part. Why are you going to your apartment?"

"I want to get a few things and see if the housekeeper left any messages. I'm expecting a call from my editor." His lips brushed hers in a brief farewell. "Don't let anyone in while I'm gone."

"Blade, you don't have to stay with me," Rori protested. He'd earlier said he wasn't going to let her out of his sight. "I'm safe in my own apartment. Really, I am—"

"I'll be back in a little bit," he interrupted, repeating, "don't let anyone in."

She didn't argue about his returning, since it was precisely what she wanted him to do. She spent the time unpacking, gathering the newspapers that had collected at her door, watering plants that had grown thirsty over the weekend. Blade spent the time scowling over the fact that his editor hadn't called. The housekeeper had left a note to that effect. She'd scrawled it across the hotel address Blade had left saying where he could be reached. Blade wondered if he should call Detective Pinchera and report what had happened the evening before. Rori had deliberately avoided discussing the incident again. What could he tell the police-man? That Rori may or may not have been purposely pushed off the curb? The truth was, the street was crowded. Even he'd been shoved around. Yet... Hell, he didn't know what to do! He'd think about it...and in the meantime he'd stick to her like glue.

The last thing Blade did after assembling a few personal articles to take with him was to douse his roses in beer. That is, what beer he didn't swig. As he was dumping the last of the brew into the flowers, he heard a slight sound and glanced in the direction of Rori's apartment. She was just stepping onto the balcony, a watering can in hand. As they'd done a hundred times since the advent of the summer, they stared at each other. This time, the sparks shooting back and forth were so hot that they made all the previous hot glances seem like nothing more than the chill of an Arctic blizzard.

Unable to take her eyes from him, Rori soaked in his every detail. He was as charismatic as always. As sexy as always. As mysteriously intense as always. It suddenly dawned on her that she still knew little about this man. What she did know, though, were the important things—that he was the one who'd freed her from her sexual bond-age, that it was him she loved. All else would come in time. After one last parting look, he disappeared inside his apartment. Minutes later, he entered her apartment as he'd left it—with a long, slow, wet kiss.

That night they ordered pizza. When it came, they ate it sprawled on the sofa, she at one end, he at the other, their feet laced together cozily. She was engrossed in his book, he in catching up on the news via the newspapers that had col-lected in their absence. In a typically male way, he started with the sports section. Rori, knowing she was acting cow-ardly and not caring one whit, avoided the newspapers. She knew they'd be filled with information regarding the recent slaying.

"Does Freeman get killed?" she asked, referring to a character in the book.

"I don't know," Blade answered, taking a bite of pepperoni and mushroom pizza.

"What do you mean you don't know? You wrote the book," she said, munching on a pizza crust.

"You paid $19.95 for the opportunity to find out for yourself."

She grinned. "I paid $18.95. It was discounted."

"There go the royalties."

"How come you write under a pseudonym?"

"I like anonymity. Besides, I didn't want my investigative career to come into conflict with my fictional career."

"Why Nichols?"

"My mother's maiden name."

"I guess this anonymity thing is the reason your picture's not on the jacket?"

"Yep. Plus I hate publicity."

"Then how can I be certain you're B. J. Nichols?" she asked, her grin growing.

"I'm not," he said, dangerously. "I only tell women that to get into their bedrooms."

"If you tell one other woman that, you're gonna be as dead as Freeman."

"What makes you think Freeman gets killed?"

"He's too trusting, too naive. Believe me, he'll get killed."

Shortly, on page one hundred forty-three, Freeman got killed . . . in grim and gory detail.

"I knew it!" Rori announced triumphantly.

"Knew what?" Blade asked absently as he thumbed through the pages of the Sunday paper. His eyes gravitated to an article on the stranglings.

"That Freeman was going to buy the farm. Gee, did you have to make his death so graphic? An ice pick to the base of the skull? Why couldn't it have been a simple gun—"

"My God!" Blade said suddenly.

Something in his voice told Rori he wasn't lamenting the brutal death of Fred Freeman.

"What is it?" she asked, studying Blade's blanched face.

"The last prostitute who was killed—" He stopped as he read something else.

"What about her?"

Blade looked up, disbelief scoring his gray eyes. "She was Savannah Brown."

It took Rori a second to grasp the significance of what he was saying. "You knew her?"

"I had just interviewed her. That morning."

"Interviewed her?"

"Yeah. For the book. I thought it would be a neat approach to tell some of it from a prostitute's point of view. I had seen her once when I was out walking. In front of the Happiest Hour." He stood, his agitation preventing him from remaining seated. "My God, I may have been the last person to see her alive. Certainly I was one of the last." He thought of how she'd looked, staring at him with eyes that had lost all their innocence despite the fact that she was still young. He thought, too, of the moment's camaraderie they'd shared, but then he forced the thought aside. It was too painful. "I can't remember what time we parted... somewhere around twelve-thirty or quarter to one, I guess. You think I ought to call the police? Yeah." He answered his own question, walked to the phone and picked up the receiver.

As he did, Rori angled the paper so she could read the headlines. LATEST VICTIM KILLED BETWEEN FOUR O'CLOCK AND EIGHT. From out of nowhere came the memory of Blade's phone ringing repeatedly, without an answer, at six o'clock that Friday evening.

Rori frowned.

Now why in the world had that thought crossed her mind?

Monday morning, after a restless night during which both had tossed and turned, Rori awakened in Blade's arms. Tuesday morning, Rori awakened to the sound of... Of what? A typewriter? It took her a moment to orient herself. She was in a strange bed. No, it was Blade's bed, and she was in Blade's bedroom. She remembered he had wanted to spend the night in his apartment because he needed to let the housekeeper in. She remembered, too, how they'd stayed awake half the night making love. Stretching like a lazy feline, she made a throaty noise comparable to a contented purr. Her eyes roved to the bedside table, to the spot where Anna Marie's picture had once stood. A warm feeling scurried over her at the realization that Blade had removed it. Rori could feel that the negative ties binding him to his dead wife had been severed... or at least they'd been severely enough frayed that time would eventually sever them.

The sound of the typewriter might also be a sign that Blade was in a state of emotional recuperation, Rori thought, rolling from the bed and slipping into a pair of shorts and Blade's oversize shirt. According to him, he hadn't written in months. He was pounding the keys in a hell-bent fashion. Dare she hope it was the book he was working on?

She stepped into the hallway and stopped the moment he came into view. Wearing only jeans and a rugged stubble of beard, he sat at the dining room table. His hair, only a little less than wild, looked as though it suffered from more than one quick run-through of his fingers. Two stacks of paper rested on the table, one stack at each elbow. One held blank sheets, while the other stack was comprised of pages overflowing with typewritten words. A few sheets lay crumpled on the floor, along with his sneakers, which rested on their sides like beached whales. Even as she watched, he removed a sheet of paper from the typewriter, put it in the completed stack and reached for a blank sheet. He rolled it into the typewriter and was typing before it had time to fully curl around the cylinder.

Rori noted idly that he used an old manual typewriter.

She also noted that he was as sexy as the devil searching for a sinner. She smiled, thinking that he could lead her astray any time he liked. The smile faded as her heart filled with love. He was such an enigma, a man of such polar contrasts. On the one hand he wrote about gory violence as if he knew about it personally, while on the other hand he made love so gently it took her breath away. Then, too, he had a power about him, a mysterious power that could be mesmerizing and a little frightening.

There was also a nut-hard shell protecting his emotions from exposure, emotions that had been wounded by his wife as surely as if she'd plunged a knife into his heart. Yet Rori sensed that his emotions ran deep and pure. He wasn't a man to love by half measure. Just as he wasn't a man to feel the darker emotions with any less intensity. She'd felt his anger over the useless death of Savannah Brown. That anger had coursed like a black, turbulent river though his soul, primarily because he seemed to blame himself. If only he'd interviewed her later, if only he'd noticed someone following her...if only...if only...

Detective Pinchera, who agreed that Blade's association with the woman was an extraordinary coincidence, had tried to make him see that it hadn't been his fault. Rori knew, though, that knights in shining armor, of which Blade Cavannaugh was a card-carrying member, felt it their responsibility to save the world. He'd tried to save his wife, but couldn't. He felt he should have saved Savannah Brown, but hadn't. The only thing he was batting a hundred on was Rori. There was no question that Blade Cavannaugh had saved Rori Kelsey—from loneliness, from sexlessness, from a solitary, loveless future.

Padding barefoot and unnoticed across the carpet, Rori stepped behind Blade, slid her arms around his neck and tunneled her fingers through the swath of hair on his chest. She placed her lips at the nape of his neck. Blade moaned, as though in deep satisfaction, yet he never broke stride with the typing. For long minutes he continued to strike the keys. Suddenly he stopped and covered her hands with his.

"Good morning," he said. "Did I wake you?"

"Good morning," she answered. "Yes, you did wake me, but it's time I got up. I wouldn't want to shock your housekeeper by having her find me in bed. Naked, I might add, since you wouldn't let me pack a gown."

He yanked her into his lap. She gave a tiny yelp of surprise. His mouth instantly found hers, his beard sexily abrading her soft skin, while his hand, as though it knew the way perfectly, eased beneath her shirt and cupped a bare breast. She moaned and arched into his palm.

"Forget the gown, forget the bed," he growled. "I'm going to take you right here on the table. She can just dust around us."

Rori giggled at the outrageous image that formed in her mind. But then the giggle disappeared as ribbons of desire darted through her belly. The table was really no more outrageous than what they'd done the night before. Standing in the shadowless dark of the patio, the nectarous scent of roses floating around them, he'd run his hand beneath the folds of her sundress, caressing her in a sweet, swollen place until she'd had no option but to shatter into a million sensual pieces. He'd then discreetly rearranged their clothing and slid into her while her body was still pulsating with pleasure. In minutes, she'd shattered again, this time with him stroking deeply inside her. Then, as now, she found it hard to believe the miracle this man had wrought in her life.

"It was nice, wasn't it?" he whispered, knowing precisely what she was thinking of and grinning decadently.

"It was wicked, Cavannaugh," she responded with a matching grin.

"That, too," he agreed, his mouth finding hers again. When he pulled his lips from hers, his mouth only a breath away, he announced, "I'm writing."

There was such happiness in his voice that Rori felt her heart swell with pride. "So I've noticed. Does this mean the writer's block has ended?"

He shrugged. "All I know is that I talked to my editor yesterday. He liked the approach I want to take—that is, after he came to from the shock of realizing I hadn't started the book yet. Then, this morning at five o'clock, I woke up with a million words pouring out of my mind. I can't get them down fast enough," he added disbelievingly.

"What do you think happened?"

He ran a bent finger across her chin. "Not what. *Who*." She had given him so much—the easing of his guilt. It had been Rori who made him see that Anna Marie had betrayed him, not he her. Maybe the psychiatrist had been right. Maybe once he'd realized that Anna Marie had killed herself, that he hadn't killed her with his success, he'd been able to write again. Then again, maybe it was Rori's love, the trust she gave him so unequivocally. He lowered his lips to hers, his tongue swirling slowly within the sweetness of her mouth. Suddenly that mouth was too sweet. Wrenching from her, he stared at her passion-flushed face. "We either cut it out now, or Mrs. Yearwood *is* going to find us on the table."

Rori sighed. "I guess that's too wicked even for us." She pulled from his lap as he pushed against her bottom.

"I'll get us some coffee," he said, shoving back his chair and starting for the kitchen.

"Can I read what you've written?" Rori called after him. "I mean, you're not superstitious or anything?"

"Yes, you can read it. No, I'm not superstitious. And you're still going to have to fork over $19.95 when it's in the bookstores."

"Whatever happened to your telling me the story?"

"I'll need the money. I'll have a wife to support by then," he said as he disappeared through the door.

Surprise and joy flooded Rori's heart. How like him! she thought. How like him to propose by not proposing at all. How blatant, how presumptuous, how...how like him! She could remember the audacity with which he'd announced that they would be lovers. She'd just seen and heard that audacity again. That endearing audacity. She gave herself up to thought of what it would be like to be married to this mercurial man. She was in the middle of some wonderful fantasies when he called from the kitchen.

"What do you think of the book so far?"

Book? What book? She forced her feet to the ground. "Give me a minute, will ya?"

Leafing through the stack of typed pages, she found the beginning of chapter one. She started to read. *She sounded like an angel, but there was something evil in the sticky-sweetness of her voice.* Three paragraphs later, the woman with the evil-sounding voice was strangled to death—in such vivid detail that Rori's heart pounded and her breath shallowed in abject empathy. She read on. Slowly, like the gauzy beginnings of a nightmare, however, she began to feel a new level of discomfort, of fear. Her attention shifted from the story to the written page itself. Why? She didn't know, except that she felt... What? As if she should be noticing something. As if the typed letters were trying to tell her something. As if she'd seen these typed characters before. But where?

Suddenly Rori's heart stopped. Her gaze flew to the manual typewriter. Underwood. The brand was Underwood. An old Underwood, probably a 1960s model. No! something inside Rori screamed as a sick feeling churned through her stomach. She went numb. Stone-cold numb. She forced herself to lower her eyes to the typed page, knowing what she'd find there. She found exactly what she feared, exactly what she would have sold her soul not to see, exactly what Detective Pinchera had said she'd see when she found the typewriter that had typed the threatening letters—the *o* key didn't quite close at the top.

Chapter Twelve

So, what do you—?''

Blade, a steaming mug of coffee in each hand, halted midsentence and midstep as he took in Rori's face. Her cheeks had bleached to a stunned, ashen color, and her eyes seemed to have grown too large for her heart-shaped face—too large and unmistakably filled with pain and... And what? The emotion, though it made no sense, looked remarkably like fear.

"My God, Rori, what is it?" he asked, setting the mugs on the table.

At his entrance, she'd looked up, seeing him yet not seeing him, recognizing him yet not recognizing him. Suddenly this man who was her lover, who had professed to love her—the man she loved—seemed like a complete stranger. A part of her brain thought how odd it was that one's life could change so drastically in the span of seconds, how odd that a defective *o* key on an outdated typewriter could bring one's life crashing down around one. Another part of her brain refused to think at all.

"Rori?" he repeated.

"The typewriter," she said in a strangled voice that sounded foreign to her own ears. "It's the one."

Blade frowned. Whatever reply he'd been expecting, that wasn't it. That she'd turned ill, perhaps, or that she hated the manuscript—or had suddenly heard a voice from outer space. But not something as mundane as the typewriter!

"I don't understand—"

"It's manual, it's an Underwood, it has a defective *o* key." Rori's voice was bland with shock.

Blade asked, "So what?"

"It's the one," Rori repeated, her words coming out with a deceptive calmness, a false peace.

Blade's voice expressed his growing exasperation. He sensed that something was wrong. Terribly wrong. And she wasn't giving him any clue as to what that something was. "It's the one what?" he asked, the question inflamed with impatience.

"It's the one that typed the threatening letters I received."

It was Blade's turn to look thunderstruck. Finally, hand on hip—his incredibly lean, sexy hip, Rori thought, despite the storm raging around her—he said, "If this is your idea of a joke, Rori, I'm not amused."

Rori's anesthesia wore off instantly, and a fear-ridden anger took its place. "Neither am I!" she cried.

Something told her that she might regret so flagrant a casting of caution to the four winds. Something told her that she might have been as foolishly trusting, as naive as B. J. Nichol's character Fred Freeman, dead Fred Freeman, and that she might come to the same grim end. Somehow she didn't give a damn about caution or grim ends. All she wanted to do was confront Blade with the evidence, because she was hurting so badly that she'd willingly take any risk that might end the pain she was feeling. She looked frantically for her purse, found it on the floor at the edge of the sofa and rummaged through it for the photocopies of the letters she'd felt compelled to keep with her.

She unfolded the single sheet of paper on which all four messages appeared and slapped it on the table beside the manuscript. "Look at it!" she demanded. "Look at the letters! Look at your book!"

The blisteringly shouted command gave Blade little choice, so he lowered his gaze from Rori's flushed face to the table.

"Detective Pinchera said the lab determined the typewriter is a manual, an Underwood, and that it has a defective *o* key," Rori said, smoothing the tumbled tangles of her hair. "Try to tell me this typewriter wasn't used to type these messages!" she ordered defiantly.

She glanced down, hoping beyond hope that she was wrong, that the two types would look dissimilar when laid side by side. But they didn't. And Stony's cliché—"—If it walks like a duck, if it quacks like a duck"—came inanely to mind.

Blade looked at her, the expression on his face totally blank. "I...I don't understand," he said, perplexity weighing each word. "It can't be."

"But it is. And you know it," she whispered, the anger gone, replaced by a dull ache in her heart. Despite what she knew to be true, she'd wanted him to make her believe it wasn't the typewriter...or that he had a perfectly logical explanation for why the type matched.

"Surely you don't think I..." he began, taking a step toward her, wanting at some basic level to comfort her, protect her.

She took a step backward.

It was only one step, one small measure of distance, yet a pain so profound it flooded into every pore of his being tore through Blade, as if a rusty knife had been plunged into his tender flesh. A horrible, sickening feeling of déjà vu swept through him. He laughed, a mirthless, sarcastic sound.

"Tell me, Rori, what is there about me that inspires such confidence in women? Anna Marie thought I was an adulterer. You think... What exactly is it you *do* think?" Before she could answer, he said, "No, no, I'm the one with the creative talent. Let me tell you what you believe. Obviously you believe I sent you the threatening messages, so therefore I'm the one stalking you, right?"

Rori didn't answer. She didn't know what she believed. The only thing she knew at the moment was that her heart had never pounded this hard. Its agonized thrashing against her chest made her feel faint.

"Right," he answered for her, adding, "I did insinuate myself into your life in a pretty bold way. That's gotta be suspicious. Oh, and speaking of suspicious, I *was* present at the elevator incident. Hey, wait, I was also there when you were pushed from the curb! I must be responsible for both, huh?"

Again she didn't answer, but although she hated herself for it, images flashed through her mind of how easily he could have been responsible for both incidents. She also remembered the afternoon she'd received the last threatening letter, the one that had been slipped into her mailbox. She had thought she'd seen Blade in her building, and discovered minutes later that he had been walking in the rain. His clothes had been soaked, she'd noted when she'd seen him on the balcony. How ironic that she'd had a heavy-duty lock installed, then given a key to the one man she wanted to keep out—the key to her heart.

"Probably what I did," Blade said, warming to the scenario with an unhealthy enthusiasm, "was wedge something in the elevator to stop it, then scurry down just in time to rescue you myself. Neat ploy, huh? Forget how hard I struggled to open that damned elevator door, forget how I practically ripped my arm from its socket pulling you up, forget how we both collapsed on the floor in total exhaustion. It was all part of my elaborate and diabolically devious plan. Just as it was my plan to go back after you'd fallen asleep and remove whatever I had wedged into the elevator. It would have been simple to do. You were out like a light."

Once more an image formed in Rori's mind. An image of a naked Blade beside her the following morning. She hadn't known he'd gotten out of bed. Perhaps he'd done more than remove his jeans. She could hear him telling Detective Pinchera that maybe the reason the police hadn't found anyone suspicious hanging around was because whoever had tampered with the elevator had belonged on the scene.

"And, of course," Blade said, dragging her to the present, "it would have been easy to push you from the curb in front of Preservation Hall, then dash to your rescue. As I remember, you told me you had been so certain it was me placing a hand on your shoulder. I was probably relieved when you were willing to accept the incident as a accident. Of course, that sick feeling in my stomach was all put-on. And telling you I loved you was just a charade to lead you off the track."

Although everything he was saying was what she was thinking, she couldn't bear to hear it spoken out loud. Especially not the part about him saying he loved her. "Stop it," she whispered.

Ignoring her, he frowned. "One thing doesn't make sense, though. Why do I keep rescuing you if I'm trying to do you in? Unless," he said, "I'm just trying to torment you without really harming you. But why would I do that, Rori? What would be my motivation? What kind of sick game am I playing? What kind of perverse pleasure am I getting out of playing it?"

Rori startled herself with her response. On the surface it was a complete departure from the subject. Below the surface it was more of the same—just uglier, blacker. "I called you Friday evening...about six...to tell you I missed you, but...you didn't answer the phone."

The relevance of what she'd just said escaped Blade completely. It was obvious from the way his brows knitted into a confused V that he thought she'd just spoken in a foreign language, one he had no skills in interpreting. It was also obvious he couldn't explain why he hadn't answered the call. Somehow he felt compelled to try, through, as if he sensed he had to defend himself against unmade allegations.

"I, uh, I don't know... Wait a minute," he said, remembering why he hadn't. "Friday was the afternoon I worked on the notes I'd taken from the Savannah Brown interview. I was kind of stir-crazy." *And restless from the hot-as-sin kiss we'd shared earlier,* he could have said, but didn't. "I went out walking." His frown deepened. "But I don't understand. What does Friday and my not answering the phone have to do with..." Suddenly he stopped. Suddenly he did understand. Suddenly he wished, more than he'd wished anything, that he didn't understand...and that he didn't have this awful, hollow feeling in the middle of his stomach. Was it possible to die from a hollow feeling? No. If it was, he would have died a thousand times over his wife's accusations of infidelity. "My apologies," he said softly, tonelessly. "I underestimated your accusation."

The pain that streaked across Blade's eyes, the emptiness in his voice, slashed at Rori's heart. "Blade, I'm not accusing—"

"The hell you're not!" he interrupted, his voice thundering with an ominous quiet. His gray eyes, always intent, pierced her with their directness. "C'mon, Rori, admit it. What you want to hear me say is that I didn't kill Savannah Brown. And that I didn't strangle those three other prostitutes, as well. You'd love to hear me say that I didn't send you those letters, that there has to be some logical reason that they were typed on my typewriter, that I'm not trying to kill you. Wouldn't you, Rori? Wouldn't you love to hear me deny all that? Or are you already so sure of everything that you don't need my denial?"

"No!"

"No, you're not sure, or no, you don't need my denial?"

"No! No, I'm not sure," she said, pushing her hair from her pale face. "I'm not sure of anything."

"Then you want to hear me deny it?"

She hesitated.

"Do you, Rori?"

Still she said nothing.

"Dammit, Rori, do you?"

"Yes!"

"All of it?"

"Yes! I want you to deny it!" Her voice lowered, and she was aware of the urgency in her plea as she added, "All of it."

A flicker of some bleak, bleeding emotion flashed across Blade's face, but then it was gone, buried deeply behind an unreadable expression. "I'd love to, Rori," he said, the words as sheer as silk, his bare footsteps as silent as death as he stalked toward her with a rolling sway of his hips that seemed to define masculinity, "but there's just one little problem. What good would it do if I did? Surely you wouldn't expect a murderer...that is what you're accusing me of being, aren't you?" he whispered as he grazed the crest of her cheek with his finger.

"No," she whispered, knowing she was lying. A murderer was exactly what she was calling him. At least it was what she was asking him to deny he was.

"Sure you are," he countered, his finger gliding slowly, sensuously along the curve of her jaw and to the tip of her pointed chin. "But if I was...am...a murderer, how likely is it that I wouldn't lie about being one? Would you really expect me to admit it?"

"I'll believe what you tell me," Rori said.

"Ah, that's what Anna Marie said, too, but she never did believe me. No matter how many times I told her."

"I'm not Anna Marie."

"No?"

"No."

"Maybe not. Then again, maybe you are," he said, the words as sweet as slow-flowing syrup. The finger stroking her chin slid into the flaxen fall of her hair to caress a curl. He did so as though he were making love to it. "Maybe that's what this is all about. Maybe you remind me of Anna Marie. Maybe I'm obsessed with blond hair. Maybe that's why I'm killing blond-haired prostitutes."

"Don't, Blade—" Rori whispered, protesting what he was saying. Primarily because similar thoughts were crossing her mind.

"Maybe she was right," Blade continued. "Maybe I *was* unfaithful to her. With blond-haired prostitutes. God only knows, Anna Marie made me feel guilty for wanting to touch her. But maybe I felt just as guilty relieving myself with prostitutes. Maybe I grew to hate Anna Marie...and the women I cheated on her with. Maybe everything ran together in my mind. Maybe the prostitutes became her, she them. Maybe you're just another facet of my blond-haired obsession.''

''Don't, Blade,'' Rori pleaded.

''What's wrong? Am I frightening you?''

''No,'' she denied, but some traitorous part of her heart admitted that it was coincidental that Blade's wife had hanged herself and that the prostitutes had been strangled. Just as it was coincidence that he'd interviewed Savannah Brown shortly before her death. Was there one coincidence too many? ''No,'' she repeated, uncertain whose benefit it was for—his or hers, ''you're not frightening me.''

''Oh, yes, I am. I can feel the fear racing through you. I can feel it here—'' he touched her behind her ear ''—and here—'' he brought his thumb to the pulse point in her throat ''—and here,'' he whispered, slowly, sexily sliding his thumb to the hollow of her throat. His hand curled, like a bronzed serpent, around her neck. ''Or is it possible that what I'm feeling is just plain, common, garden-variety lust? Does your body want me...regardless of what you think I'm capable of?''

Rori stared at the man looming before her. With the dense darkness of his morning beard, with his hair wild from sleep and rambling fingers, he looked rugged, barbarous and so blatantly sensual Rori had to concede that he was right. She did want him. No matter what he might be. She wanted him so badly that her lips tingled with need, her breasts knotted against the fabric of his shirt, as if straining toward the nakedness of his heated chest, while her femininity throbbed with hot and heavy pulsations.

Blade's head lowered.

Rori's heart skittered.

''Maybe this is how I killed them,'' he whispered.

Of its own accord, Rori's head raised to better receive his lips.

This time it was Blade's heart that skittered.

"Maybe I seduced them first," he breathed, his lips brushing hers.

Rori whimpered.

"Maybe I wasn't teasing when I said I tell women I'm B. J. Nichols just to get into their bedrooms." His teeth bit her bottom lip, gnawing gently, provocatively, pulling the sensitive flesh into his mouth, where he sucked it.

Rori moaned, not giving a damn who he was as long as he didn't stop what he was doing.

Suddenly, as though tortured by his game, he pulled his mouth from hers and ordered, "Tell me you want me! Tell me if I pulled you to the floor right here, I could have you!"

Rori was dimly aware that his demand was punitive. She had made demands of him, demands of denial, and now, though what he was asking of her in no way measured up to what she'd asked of him, he was demanding his own pound of flesh.

"Tell me!"

"Yes," she breathed.

"Yes, what?"

"Yes, I want you."

"And could I have you right here...now...this minute?" When she didn't answer, he rubbed the swollen front of his jeans against her. She whimpered. "Answer me!"

"Blade—"

He rotated his hips in a upward motion, thrusting himself into the soft valley of her body. "Could I have you right here?" he growled.

"Yes!" she cried, the tormented admission wrung from her. "Is that what you want to hear? Yes. Yes. Dammit, yes!"

For a second it was as though the world stood still. Rori's eyes had hazed to the aquamarine color of the sea at twilight. Blade noted this, just as he noted her ragged breath and the rapid pulse fluttering against his hand, which still lay curled around her throat. She looked wholly vulnerable...and more desirable than any woman he'd even known. With a deep groan, his lips slammed into hers, casting them both off the face of the planet. Her mouth parted at the rapid, piercing penetration of his tongue, her own meeting his with a matching fervor. Heat to heat. Need to need. Her hands splayed against the hard warmth of his chest, her fingers lost in the forest of thick brown hair. She could feel his thighs flush against hers. She could also feel his hand at her throat. It began to tighten...tighten...tighten...

Is he going to kill me?

The question flitted through her mind, and on the heels of it was the answer. She didn't know. She didn't care. The truth was that he killed her with pleasure every time he touched her. And if he was going to kill her, if he was going to strangle the breath from her, she could think of no better way to leave life than with her lips branded with his kiss.

Slowly his hand eased its pressure; slowly he tempered the runaway kiss; slowly his mouth pulled from hers. His uneven breath fanned against her face and his eyes met hers.

Tell me you believe I'm not guilty, he pleaded silently.

Tell me you're not guilty, she answered.

Blade saw the doubt lingering in her eyes. It was there amidst passion, it was there amidst some strong feeling that she'd once—now eons ago, it seemed—called love, but it was there. Like a cancer. And like a cancer, doubt multiplied and spread until all in its path was destroyed. It was a sickness, a death, he could not live through a second time.

Drawing his hand from her neck, he edged his body away from hers. "Needing me, wanting me, isn't good enough," he said in a tone that suggested he wished he could settle for less. "I want you to believe in me. Totally. Completely. I want you to be willing to stake your life on me. And I won't make it easy for you, Rori. I won't deny a thing. In fact, I'm through begging you, and the rest of the damned world, to believe in me."

With each word, anger grew until it flashed hotly in his eyes as he bent to snatch a T-shirt off the floor. He headed for the door. Flinging it open, he turned, his stormy gray eyes finding hers. He was once more that mysterious, mercurial stranger she'd spent weeks staring at from her balcony.

"Goddamned through!" he said with such force that the floor seemed to shake beneath her. The door slammed behind him, shaking the apartment's windows and Rori's soul. And then came the rush of a roaring silence.

Beads of sweat popped across Blade's chest, tunneling in and out of the copious coils of hair. How in the world, he thought, squinting at the sun, could a before-eight-o'clock sun be so ruthless? Unquestionably it was going to be another sweltering day, although the pace at which he walked, as if he was headed for hell in a hurry, was adding to the heat. He slowed. Only then did he realize that he was barefoot...and that he was still carrying his T-shirt. He stopped, hung his head and, hands on hips, exhaled a deep sigh.

He felt the warm, grainy concrete beneath his feet.

He felt the warm sun raining down on his bare shoulders.

He felt a weight in his chest that threatened to smother him.

An image of Rori formed in his mind—disheveled, confused, frightened Rori. It was the wide-eyed, hurt-eyed Rori he'd so dramatically left behind. Despite his resolve, the image pricked at his heart.

Stop it, Cavannaugh! You're not going back to defend yourself, so don't even give that crazy idea a thought. You're through begging for people's leftover scraps of trust. You're through, man. Through, as in fini, caput, over and done with. You got that?

Yeah.

Right.

Damned straight!

Blade wiped the T-shirt across his sweat-dampened chest, then mopped his hair-laden armpits. Slinging the soft, cotton shirt around his neck, he began to walk again, his stride more reasonable.

There was still warm, grainy concrete beneath his feet.

The sun still bore down on him.

The painful weight on his chest threatened to suffocate him with his every breath.

God, how fatally could a man be wounded and still keep going? He'd thought Anna Marie had hurt him as deeply as he could be hurt, but he'd been wrong. Dead wrong. Her lack of faith in him had been nothing compared to Rori's...because, as much as he'd cared for Anna Marie, what he felt for Rori was a thousand times greater, a thousand times stronger. He'd never felt with another woman what he felt with Rori—a subliminal peace that seeped into his soul.

Sweet God, he cried like an injured beast, *how could she do this to me? How could she believe that I'd hurt her? Doesn't she know that I'd die before I let anything, anyone, harm her?*

Part of him wanted to blame her, without benefit of mercy, while another part had to admit that her lack of faith was not unjustified, as his wife's had been. Anna Marie had

had no reason to distrust him. Rori had a good reason—a reason with twenty-six plus keys, one of them a defective *o* key. He frowned. How was it possible that his typewriter had been used to type the messages? He knew he should ponder that question, that it was a question of magnitude and importance, but nothing would compute beyond the fact that, when push had come to shove, Rori hadn't trusted him.

He remembered the doubt in her passion-hazed eyes.

He remembered the way her body had clung to his despite the fact that she thought he might be guilty of the foulest of deeds.

Her body had trusted him days before in a way she'd never trusted her husband. Why couldn't people listen to instinct? Why were they always so certain that logic and reason were better guides to behavior? And was he entertaining the notion of telling her he wasn't guilty... because that was exactly what instinct told him to do?

No!

He didn't care what instinct dictated. A man had his pride. And, with God as his witness, he wouldn't humble himself with a denial that he shouldn't have to make in the first place! Love believes. She'd said so herself. Hadn't she? Yeah, but...

He stopped, sweat dripping from his brow, his tanned chest glistening with a fine sheen of moisture. But what, Cavannaugh? But love also had to make concessions, didn't it? Hadn't he always regretted that he hadn't tried to convince Anna Marie just one more time of his innocence? Was he going to make the same mistake twice? Besides, Rori was in danger from some unknown source. She was scared. Hurting. Thinking that he might have betrayed her. Under the circumstances, mightn't he have thought the same thing? Under the circumstances, couldn't he give an inch?

He closed his eyes and raised his face to the sun, breathing out a stream of air that fluttered the hair falling across his forehead. Who could have had access to his typewriter? Nobody came to mind. Think, Cavannaugh! Somebody typed those letters on your old, dilapidated machine. Okay, let's start with the obvious. There's Donald Weiss. He has a set of keys. Good, good, who else? Suddenly a thought crossed his mind. It was a bizarre thought, but nonetheless this man would have had access to the typewriter. The phone repairman. Lord only knew he'd been at the apartment. In fact, he'd been there the afternoon Rori had received the last letter, the afternoon of the evening of the elevator incident. Neither the phone repairman nor Weiss would have drawn any attention. Both would have blended unnoticed into the scenery. Both . . .

Abruptly another image crossed his mind. A half grin formed at the image's ludicrousness. But then the grin fell away. It *was* ludicrous, wasn't it? Yes, preposterous, even. Yet . . . A dark coldness swept through him, chilling him to the bone despite the searing sun.

He checked his watch. It was seventeen minutes after eight o'clock. He knew he had to be wrong. There'd come a time when he'd laugh at this. He and Rori would laugh at this, he thought, unconsciously reconciling them. But in the meantime, he started to run. Pebbles gouged his bare feet as his legs pumped out a racing rhythm. The T-shirt draped around his neck sailed unnoticed to the ground. A dog barked furiously and ran with him for almost a block before falling by the wayside from exhaustion. Two joggers looked at Blade as if he'd lost his mind in the morning heat.

And he wasn't altogether certain he hadn't, either. But one thing he did know for sure, and even had the presence of mind to marvel at. At the moment he'd gladly bury his masculine pride. At the moment he'd humble himself in whatever way he had to. And all for one thing: to know that Rori was safe.

For a long while after the door had slammed behind Blade, Rori stood in one spot, watching the door and listening to the silence around her. She felt as if a button had been pushed, throwing her into an emotional overload. Disbelief, hurt, fear, confusion—all vied for existence, but mostly she felt empty. As though, when Blade had closed the door, he had shut off a chamber of her heart.

She had seen the hurt in his eyes, a hurt she'd put there. But, dear God, could anyone blame her for wanting to hear him say he was innocent? That was all she'd asked! She'd told him she would believe what he told her. But would she have? Yes, unlike his wife, she would have believed.

"You don't know how it hurts to be accused of something you're innocent of...especially by someone who's supposed to love you."

"You didn't betray your wife. She betrayed you. Love believes."

The last words, her words, came tripping through the stillness, haunting her, taunting her with their simplistic yet complicated litany. Like his dead wife, she hadn't believed in him enough to trust him. But then, could anyone blame her for not believing in the face of such overwhelming evidence? Yes, came the immediate answer. One someone could. She blamed herself.

Tears stung her eyes and she turned from the door. Her gaze fell to the typewriter, to the photocopied letters, to the manuscript. There was no doubt that this typewriter had produced the messages. Even Blade recognized that it had. But did that necessarily mean *he* was guilty?

"Love believes."

Did she really believe he could be guilty of the heinous crime of murder?

"*Needing me, wanting me, isn't enough. I want you to believe in me.*"

Did she really believe he could harm her? Did she really believe that the man whose kiss could be as gentle as starlight could kill her? She'd trusted him . . . from the beginning . . . in ways she'd never trusted another man. She'd sought the safety of his arms. Had she been wrong?

"*Love believes.*"

Rori swiped at a tear, feeling in that moment like the murderer she'd accused him of being. She'd murdered him with her betrayal. Just as his wife had. Yet Rori knew her crime was greater, far greater. His wife had been emotionally ill.

Suddenly the emptiness inside her swelled with a punishing, painful need. She had to find him. She had to apologize. She had to beg him to forgive her. Starting for the door, she realized she wore no shoes. A quick dash to the bedroom, and she was hopping, skipping, slipping her feet into a pair of canvas wedges even as she ran for the door.

Don't let it be too late!

Don't let him hate her!

Don't let him turn his back on her the way she had on him!

With this trio of fervent prayers, Rori opened the door . . . and plowed straight into a wall of flesh.

Chapter Thirteen

Mountain.

For a stunned second, Rori had the impression that she'd just run into a mountain. Behind an ample bosom, which reclined on the woman's chest like a crowded shelf, lay a rock-hard strength. Her shoulders were wide and square. In height she matched Rori eye to eye—brown eye to Rori's blue. No, Rori thought fleetingly, the woman's eyes weren't brown, but black. Like midnight. Like her hair, which was the color of coal and cut close and straight, the longest strands no more than a few inches long. There never would have been a time when the woman was pretty—her complexion was too chalky, her features too coarse—yet in her youth she might have had a vibrancy that would have translated into attractiveness. Rori thought she looked tired, tired of hard physical labor, tired of life's incessant ups and downs. Rori sensed that this woman had seen far more downs than ups.

Rori also knew who the mountain was. Even without the white uniform, starched as crisp as an early morning, and the fact that Blade's housekeeper was expected, she would have known. How, she wasn't sure. Intuition, perhaps. The same intuition that told her Blade could never harm her...or anyone else, for that matter.

"I'm sorry," both women mumbled in that split second of contact.

The housekeeper swiftly took in Rori's sleep-mussed hair, her love-kissed lips still swollen from Blade's hungry mouth, his baggy shirt clinging to the curves of Rori's body and hiding her shorts except for an occasional peek at the edges. Something in the way her gaze came to rest on Rori's said she knew that Rori had spent the night. Something in the pious tilt of her chin said she didn't approve. Rori couldn't care less. The truth was, she cared about only one thing: finding Blade.

"Excuse me, but I was just on my way out," Rori said, stepping around the mountain and into the hall.

"Is Mr. Cavannaugh up?"

If Rori had had any doubt as to Alice Yearwood's disapproval of Blade and her being lovers, the issue would have been settled the moment the question was asked. Though it was posed politely enough, censure lay below the query's surface, a fact evinced by the brittle tone in which it was delivered.

Any other time, Rori might have found the situation amusing. Now she found it a deterrent. "Mr. Cavannaugh is out," she said, starting to step down the hallway.

"Wait!"

The brittle tone cracked like a dropped mirror, compelling Rori to obey the command. She turned. For a heartbeat, she had the oddest feeling, as if somehow it mattered that Blade wasn't there. The odd feeling had everything to do with the way the woman was looking at her—with a dark, singular intensity that was unnerving. But then the woman spoke and the odd feeling ebbed away.

"Mr. Cavannaugh said that you were interested in hiring a housekeeper."

"Yes. Yes, I am. Why don't we talk later—"

"I have a list of references," the housekeeper interrupted.

"Good. Just leave it on the table and I'll—"

"Wait!" the woman said again, this time clasping Rori's forearm to stall her.

Startled, Rori glanced at the large hand clamped around her arm. Alice Yearwood, as though startled by what she'd done, removed her hand . . . but not before Rori confirmed that the woman was strong. Though she hadn't hurt her, she'd left the red imprint of her fingers in Rori's flesh.

"I'm sorry," the housekeeper said, "but it'll only take a moment. I went to a lot of trouble to make out my references." She started to dig through her black shoulder bag. "Maybe you could just look at them quickly . . . and I could answer any questions you might have."

She pulled out a neatly folded sheet of paper. At Rori's hesitation, Alice Yearwood took a step toward the apartment door. Then another. In response, as though following a silent Pied Piper, Rori, too, started toward the apartment. The odd feeling returned. She felt as if she was being manipulated. Don't be stupid, she told herself, you're just being prudent. The easiest way out was to take a look at the darned references then leave. After all, the housekeeper had been right in one respect. It *would* take only a moment.

At the door, the woman eased aside, allowing Rori to enter first. Rori edged past her and into the room. Alice followed, closing the door behind her. Though not in the least claustrophobic, Rori had the feeling of being hemmed in. Because of that, she reached for the list of references and moved deeper into the room. Away from the housekeeper, who remained in front of the door. Rori walked toward the end of the coffee table. She wondered if she had moved to that spot because that was where the telephone sat. Why had that thought crossed her mind? The truth was, she did feel... What? Comforted? Yes, she felt comforted by the telephone's nearness. A fact that brought back the odd feeling.

"Aren't you going to look at them?" Alice asked.

"What?"

The woman nodded toward the paper Rori still held—unopened. "My references. Aren't you going to look at them?"

Rori shifted her attention to her hand. "Yes. Yes, of course," she said, unfolding the sheet of paper.

On some plane of acknowledgment, she recorded the unexpected fact that Alice Yearwood could type. Allowing her gaze to roam down the listing, Rori noticed that the heading—References—was precisely centered. She frowned. For a reason she couldn't identify, it struck a familiar chord. Just as did something else about the script, something she couldn't put her finger on. She did feel a tightening of her stomach muscles, as if on some unconscious level she perceived something she couldn't yet consciously cope with. The page was filled with names, personal and commercial. The number of references surprised her.

"You must work all the time," Rori commented, glancing up. The housekeeper, who moments before had been across the room, now stood at the opposite end of the coffee table. The proximity startled Rori. She fought the urge to move away.

"Being a responsible person doesn't leave much time for rest. I have a grandson to support . . . and a daughter I keep having to bail out of jail." At the mention of her daughter, Alice Yearwood's face filled with sorrow, aging her with the weight of unflattering years. "She's not a bad girl. The devil just keeps working his wicked ways on her. You do believe in the devil, don't you, Ms. Kelsey?"

Rori was uncertain which unsettled her more—the macabre subject matter or the way the housekeeper was staring at her. Intently. With an unnatural light in her ebony eyes.

Ignoring the question about the devil and determined to hasten the interview, Rori looked at the references. She scanned the personal names, which included several prominent doctors, then rushed through the listing of commercial establishments—the Night's End, Mischief, Inc., the Happiest Hour. The Happiest Hour? Something about the name was familiar. But what? She could feel the answer poised at the edge of her mind. Dammit, everything seemed familiar. Frighteningly familiar!

"You, uh, you work at nightclubs?"

"God sends me there," Alice Yearwood said calmly, matter-of-factly, as if she were making the most ordinary of statements. "I'm like a missionary going into a heathen land. I save souls."

The odd feeling was back, this time raising the hair on Rori's neck. She looked at the telephone, not sure why—

except that knowing it was there was... There was that word *comforting* again.

"God sends me there to save the prostitutes," Alice volunteered. "They're really good girls. Decent girls. But the devil has gotten inside them, Ms. Kelsey, making them live in hell, making them do vile and vulgar things." Her voice lowered. "Making their mothers worry about them."

Prostitutes.

The Happiest Hour.

Hadn't she heard Blade say that was the club where Savannah Brown had worked?

"It's my mission to save them from the devil, from themselves," the housekeeper said, her voice a strange monotone. "Sometimes the only way to do that is to free them from life, to cast them into an eternal peace, to send them to God, who can purify all evil. They thank me, Ms. Kelsey. I can see it in their eyes as they're being purified."

Eyes.

Alice Yearwood's eyes, like pools of black, stagnant water, had grown opaque, reflecting nothing. They were eerie, frightening. But nowhere near as frightening as what the woman was saying. Fear, like a heinous beast, crawled over Rori's flesh. Conversely, paradoxically, she felt a benumbed calmness.

"You're the one, aren't you? You're the one killing the prostitutes."

"Oh, no, I don't kill them," Alice Yearwood said, eager to correct Rori's misunderstanding. "I send them to God to be purified. Don't you see they're reborn with cleansed souls?"

Yes, she did see. Regrettably, she saw everything. She looked at the list of references that she still held. Searching out the Happiest Hour, she saw what she knew she would see, what she'd seen from the beginning but hadn't accepted. The *o* in the word *Hour* didn't close completely. Even the precisely centered heading made sense. A grisly, gruesome sense.

"You sent me the letters, didn't you?" The letters, she thought, that had been typed on the typewriter sitting on the dining table a few feet away. The letters she'd accused Blade of writing. The letters she'd demanded Blade deny he wrote. Oh, God, where was he now?

"God told me to," Alice Yearwood said simply.

"Why?" Rori whispered, her heart hammering against her chest like the wings of a giant bird.

"Because the devil's in you, Ms. Kelsey. He's using you just like he's using the prostitutes. Don't you see that? Only he's using you to corrupt them. He's making you say filth on the air. People listen to you and then they go and fornicate."

"It's only a radio show!" Rori cried. "I'm only playing love songs. I'm only talking about romance. People fall in love, for God's sake!" *Oh, God, Blade, where are you?*

"Sex is only for procreation. Its enjoyment is sinful." Alice let her eyes trail the length of Rori, revulsion forming on her face. "Look at you. You're still wearing last night's sin as though you're proud of it."

"Get out!" Rori said softly. The words vibrated with anger.

"You did spread your legs for him, didn't you?"

"Get out!"

"You did twist beneath him in pleasure, didn't you?"

"Get out! Or I swear I'll call the police!"

"I'm a messenger of God. The police can't hurt me."

"We'll see," Rori said, throwing the references to the floor and reaching for the phone. She drew it to her ear. For the second time in minutes, a hand clamped around her wrist. This time, the fingers of the hand dug cruelly into her flesh. Rori grimaced, whimpered and dropped the phone. But not before she realized that the phone was dead. Dead. As in on the fritz again. Blade wasn't going to be happy that the phone was out again, she thought foolishly as she rubbed at her wrist in an attempt to ease the sharp pains jabbing through it.

Alice realized that the phone wasn't working. She brought it to her ear, listened, then smiled. A sweet, sincere smile that looked totally out of place under the circumstances.

"It's a sign," the housekeeper announced. "God always gives me a sign when it's time. I knew it was time to purify the last one when I saw Mr. Cavannaugh talking to her. I had gone to the Happiest Hour to tell them I couldn't work that night because I had to keep my grandson. My daughter was in jail. She's not a bad girl, Ms. Kelsey. The devil just gets in her and makes her go to bed with men. But she's not a slut. She's a good girl."

Rori heard the woman's pain. She felt it in the marrow of her bones. It was the kind of bleak pain that moved through one's spirit like a cold winter wind blowing through the skeletal branches of a bare tree. "I know she is. And I don't think she'd want you hurting anyone else."

"Oh, no, she wouldn't! She's a sweet girl. But don't you see it's God who's punishing you? He told me only to frighten you with the elevator...and after I read Mr. Cavannaugh's note telling me where you'd be in the French Quarter, in case his agent called, God told me to follow you and to push you from the curb. They were warnings, Ms. Kelsey. God was giving you a chance to repent, but still you corrupt others, still you shame yourself. But now he wants me to stop you. He's given me a sign." Suddenly the look on the housekeeper's face was gentle, benevolent. "I won't hurt you. If you don't struggle, I won't hurt you. You'll thank me for saving you. The others did."

It was funny, Rori thought, how calm she felt. She'd always imagined that, under such conditions, the brain short-circuited, the heart went wild, fear pumped adrenaline into every cell of the body. But she felt none of that. Only calm. She knew it was a false calm based on shock, but still it surprised her. Utilizing the rationality she retained, Rori glanced beyond the woman to the door. Her chances of reaching it before the housekeeper were slim, yet they were better than her chances of staying alive if she didn't try.

Without giving herself time to dwell on the dismal odds, Rori skirted the coffee table and streaked for the door. Out of the corner of her eye, she noted the startled look on Alice Yearwood's face, as though she could not understand Rori's denying herself the peace she was being offered. The woman's hand snaked out, grabbing a fistful of the oversize shirt. With a grunt, Alice jerked, sending Rori thudding to the floor. A pain shot through Rori's hip and her head slammed against the edge of the dining table. Another pain, like a malevolent starburst, erupted inside her skull, spewing fragments of dark light.

The jarring motion sent the pages of Blade's manuscript flying off the table, and the two mugs of coffee tumbled over. Cold black coffee streamed onto the white carpet. Inanely, in that part of her brain not participating in the fireworks, Rori thought that someone was going to have a hell of a time getting the stain out. Not so inanely, she realized that her calmness had fled. She was scared. More scared than she could ever remember being. Her heartbeat, pounding like a drum, exploded in her ears.

The instinct for survival kicked into high gear. Her head throbbing, lights flashing, she crawled beneath the table. A hand grabbed her ankle, but Rori yanked free. She sped across the coffee-soaked carpet, feeling the cool wetness on her palms and knees. Then, she felt the smooth tile of the kitchen floor. Where was she headed? Something answered that, if she could only make it to the balcony, she could scream for help. Still on her knees, she was trying to shove the glass door open when the mountain slammed against her, sending her sprawling to the floor. Rori cried out.

"Don't make me hurt you!" Alice pleaded, her hot breath washing against Rori's cheek. "It won't hurt if you don't fight me! God's waiting to cleanse your soul. Go to him."

Rori fought to open the door. She grazed the slick glass, seeking a hold, but her fingers could find none. She tried again. Again she failed, her only reward being the breaking of her fingernail to the bloody quick.

"Don't do this!" Rori begged, trying to reason with the woman, the woman who was so effortlessly rolling Rori to her back. "You don't want to do this! God doesn't want—"

The air whooshed from her lungs as Alice Yearwood's knee found the pit of her stomach, painfully pinning Rori to the floor. Rori bucked, kicked, but succeeded only in driving the pain in more deeply.

And then she felt the rough, chunky hands slide around her throat.

No! Rori screamed silently, her hands thrashing. Her fingers scratched at glass and metal. Suddenly, miraculously, the glass door slid open several inches. Hot, muggy air blasted in. Rori tried to scream, but no sound came out except a gasping rasp as her throat closed off, as her windpipe clogged. Rori's hands frantically sought the life-threatening clamp at her neck. Crazed with the need to breathe, she tried to pull the bruising fingers away. But she couldn't. The woman's strength surpassed hers.

Rori fought...struggled...her fingers scraping her assailant's face...but already the world was beginning to grow dark. Black lights flashed behind her eyes, and the tiny bones in her neck felt crushed beneath the insidious weight of the probing fingers. The housekeeper had begun to chant something that resembled Biblical verses.

She was going to die. Here. Now. Rori accepted that fact with serenity. Her only regret, she realized, was that Blade would live the rest of his life never knowing she'd been on her way to find him, to tell him that she believed in him.

Rori's hands went limp.

The black lights blended together into a peaceful, beckoning whole.

Air no longer seemed a precious commodity.

And then there was nothing...nothing...nothing...

Abruptly, the hands were wrenched from Rori's throat. Air rushed into her lungs in a painful gush. The knee in her stomach fell away. What was happening? She heard a voice, a deep voice, a masculine voice. The voice growled a curse. Which sounded strange, mixed with chanted Biblical verses. As once more the light of life, the brilliance of consciousness, entered Rori's body, she realized, dimly, that the voice belonged to Blade. And that he'd just hauled Alice Yearwood to her feet...and that they were scuffling...and that he'd clipped her full under the chin. The woman sailed against the sliding glass door. The sound of shattering glass filled the air. As did the sound of a table tipping over as she stumbled onto the balcony. She hit the wrought-iron railing with such force that she tottered and wavered before,

grasping at thin air, she tumbled over the balcony's edge.
She screamed. A blood-curdling racket that ripped open the
sultry morning. An exquisite silence followed.

Rori heard little beyond her own breath—the magical
sucking of air that allowed life to flow into her. She was
aware, too, of Blade kneeling before her. He looked worried, scared. She tried to tell him that she was all right, but
the words hurt her tender throat. She tried to raise her hand
to his face, but couldn't find the strength.

"Oh, God, Rori," he whispered, gently pulling her into
his arms. She could feel his sweat-damp body against hers,
could feel his violent heartbeat merge with hers, could feel
his warm breath against her neck.

"I was—" She choked on the words. She had to tell him.
She had to start over and tell him. Because he had to know.
She had to make him believe her. "I . . . I was coming after
you—"

"Shh."

"—to tell you—"

"Shh."

"—that I believed you...that you didn't...have to deny
anything." She pulled back until their eyes met. "I swear
it," she said, as though it was the most important thing
she'd tried to convince anyone of. "Please . . . please believe me!"

Her hoarse voice, her passionate entreaty, the singularity
of her thoughts in the face of the nightmare she'd just lived
through, moved Blade until he, too, could hardly speak. For
long moments, they stared at each other. Then they heard
the crowd gathering below the balcony, felt the morning
heat creeping into the apartment, smelled the strong, heady
scent of fat, rich roses.

Finally, swallowing the knotted emotion from his throat, Blade brushed the hair from her face and whispered simply, unequivocally, "Love always believes."

Epilogue

New York.

It was the last of a fifteen-city, two-month tour publicizing the latest B. J. Nichols novel. To say that the book was a best-seller was a gross understatement. It had climbed the charts overnight, selling out in some bookstores before it arrived because of waiting lists that had been compiled weeks before. Critics were calling it "faction," a blend of fact and fiction told sensitively from the viewpoints of killer and victim. Readers were calling it suspense at its finest, with a spicy dash of romance thrown in. The publishing house was calling it gold. As was Thaddeus T. Abrams.

Blade's editor, his cheeks pinched by his nervous energy, had met Rori at the airport at noon and had driven her through a Spring-dappled New York City to join Blade for lunch at a posh restaurant. With Blade's tight schedule, a TV interview that afternoon then an autographing at a bookstore, husband and wife had to settle for a paltry, and very public, kiss. During the extensive, seemingly never-ending tour, they'd had to settle for a lot of hurried kisses and stolen moments. Rori had stayed in New Orleans, where each weeknight she anchored Night Spice, but then, come the weekend, she flew to meet Blade wherever he happened to be. This time they'd be going home together, to her apartment in New Orleans. To say that Rori and Blade were relieved that the tour was over also was an understatement. Not even Thaddeus's news that a movie company was interested in *Murders in the Color of Blond* could compete.

Lunch and the interview over, Rori, canvassing the aisles of the bookstore, glanced at her husband who was signing books for his adoring fans. She smiled as she selected another book to join the several she held in the crook of her arm. He hated publicity, but was giving it his most noble effort. He smiled, talked, even had his picture taken when an ardent fan requested it. That he was tired, ready for the event to be over, was obvious. The autographing had been scheduled to end an hour earlier, at six o'clock, but people kept coming. The end, however, was in sight. Only a couple dozen people were still in line.

Sensing Rori's gaze, Blade looked up. His gaze unerringly found her . . . the way it had countless times that afternoon. As always, he felt a momentary seizure of panic as he remembered how he'd almost lost her. As always, a slow, sensual heat—the heat was coming rapidly now—suffused him. He recalled another time in a bookstore when they'd spoken of kissing in front of Isaac Asimov and Robert Ludlum—a long, slow kiss that they'd ultimately decided to defer. At the moment he was in no mood for deferral. It had been a hellishly long week away from his wife. What he was in the mood for was a lot more than a kiss . . . if he could believe the ache he felt for her. If he could just hold on for another ten minutes. If he could just—

"Marilyn Davidson."

Blade cut his eyes to the person holding out a copy of his novel. He cleared his throat. "I'm, uh, sorry. I didn't catch the name."

"Marilyn Davidson," the woman repeated. "By the way, Mr. Nichols, I loved the book. It was wonderful."

Quickly scrawling an inscription to Marilyn Davidson, Blade said, "Thanks. I'm glad you enjoyed it."

Rori reached for another book to add to her collection. Her eyes brushed those of the last woman in line. The woman had rushed in only seconds before, a hurried, harried look on her face. She smiled at Rori, who was browsing at a nearby shelf. Rori smiled, which the woman obviously took as encouragement.

"I thought I wasn't going to make it in time," she confided to Rori. "I had to work late. I would have died if I hadn't gotten here in time to get his autograph. Have you read the book?" she asked, patting a copy of *Murders in the Color of Blond*.

"No. No, I haven't," Rori said. Someday she would, but the memories of that time nine months earlier were still too painful. She could remember too clearly the bruises she'd worn at her throat for weeks after the nightmarish incident.

"You should," the woman said, adding, "it's the best book I've ever read. They say it's true. What he wrote about really happened. Or at least it's based on what really happened."

"Faction," Rori said, repeating the critics' comment.

"Yeah. Right. It's the story of a disc jockey in New Orleans who's stalked by a murderer who's killing blond-haired prostitutes. The disc jockey's blond and beautiful, with a voice to die for.''

"Sounds fascinating," Rori said in a natural drawl that defined precisely the to-die-for voice the woman had just spoken of.

"This investigative reporter in the book falls in love with her and in the end she thinks he's the one stalking her..."

Rori's heart constricted. She would never forgive herself for doubting Blade...even if it had been only for a brief while. Blade, however, had forgiven her. Repeatedly, he'd told her that her wedding gift to him had been the knowledge that she'd been on her way to find him, to tell him that she did trust him. In some strange, fanciful way, Rori thought fate had arranged those few minutes of doubt so she could understand firsthand what Blade had suffered with his wife. To be innocent but judged guilty was a soul-scarring thing. Rori had hurt him once, which made her vow vehemently never to do so again.

"But he rescues her as the strangler is trying to kill her..."

It was here, Rori knew, that the story departed from reality. In the book, the villain was a telephone repairman. Out of deference to Alice Yearwood's family, Blade had altered the story. Alice Yearwood had died instantly, taking with her all the answers to the many questions the police had. The police psychologist had enough to go on, however, to piece together a probable scenario. The motivation for her murdering spree had been her nineteen-year-old daughter, a young woman with blond hair, who was supporting her drug habit by prostitution. In some convoluted act of transference, the psychologist believed, Alice Yearwood was saving her daughter by "purifying" other prostitutes. Rori knew, because she'd been instrumental in arranging it, that the daughter was in a drug rehabilitation program.

"In real life, he married the disc jockey and wrote the book on their honeymoon, in two weeks. I read it in *People* magazine. I wonder if he took time to... well, you know what I mean..."

Rori did indeed. And the answer was no. He hadn't touched her, not even as much as a kiss, for two weeks. He'd written night and day, taking time only for the bathroom and to eat junk food at the typewriter, the old, worn-out Underwood. Occasionally, when he could resist no longer, he'd lain on the floor to catch a couple of hours' worth of sleep before going back to the writing. She had slept on the sofa to be near him. When the book was finished, he'd mailed it off without even reading through it. Then he'd crawled into bed and slept eighteen hours straight. When he'd awakened, the honeymoon had truly begun... and it hadn't stopped since. She still blushed at some of their marathon lovemaking... and at the responses he could so easily draw from her. Responses that her past would never allow her to take cavalierly.

"Can you imagine being married to him?" the woman asked, the thought obviously sending her into rapture. "Is he gorgeous or what?" she whispered.

If you think he's gorgeous now, Rori thought, you should see him naked and sprawled on a bed. Instead, she said, "Yeah, he is gorgeous."

The woman sighed, as if in supreme disappointment. "But I hear he's totally besotted with his wife."

Rori's heart constricted again, this time from pure love. Her voice was a husky whisper when she answered, "I hear she's totally besotted with him."

The fan gave another sigh that said, "Ain't love grand?" Moving up in line, she said, indicating the book, "You ought to read it."

"I will," Rori promised. Someday.

While Blade signed the last of the books, Rori paid for her purchases. The sack the clerk handed her was heavy. As she started to lift it, Blade, his eyes briefly, hotly connecting with hers, relieved her of the bag and, thanking the bookstore manager for the autographing, said a hasty good night. Without a word, his hand at her back, he guided Rori toward the long limousine waiting to take them to the hotel. The chauffeur, dressed impeccably in royal-blue livery, opened the car door. Rori scooted in, with Blade right behind her. The car door closed behind him, and in seconds the pantherlike beast growled softly as it pulled from the curb. Without a word, but with a comparable growl, Blade reached for Rori.

He kissed her just the way he'd wanted to all day, just the way he'd wanted to all week. Which was to say he kissed her thoroughly, completely, leaving not so much as an inch of her mouth untouched. She moaned softly and curled her tongue with his. As his tongue danced with hers, he reached for the buttons of her blouse. He'd undone two before Rori had the presence of mind to realize what he'd done.

"Blade, what are you doing?" she whispered in a scandalized tone.

"Making love to my wife," he replied calmly, releasing another button.

"You can't do that! Not here!" she said, swatting at his hand.

"Watch me," he replied, pulling his hand from hers and unfastening another button. A pale blue teddy, with tons of frothy lace, came into view. Blade groaned low and deep at the sexy sight of her satin-draped cleavage.

"Blade!" she said, trying to stop him from easing his hand into the garment and cupping her bare breast in his palm. Her breath scattered like dandelions in a wild wind. God, his touch felt so good!

"Look," he said quietly, so they couldn't be overheard, "I fought this limousine tooth and nail, but Thad insisted. I hate all this fame-game crap, but right now this car has real potential. It has tinted glass that you can't see out of, let alone into... even if it wasn't nighttime. The partition is up and the doors are locked. It's a twenty-minute drive to the hotel. And, lady," he said, his tone far more promise than threat, "that's more than enough time, considering how I feel."

Whether it was the forbidden nature of what he was suggesting or the way his thumb had found the peak of her breast, Rori didn't know, but sparklers of feeling ignited low in her belly.

"You can't be serious," she tried one last time, adding at the sultry look in his depthless gray eyes, "you're serious." She knew he could be a man of great restraint—after all, he hadn't touched her for two weeks on their honeymoon. On the other hand, just like the stranger she'd first seen on the balcony, he also was a man of action. When he wanted something, he wanted it. Then. Not later. More than once they'd left a restaurant in midmeal when a stronger appetite had overtaken them.

"Damned straight!" he said, lowering his head to her breast, which he eased above the garment and took into his mouth. At the bawdy teasing of his lips and tongue, she sighed and laid her cheek across the top of his head. As he kissed the nipple, he ran his hand beneath her skirt and up her leg. "Help me!" he muttered.

"Do what?" she asked breathlessly.

"My belt."

"Oh," she moaned as his hand connected with its sweet target. She reached for his belt.

"That's it," he whispered feverishly. "Now the zipper."

"Blade!" she whimpered as his fingers knew her in a carnal way.

"Undo the zipper, Rori."

"God, that feels so good."

"It's gonna feel better."

"Mmm."

"Lean back."

"Where?"

"The corner."

"I can't."

"You can. Put your leg here. That's it. That's it. Wider."

"You're so hot," she whispered as her hand closed around him.

He moaned. "You're so wet, so sweet! You're so—" He groaned as he slid inside her. Seconds and mere strokes later, as the end came, he buried his lips against hers.

"I love you...I love you...I love you..." they both chanted.

Ten minutes later the shiny black limousine pulled to the curb at the hotel. When the chauffeur opened the door, two prim, properly attired individuals got out. They didn't dare glance at the other, however, for fear that their barely suppressed grins would burst onto their faces.

"Oh, my books!" Rori cried, almost forgetting her purchase. As she reached for them, the sack tilted, spilling its contents onto the street.

Blade stopped to pick up the books. At the sudden realization that they all dealt with either pregnancy or child-rearing, Blade raised his head, his gaze flying to Rori's. He felt as though he'd been poleaxed. She looked sheepishly uncertain and deliriously excited.

"There's, uh, there's something I need to tell you," Rori said. "I was going to wait until we got home."

The books forgotten, Blade rose to his feet. "Tell me now."

She stared at him, hoping to heaven that he was as pleased as she. She wished, too, that they didn't have an audience made up of the chauffeur, the hotel doorman and several passersby who'd stopped to gape at whoever had climbed from the sleek limousine.

"I . . . I'm going to have a baby," she announced quietly.

Blade said nothing, did nothing. It was as though he'd slipped into a catatonic stupor. Slowly, like a spring thaw after a miserably cold winter, his lips slid into a grin. Then he gave a war whoop that stopped half a dozen more passersby. Scooping Rori into his arms, he planted a quick, fierce kiss full on her lips before starting inside the hotel.

"Oh," he said over his shoulder to the chauffeur, "could you get the books? We're having a baby." To the doorman who was holding the door wide, Blade said, "Get me roses. Lots of roses. But only red ones."

The doorman smiled. "Yes, Mr. Cavannaugh . . . and congratulations, sir."

"Thank you," Blade replied, totally oblivious to the grinning sidewalk onlookers . . . and to the people in the lobby who looked at the strange sight of a man carrying a woman.

"You're sure?" Blade asked as he headed for the elevator.

"Yes," Rori replied.

"When?"

"Denver, I guess."

Blade grinned. "Good old Denver. I knew we had a good time there."

"You are happy? About the baby, I mean?" she asked as the people departing the elevator stared.

"God, yes," he whispered, entering the elevator and punching the number for their floor. Unhurriedly he let her slide the length of him until her feet rested beside his. His hand moved with exquisite tenderness to cup her cheek. "God, yes," he repeated, his head lowering, his lips melting into hers.

This kiss was slow and sweet and spoke not of passion, but of love. It spoke, too, of commitment. Of all the special things that can exist between a man and a woman, a husband and a wife. It spoke of trust. Eternal trust.

Rori felt all this and a thousand things more. Mostly, though, she felt a delicious gentleness. She'd dreamed of this man's gentle kisses long before he'd kissed her. Now, just as in that long-ago dream, his kiss brought tears to her eyes.

"I love you," she whispered.

Then the elevator started toward their room. Toward tomorrow. Toward home.

* * * * *

Silhouette Special Edition

COMING NEXT MONTH

#619 THE GIRL MOST LIKELY TO—Tracy Sinclair
Kate Beaumont was desperate for a man—even if she had to hire one!—for her high school reunion. And after seeing the shy, sexy scientist in distress, Garrett Richmond gladly offered his masculine services...

#620 NO PLACE TO HIDE—Celeste Hamilton
Urban refugee Carly Savoy thought she had found safety in her secluded mountain retreat—until mysterious Ben Jamison shattered her sanctuary and threatened to unravel her innermost secrets.

#621 ALL WE KNOW OF HEAVEN—Phyllis Halldorson
After seven agonizing years of grief and regret, Michaela Tanner forced herself to assume the worst about her P.O.W. husband, Heath. But on the eve of her second marriage, Heath's presence was more than mere memory...

#622 PETTICOAT LAWYER—Kate Meriwether
Camille Clark rallied all the toughness she could muster to face police officer Pike Barrett in court. But Pike, detecting softness beneath the stunning attorney's brittle sophistication, was determined not to remain her adversary for long!

#623 FREEDOM'S JUST ANOTHER WORD—Jennifer Mikels
The only thing conservative Joshua Fitzhugh shared with free-spirited Allison Gentry was his boardinghouse bathroom. But in his search for a "suitable" mate, the sensible professor was hopelessly sidetracked by his offbeat neighbor!

#624 OLD ENOUGH TO KNOW BETTER—Pamela Toth
One decade after escaping a domestic dead end, Maureen Fletcher remained blissfully single. Then her heart was hooked by handsome Bailey McGuire—but, at her age, could she handle ready-made motherhood?

AVAILABLE THIS MONTH:

#613 LAUGHTER ON THE WIND
Bay Matthews

#614 NIGHT SPICE
Karen Keast

#615 CHOICES OF THE HEART
Barbara Faith

#616 TWO FOR THE PRICE OF ONE
Madelyn Dohrn

#617 PRAIRIE CRY
Dawn Flindt

#618 MAKE ROOM FOR DADDY
Andrea Edwards

🖤 Diamond Jubilee Collection

It's our 10th Anniversary... and *you* get a present!

This collection of early Silhouette Romances features novels written by three of your favorite authors:

ANN MAJOR—*Wild Lady*
ANNETTE BROADRICK—*Circumstantial Evidence*
DIXIE BROWNING—*Island on the Hill*

* These Silhouette Romance titles were first published in the early 1980s and have not been available since!

* Beautiful Collector's Edition bound in antique green simulated leather to last a lifetime!

* Embossed in gold on the cover and spine!

This special collection will not be sold in retail stores and is only available through this exclusive offer.
Look for details in all Silhouette series published in June, July and August.

Double your reading pleasure this fall with two Award of Excellence titles written by two of your favorite authors.

Available in September

DUNCAN'S BRIDE
by Linda Howard
Silhouette Intimate Moments #349

Mail-order bride Madelyn Patterson was nothing like what Reese Duncan expected—and everything he needed.

Available in October

THE COWBOY'S LADY
by Debbie Macomber
Silhouette Special Edition #626

The Montana cowboy wanted a little lady at his beck and call—the ''lady'' in question saw things differently....

These titles have been selected to receive a special laurel—the Award of Excellence. Look for the distinctive emblem on the cover. It lets you know there's something truly wonderful inside!

Appearing in October
for a return engagement, Nora Roberts's
bestselling 1988 miniseries featuring

THE O'HURLEYS!
Nora Roberts

Book 1 THE LAST HONEST WOMAN *Abby's Story*

Book 2 DANCE TO THE PIPER *Maddy's Story*

Book 3 SKIN DEEP *Chantel's Story*

And making his debut in a brand-new title, a very special leading man . . . Trace O'Hurley!

Book 4 WITHOUT A TRACE *Trace's Tale*

In 1988, Nora Roberts introduced THE O'HURLEYS!—a close-knit family of entertainers whose early travels spanned the country. The beautiful triplet sisters and their mysterious brother each experience the triumphant joy and passion only true love can bring, in four books you will remember long after the last pages are turned.

Don't miss this captivating miniseries in October—a special collector's edition available wherever paperbacks are sold.

OHUR-1